Emily Harvale lives in Eas
You can contact her via he
Google+ or Pinterest

Author contacts:
www.emilyharvale.com
www.twitter.com/emilyharvale
www.facebook.com/emilyharvalewriter
www.facebook.com/emilyharvale
www.emilyharvale/blog
www.pinterest.com/emilyharvale
www.google.com/+EmilyHarvale

***

Scan the code above to see all Emily's books on Amazon

Also by this author:

Highland Fling

Lizzie Marshall's Wedding

The Golf Widows' Club

Sailing Solo

Carole Singer's Christmas

Christmas Wishes – Two short stories

A Slippery Slope

The Perfect Christmas Plan – A novella

Be Mine – A novella

***

The Goldebury Bay series:

Book One – Ninety Days of Summer

Book Two – Ninety Steps to Summerhill

(This is an ongoing series)

Ninety Steps

to

Summerhill

Emily Harvale

ISBN 978-1-909917-09-5

Published by Crescent Gate Publishing

Print edition published worldwide 2015
E-edition published worldwide 2015

Editor Christina Harkness

Cover design by JR, Luke Brabants and Emily Harvale

Acknowledgements

Goldebury Bay is loosely based on my home town of Hastings as you'll know if you follow me on social media. Hastings is a beautiful seaside resort on the East Sussex coast of the UK. It has many tourist attractions, several of which are similar to those in my fictitious resort of Goldebury Bay. However, the attractions in this book are purely fictional and therefore, should not be confused with any real tourist attractions either in Hastings or in any other resort.

My special thanks go to the following:

Christina Harkness for editing this novel. Christina has the patience of a saint and her input is truly appreciated.
My webmaster and friend, David Cleworth who does so much more for me than website stuff.
Luke Brabants and JR for their work on the gorgeous cover. JR is a genius in graphic design and Luke's a talented artist. Luke's website is: http://www.lukebrabants.com
My fabulous friends for their support and friendship.
My Twitter and Facebook friends, and fans of my Facebook author page. It's great to chat with you. You help to keep me (relatively) sane!
And finally, you – for buying this book. Thank You. It really means a lot to me. I hope you enjoy it.
Love,

Emily xx

This book is dedicated to May Millgate: a true inspiration.

Chapter One

Sophie Summerhill firmly believed in Fate; she just wished it would leave her alone for a while and go and play with someone else's life.

'Everything happens for a reason,' she could almost hear her mother say although even Julia Summerhill would have difficulty finding a reason for this latest little twist, and it was yet another one that Sophie could very well have done without.

She closed the leather-bound menu and wondered if she should look for somewhere cheaper than this quintessential English tearoom but as raindrops the size of garden peas splattered against the leaded glass panes, she acknowledged that comfort came with a price.

'May I have a coffee and some toast, please? With butter,' she said, managing a smile for the white-haired woman in a paisley dress who was re-arranging postcards – rather optimistically in Sophie's opinion – in a swivel-stand near the door.

She hoped the cheerful-looking woman actually worked in Betty's Pantry or this would be the second person she'd offended in less than fifteen minutes, the first being at the garage where her Ford Fiesta had just died.

She should have been thankful that her car had made it that far. For several long, nerve-racking minutes before it coughed and spluttered its way down the steep, winding hill leading into Goldebury Bay, she had visions of it stopping dead. Right in the middle of nowhere. In the pouring rain. With all her worldly goods bundled on the seats and in the boot and where not even one bar was visible on her mobile phone and another human being was a rarer sight than an Osprey. Not that there were any Osprey on the south-east coast of England. At least, not as far as she was aware.

And she should also be thankful that not only was there a garage of the foot of the hill but that it was open and the forecourt empty so that her car could glide… well, more like chug the last few feet before coming to a halt with the mechanical equivalent of a fart, slap bang in the middle of the wide, concrete frontage.

But she wasn't thankful; she was cross. Why couldn't it have made it the final three miles or so to the house? Was that really too much to ask? Why? Why? Why?

It was the proverbial straw that broke the camel's back and the last thing she had needed at that precise moment, was a car mechanic on the make.

As she had dashed from the car to the shelter of the open-fronted workshop, a middle-aged man in oil-covered overalls had shaken his balding head and pronounced: 'This is going to cost a pretty penny.'

Without even lifting the bonnet.

Sophie had fought back tears of anger and frustration. 'You can tell that just by looking at it from several feet away? You're obviously psychic.'

'And you're a cheeky miss,' said the man. 'You're welcome to take it somewhere else if you can get it started. But I don't need to be no psychic to tell you that the only one here who can do that, is me.'

Sophie knew she had no choice. She'd let her breakdown cover lapse.

'I'm sorry,' she had said, swiping away an escaping tear.

'Things haven't been going well lately. Is there any chance you could give me a rough idea of what's wrong and how much it's likely to cost, please?'

The man had cleared his throat. 'There, there. No need for waterworks. I'll take a look-see. Maybe I can work some magic. Give me half an hour. Unless there's somewhere else you'd rather go, there's a nice little tearoom a few doors down called Betty's Pantry.'

Sophie thanked him and sprinted through torrential rain towards a sign, which was swinging wildly from an ornate, iron bracket and bearing an image of a teapot and a plate of cream scones.

The door of the bow-fronted, 18th century building rattled open when Sophie pushed it and as she stepped inside, she felt as if someone had wrapped her in a coffee-scented blanket. She sat at a table nestled in the curve of the window and experienced an overwhelming sense of relief. Although she had no idea why and it vanished the moment she had seen the menu prices.

Oh, why couldn't the car have made it to the house?

She'd stopped at a supermarket on her way and there was a boxful of groceries in the boot. Now she'd have to pay for coffee and toast and after that, she'd probably still end up having to drag her suitcase... and the box of groceries for two miles along the coast. It was another mile up that bloody hill and down again on the unfinished, but now mud-caked road. Unless she used the steps. They were only half a mile away. The ninety steps to Summerhill. She'd counted them as a child. Could she drag her suitcase – and the groceries – up the steps? She'd have to leave the rest of her belongings in the car and collect them later.

She placed the menu back in its stand on the rose-patterned tablecloth and sighed. She really hoped the mechanic could work some magic, and cheaply, but the way things had been going lately, he'd probably tell her the damn thing was a write-off.

In the past eight weeks her life had been turned upside down, inside out and trampled on by Fate's running shoes. There seemed to be no respite. It had been one bad thing after another. And she couldn't even turn to her mother for a comforting hug. Julia Summerhill and her latest boyfriend had sailed to the Cayman Islands in January – with Sophie's blessing at the time – to start a new life.

But Sophie had been happy then, or relatively so. She had no idea she'd be alone, unemployed and homeless just a few shorts weeks after telling her mother: 'Bon Voyage and see you soon.'

There had only been one glimmer of hope in Sophie's life since then, and that had arrived just yesterday, by post. Whether one should see a formal notification of the death of a relative as 'hope' is debatable in many people's opinion. But probably only by those who hadn't met Silas Summerhill.

'Terrible morning, isn't it?' the white-haired woman in the tearoom was saying. Her thin, bright pink lips exuded a broad smile. 'You here on holiday?'

'No.' Sophie shook her head, sending yellow-gold lengths of wet hair swishing around her shoulders like rapeseed in a windswept field.

'Just passing through?'

'You could say that.'

Sophie forced another smile whilst she draped her dripping, denim jacket across the back of her chair. She turned her face towards the window, hoping the woman would realise she wasn't in the mood for conversation. She could feel another wave of tears rising to the surface and she didn't want a second person to witness her self-pity.

'You should have some of my home-made marmalade

with your toast. I'll bring you a pot. I'm Betty, by the way.'

'Thanks,' Sophie said, 'but I'm not a lover of marmalade.'

'Ah, but you haven't tasted *my* marmalade. There's none quite like it for miles around. You're not from around here, are you?'

'No, I'm not.' Sophie rummaged through her oversized handbag and as she pulled out her mobile phone it seemed Betty finally got the message. From the corner of her eye, Sophie saw her shuffle towards the door marked 'kitchen' and a moment later, the mouth-watering smells of baking bread and sizzling bacon wafted into the tearoom, fanned by the swinging door before it finally clattered shut.

Sophie breathed in the heavenly aromas and suddenly felt very hungry. She hadn't eaten since lunch yesterday and that was only a sandwich and an apple. She wondered if her funds would stretch to a 'bacon butty' or better still, a full English breakfast but she remembered those groceries in the boot. She mustn't spend money on something she didn't need, especially now that her car had broken down.

Licking her lips and trying to ignore her rumbling tummy, she checked her messages – there weren't any – then watched as people raced past the window, fighting the wind and rain with their umbrellas. The little town was busier than she expected but it was a Saturday and the tourist season, even if it felt more like November than June. She felt sorry for anyone on holiday in Goldebury Bay in weather like this.

She also felt sorry for herself but she must try to be positive and pull herself together. Spurting tears every five minutes wasn't good for her self-esteem.

It was simply because she was tired, she knew that; and anxious about her future. She hadn't slept well recently and leaving London at six-thirty this morning in a vain attempt to avoid traffic jams, hadn't worked out as she had hoped. Why did the powers that be always carry out road works on main roads and motorways at the busiest times of the year? It was one of life's annoying little mysteries.

But if things went according to plan, this miserable state of affairs wouldn't be for long. Hopefully before the summer was out, she'd be joining her mother in the Caymans and living a life of luxury on a sun-drenched island instead of a life of near-poverty in a tiny, rain-soaked, seaside resort. She just had to get through the next few weeks, solve the mystery of the ancient feud between the Beaumonts, the Suttons and the Pollards and find the fabled, long-lost treasure. Simple! After that, her life would be perfect.

Her old life was gone; a much better one was just around the corner. If she told herself that often enough, perhaps she would begin to believe it.

The kitchen door swung open and Betty reappeared with Sophie's coffee. It was in a delicate-looking, china cup and Sophie tried to hide her disappointment. She was hoping for one of those giant cups most of the coffee shops used but she should have guessed from the décor, both inside and out, that this place specialised in 'dainty'… with the exception of the prices.

'You're not one of those journalist types, are you?' Betty asked, placing Sophie's coffee on the table.

The seemingly glued-on smile on Betty's lips came unstuck for just a second and for some reason, Sophie was rather thankful that she could say, in all honesty, that she was not. Nor anything close to one. In fact, she was currently unemployed and almost broke. But that was far more information than she intended to divulge.

'I'm not a journalist.'

'Well, thank heavens for that. We've had more of those

than our friendly, little town can cope with, thank you kindly. They've been here on and off since last September, you know.'

Betty clearly wanted to talk, or gossip more like, Sophie thought. She hadn't been in Goldebury Bay since she was nine years old but all small towns were the same: full of people minding everyone else's business.

'Hordes of them came after the arrests,' Betty continued, 'and back for the trials, and now the verdicts are expected any moment, there'll be more. Then there's the sentencing. You've probably read about it. It's been in all the papers and even on the news. And not just local, mind. National too. None of us could believe it at first. Although I always knew the Beaumonts weren't all they pretended to be.'

'Jeremiah was a pillar of the community before he was arrested,' Sophie said without thinking, the moment Betty stopped for breath.

'You know the Beaumonts?' Betty's eyes narrowed momentarily.

Sophie fidgeted in her seat, annoyed for letting that slip. But perhaps it wasn't such a bad thing. The trials of alleged drug-smugglers, Jeremiah Beaumont and his niece, Hermione, were one twist of Fate that she hoped might actually work in her favour. Everyone was so wrapped up in the proceedings that no one would find it at all odd that a stranger would come to Goldebury Bay and start asking questions about the Beaumonts. Or their ancestors. Or even about the ancient feud between the Beaumonts, the Suttons and the Pollards.

Even Sophie had been vaguely interested in the trials until yesterday. Now she had far more important things to think about than whether or not Jeremiah and Hermione Beaumont would be found guilty. And she may as well start sowing the seeds of her cover story right away.

‘No,’ she said. ‘Only from what I’ve read and heard. As you say, the story’s been widely reported. You’d have to live on Mars to miss it. They’ve lived in Goldebury Bay for centuries, haven’t they? The Beaumonts. I’m interested in the Tudor period – particularly art from that era – and I read about a Barnabus Beaumont, a 16th century pirate – or should I call him a privateer? He helped defeat the Spanish Armada, I believe. I’d love to see a portrait of him, if there is one.’

Betty nodded, apparently satisfied. ‘That’s right and there’s more than one picture of Barnabus. Captain of *The Sea Witch*, he was. Both man and ship are famous around these parts. And not just these parts, mind. Barnabus Beaumont’s adventures are known of far and wide. A real hero he was. Not like the current Beaumonts. They’re a bunch of villains. Apart from Thaddeus, of course. He’s a darling. Although he was a little monster as a boy. And Mercedes – she’s an angel. Her husband’s a hero too, you know. Got a medal and everything. The mother’s foreign and never quite fit in but she tried, bless her. Couldn’t cope with all the press poking their noses in her business though, especially when she discovered she’d lose the house. Ran off back to Spain she did and dragged Mercedes and the children with her. Wanted Thaddeus to go too but he wouldn’t budge. But listen to me running my mouth off, when all you want is some breakfast. Oh! Speak of the Devil. Here comes one of those journalists.’ Betty tapped the side of her nose and bobbed her head towards the door but Sophie noticed she was still smiling despite her previous comments about journalists.

A tall, lean man, in his thirties by the look of his clean-shaven, lightly tanned face, shoved the door open and almost fell over the threshold as he shook rain from his tousled, dark brown hair and black, leather jacket.

‘Morning Betty,’ he said, a cheeky smile plastered across his rather handsome face. He grabbed her by the shoulders and planted a kiss on her flushed cheek. ‘How’s my favourite girl this morning?’

Betty giggled and gave the man a playful shove. ‘Get away with you, Timothy. You’re soaked through. The usual, is it?’

‘Yes please. And a *mug* of coffee. Not one of those tiny, posh little cups.’

‘I know, I know.’ Betty shook her head but her smile stretched from ear to ear.

Timothy winked before Betty shuffled away, and immediately arched his brows as his gaze landed on Sophie.

‘Hello! I haven’t seen you before. Do you live around here and if so, how come I’ve missed you till now? I’m Timothy... Timothy Richards. May I? So much for “Flaming June”, eh? It’s a deluge out there.’

Before Sophie had a chance to respond, he’d removed his jacket, tossed it over a chair and plonked himself on the vacant seat opposite her, at the same time, tugging at the saturated legs of his jeans.

She was annoyed by his temerity. ‘Do you usually just barge into people’s lives without waiting to be invited?’

He raised one brow. ‘Yes,’ he said, before leaning forward and giving her a seductive smile. ‘I’m sure you’ve heard this a hundred times before, but you have really pretty eyes. Are they blue or grey? Or a mixture of both?’

Sophie looked away, blushing uncomfortably under such intense scrutiny from such a good-looking man, whose own eyes, she couldn’t help but notice, matched the dark blue T-shirt he was wearing. ‘It depends on my mood,’ she replied, truthfully.

‘And what mood are you in right now?’

'Not a good one. And I'd rather like to be on my own, if you don't mind.'

'But I do mind.'

Sophie darted a look at him and was cross to see him wink.

'Look,' he went on. 'It's been a shitty morning so far and it's only nine o'clock. A pretty face and some friendly conversation on this wet and windy Saturday is exactly what I need.'

'But it's not what *I* need. What *I* need is to be left alone. And believe me, your morning is probably nothing compared to mine.'

She glowered at him but he leant closer and smiled.

'Sorry to hear that. Let's compare. I'll tell you mine if you'll tell me yours.'

Sophie gasped. 'I don't want to be rude – although clearly you have no such qualms – but I really would like to be alone.'

He shrugged as if he was used to this response from people he accosted.

'Okay,' he said. 'I'm sorry if I've upset you. That wasn't my intention. But you really do have the prettiest eyes I've seen in a very long time. I hope your day improves.'

'Thank you. I hope yours does, too.'

She had a sudden pang of guilt and wondered whether she should tell him to stay, but a handsome man was the last thing she needed right now. Especially a handsome journalist. Journalists asked questions and she didn't want to answer any.

He shoved the chair back and leant over to grab his jacket but stopped; instead, he stared out the window and swivelled round to look at the door, leaving his jacket where it was.

Sophie glanced towards the door as it rattled open and

two young women followed by two young men, dashed in. She wondered why such an *olde-worlde* tearoom should attract so many people in their thirties. Perhaps it was the only one in Goldebury Bay. Surely not. She was certain there used to be three or four, at least. Although that was a long time ago and small resorts such as this hadn't fared well over the years. Besides, the last time she was here, she'd been more interested in ice cream parlours than tearooms and coffee shops.

She also wondered why Timothy seemed transfixed. The women were certainly attractive; the one with long, blonde, wavy hair more so than the one with the jet black bob, but he appeared to be staring at the men. And one man, in particular.

'I don't care what you say,' the blonde woman was saying. 'It isn't over until the fat lady sings – or in this case, the jury. I… oh!'

Sophie saw her scowl at Timothy.

'Morning all,' Timothy said. 'How are you all this morning?'

'As if you care,' the blonde woman hissed.

'Leave it, Poppy,' said the man whom Timothy was staring at. His deep, throaty voice sounded as if he carried the troubles of the world on his shoulders.

'But the man's a shit, Thaddeus,' the blonde said, looking at Sophie as if she were something not even a cat would drag in.

Sophie recognised the name immediately. Was this Thaddeus Beaumont? There couldn't be more than one Thaddeus in Goldebury Bay. She studied his profile intently.

He wasn't quite what she'd expected – although in many ways he was. She'd expected him to be tall but he seemed taller and broader in his faded jeans and blue and white

Gore-Tex jacket. He was definitely more handsome than she'd imagined. His thick, dark hair shone inky blue-black in the light from the wall lamps but as he turned his head in her direction, she noticed his olive skin showed signs of weariness. So did his serious-looking, chocolate-brown eyes. He definitely needed a shave, although the stubble added a certain something, she had to admit. For a split second, she could actually picture him, dressed head to toe in black, standing on the prow of his ancestor's pirate ship with the wind ruffling his hair, and an arrogant smile on his perfect lips. His long legs astride, his strong arms crossed and his loose-fitting shirt open to reveal a tanned, muscular chest…

'He's just doing his job, Poppy,' Thaddeus said. 'Don't let him provoke you.'

His gaze settled on Sophie, interrupting her thoughts. As his eyes met hers, a furrow formed between his brows. He looked away after just a moment and walked towards the table farthest from where she and Timothy sat. And she understood precisely why.

What she didn't understand was why she'd blushed and held her breath as he'd looked at her. It wasn't as if he could read her thoughts and he couldn't possibly know who she was. More importantly, he couldn't know why she was in Goldebury Bay, and she needed to keep it that way for as long as possible. Preferably until she'd found what she'd come here for. Or better still, until she'd left Goldebury Bay far behind her.

Chapter Two

'I'll move,' Timothy said, reaching for his jacket once again.

Now though, Sophie wanted him to stay. She leant towards him and keeping her voice low, said: 'They don't seem to like you much. Is that Thaddeus Beaumont?'

Timothy frowned. 'You're not a reporter, are you?'

'No. Just curious.'

He abandoned his jacket and leant forward placing both arms on the table, his face just inches from hers and grinned. 'So your eyes turn grey when you're curious?'

She tutted. 'I have no idea. Is it him?'

She tried not to look but her gaze turned towards Thaddeus. She felt the red hot flush fill her cheeks as their eyes met for a second time. Hastily she looked away, fiddling with a lock of yellow-gold hair, first pushing it behind her ear, and then tugging it loose to hide the blush of her cheeks and the small, but noticeable, crescent-shaped birthmark.

'It's him,' Timothy said. 'And now your eyes are blue … with flecks of silver and—'

'Will you please stop talking about my eyes!'

'Sorry,' Timothy said, the grin growing wider.

Betty headed towards their table, carrying a large tray. 'Here's your toast, dear, and your breakfast, Timothy. Just the way—' She stopped in her tracks. 'Oh! Good morning, Thaddeus. I didn't see you come in. And Oliver, Cleo...

Poppy. How lovely.'

For a moment, uncertainty overcame her but her waitressing skills soon kicked in and, with her smile glued back on, she delivered the toast, English breakfast and a large mug of steaming coffee to Sophie and Timothy.

'Thanks, Betty,' Timothy said. 'Would you bring us a pot of coffee, please? I think this young lady needs a refill.' He nodded towards Sophie's dainty cup.

'Of course,' Betty said as she shuffled towards the table where Thaddeus sat with his friends.

Timothy stared at Sophie's plate. 'Don't you want more than toast?'

'I'm not that hungry,' she lied. 'I'm just waiting for my car to be fixed.'

'Oh, what's wrong with it?'

'No idea. I'm not a mechanic. I'm hoping the guy at the garage is though.'

'At Mike's Motors? Mike's the best. That man can work magic. He fixed my car in no time, a couple of months back. And cheaply too,' Timothy said, tucking into his breakfast.

Once or twice as Sophie ate her toast, she felt her gaze drift towards Thaddeus and had to check herself. Was it guilt that made her keep looking at him? Or something else entirely?

She had to ask: 'Is that his girlfriend? Thaddeus, I mean and the beautiful blonde.'

Timothy's knife hovered over a thick rasher of bacon as he looked across at her. 'I didn't think you wanted friendly conversation. What's changed?'

Betty reappeared at that moment with the pot of coffee and they waited in silence whilst she placed it on the table.

'Let me know if you change your mind about the marmalade, dear or if there's anything else you need,' she said with her usual smile.

'Thanks Betty,' Timothy said, still looking at Sophie, and when Betty was out of earshot he continued: 'Don't tell me. That was before you saw Thaddeus Beaumont.'

'No I… What's that supposed to mean?'

He sighed and shook his head. 'Don't worry, he has that effect on most women. Of course, it probably worked out better for him when he was rich. Now that he's broke and unemployed – not to mention, homeless – he's not the catch he once was. But they're still attracted to him and he'll never have a problem finding a bed for the night, that's for sure.'

'I'm not attracted to him! I'm just curious, that's all. What with the trial and everything. He was suspected of involvement in the smuggling, I think I read, but they didn't have any evidence to charge him. What did you mean about him being broke, unemployed and homeless?'

She knew that feeling and instantly lowered her eyes, not wanting to give anything away. Timothy seemed to be studying her face a little too intently.

'Hmm,' he eventually said, pouring her a cup of coffee. 'If I'm going to tell you everything I know – and I suspect I'd willingly do that and a whole lot more – I think I should at least know your name.'

Sophie's face burned but she knew she had to give him that. 'It's Sophie.'

'Sophie…?'

'Just Sophie.'

'O-kay, *Just Sophie*, to answer your original question, the beautiful blonde, whose name is Poppy Taylor, would like to be his girlfriend from what I hear but Thaddeus seems a bit reluctant to commit, if you know what I mean. One-night stands are more his style, I gather. I suspect he and Poppy are 'friends with benefits' though. Rumour has it that he's still carrying a torch for Cleo, the other girl over there. They dated last year before this whole smuggling thing blew up. She's Cleo Merrifield and she lives with the other guy, Oliver Sutton, and to—'

'Sutton? Did you say, Oliver Sutton?' Sophie darted a look at the man with chestnut-brown hair who sat with his back to her. Thaddeus caught her looking and she hastily looked away.

'Y-es. Why?' Timothy frowned. 'Oh. You probably read about him in the papers, too. That he helped the police, leading up to the arrests and then that Hermione Beaumont accused him of being involved in the smuggling operation. It was touch and go whether he'd be charged because they found some of the stash hidden in the restaurant he owns. Everyone believed he was innocent though – including me oddly enough – and that Hermione had set him up. That was proved to be the case fairly quickly, fortunately for him. Although the rag I worked for at the time did drag it out a bit.'

'No I… I mean, yes. Yes, that was it. I read about both of them in the papers.'

'What amazes me is that they still haven't caught the other guy who actually was involved. That Geoffrey Hadleigh – the accountant. You'll have read he was arrested but released on bail and subsequently absconded. And there's another funny thing. He and Poppy were dating at the time.' Timothy shook his head and chuckled as if he found the whole story rather amusing.

'That's interesting. But you were going to tell me what you meant about Thaddeus being broke.' Sophie leant closer, forcing herself to look at Timothy and not let her gaze wander, yet again, in the direction of Thaddeus and his friends.

'Well, whether or not his dad, Jeremiah, is guilty of

drugs and tobacco smuggling, the old man has lost the lot and that means Thaddeus has, too. Thaddeus worked at Beaumont Boats, one of Jeremiah's businesses and virtually everything Thaddeus had, from the roof over his head to his car… oh wait. Not the car. I think he does own that. But everything else was owned by one or other of the family businesses. It seems Jeremiah had a bit of a gambling addiction. He'd been losing money hand over fist for years and he borrowed heavily against all the businesses. When his losing streak got worse, he simply siphoned money from anywhere he could. The banks were taking action even before he was arrested and the accounts were frozen. Between the gambling, the banks and... assuming he's found guilty, which is a foregone conclusion if you ask me – the possible confiscation orders under the Proceeds of Crime Act there'll be absolutely nothing left.'

'Nothing?' Sophie was horrified. She hadn't realised things were that serious for the Beaumonts. Her throat suddenly felt very dry and she took several gulps of the coffee Timothy had poured for her.

'Not a single penny. Unless they've got something stashed away somewhere and nobody knows about it.'

Sophie nearly choked on her coffee and silently cursed Timothy Richards. That was the problem with journalists: they had a way of getting to the truth. Sometimes without even realising.

Chapter Three

'Sorry, love. It's your fuel pump,' Mike of Mike's Motors informed Sophie on her return to the garage. 'Petrol wasn't getting to the engine. That's why it cut out.' He clonked shut the bonnet of a Toyota Land Cruiser he was working on and wiped his oily hands on an equally oil-ingrained, cloth.

The torrential rain had stopped and a warming sun popped up intermittently like a jack-in-the-box amongst the clouds but Mike's words left Sophie cold.

'That… that sounds expensive.'

'You won't get much change from five or six hundred quid. And that's just the part. There's my labour on top of that. Now don't start them waterworks again. That's the cost of a new one. My brother owns a vehicle scrapyard and we might be lucky enough to find you one for a fraction of that. But it might take a few days. I've called him and left a message.'

Sophie rubbed her tearful eyes. 'Thank you. And I'm not crying. It's the sun. I… I left my sunglasses in the car.'

'And not just them by the look of it. You doing a boot sale or something? Or are you like the wife? She packs everything bar the kitchen sink when we go on holiday.'

Sophie shook her head. 'I'm… moving. So, what will it cost if you're able to find a second-hand one?'

He rubbed his chin, leaving a grey smear just below his lip. 'Hmm. With parts and labour? Somewhere around two hundred, I should think. But I might be able to work some magic and get it done cheaper.'

Sophie seemed to have a lump in her throat, making it difficult to talk. 'That… that would be… great if you could. Thank you.'

It was a huge chunk out of her dwindling funds but what could she do? Her only alternative was to ask if he could arrange to tow the car to the house but that would probably cost almost as much and she'd still have no car. Did she really need one? She was reasonably fit, although Goldebury Bay was one of the hilliest places she'd ever been, but even this tiny resort had public transport. Not much she suspected but she'd seen at least one bus pass the window of Betty's Pantry when she was inside.

'You staying local? Or were you on your way somewhere else?' Mike asked. 'If you're local, you can leave it here for the weekend and think on it. There's room. Or you can get it towed to somewhere else. I close at twelve mind, so it'll be locked up tight till eight a.m. on Monday.'

'That's very kind. I'm staying locally. Um. You said your brother owns a vehicle scrap- yard. Does he – or do you – know anyone who might be interested in buying my car as it is? I know it'll be worth more once the repairs are done but… my funds are tight and I don't really need a car.'

Mike frowned. 'That's a bit drastic, love. You saying you can't scrape together a couple of hundred quid? Don't think I can do it much cheaper but I'll try. Things really that bad?'

Sophie saw genuine concern in his eyes and she shook her head. 'Just a thought. I may be here for several weeks and a car's not essential. Most things are within walking distance in a place like this. I'll probably be selling it at the end of the summer anyway, so…' She shrugged. 'It was just an idea.'

Mike nodded. 'Come back Monday after lunch and I'll let you know if we've found the part. And what you'd likely get for it, as is. Then you can decide what you want to do. Best not make any hasty decisions, as the wife's always telling me. Fair enough?'

'Thank you so much. I really appreciate everything you're doing.'

'It's no trouble, love. What're you doing about your things? They'll be safe here but you'll want to take what you'll need between now and Monday. Got the number of a cab firm if you need one.'

Could she afford the luxury of a cab? Not if she'd got to find two hundred pounds to repair her car. And a cab wouldn't take her all the way. It would stop when the tarmac ran out. She'd still have to drag her things through a quarter of a mile or so of mud. She resigned herself to the fact that this was yet another little twist of Fate and she was going to have to haul what she needed, to the house, on foot.

'Thanks, but I can walk. It's not that far. I may need to do a couple of trips though, if that's okay with you.'

'That's fine with me. But you sure you want to walk? Where're you staying?'

Mike had been so helpful and Sophie didn't want to lie. Not unless she had no choice. 'At a place called Summerhill,' she said, wondering what his reaction would be.

'Summerhill! You sure? Must have the wrong address, love. Old Silas isn't one for visitors.'

So Mike hadn't heard? She wondered if anyone in Goldebury Bay knew. If not, she could keep quiet about it for now. But was that just another form of lying? She decided it was. Everyone would know sooner or later in any event.

'Silas Summerhill passed away on Monday,' she said. 'I… I'm here for the funeral, next week. His solicitors have kindly allowed me to stay at the house.'

She'd expected Mike to react as he had – with astonishment and disbelief – when she'd mentioned she was staying at Summerhill. She hadn't expected open-mouthed silence.

'I'm sorry,' a deep male voice said. 'I couldn't help but overhear. Did you say Silas Summerhill is dead?'

Sophie spun round; now it was her mouth that fell open. Thaddeus Beaumont was standing just outside Mike's workshop, his brows furrowed and a look of something akin to sadness in his eyes.

'How long have you been there?' She hadn't meant to shriek but it suddenly struck her that he may have overheard a great deal more.

'Not long. Was someone with him?'

'What?' She couldn't take her eyes from his.

'At the end. Was someone with him when he passed? I'd hate to think he died alone. But you may not know, of course. Sorry. I'm rambling. It's a bit of a shock. I thought the old goat… I mean… I'd thought he'd live forever.'

'You and me both,' she said.

'Are you a relative?' Mike had found his voice.

Sophie's instinct for self-preservation kicked in. Ignoring Mike's question, she snapped out of the seemingly trance-like state Thaddeus' presence appeared to have induced and stared at Thaddeus.

'Forgive me for asking,' she said, suddenly fearful that he had followed her, 'but what are you doing here? Do you want something?'

He looked confused. 'I've come to collect my car,' he

said, nodding in the direction of the Land Cruiser that Mike had been working on. 'But you were here first so I waited. I didn't mean to butt in but when I heard Silas' name I—'

'Had to poke your nose in.' She turned her back to him and forced a smile at Mike. 'I'll give you the keys when I've taken what I need from my car. Thank you again for everything.'

Mike scratched his balding head as if he wasn't at all sure what was going on. 'Right you are.'

She spun round again and met Thaddeus' look of astonishment. She could easily have walked around him in the open frontage of the workshop but she stood her ground. 'Excuse me,' she said, holding her head high.

He stepped aside without a word but as she headed towards her car which was still on the forecourt exactly where it had broken down, she heard him say: 'Well that told me, didn't it? She's obviously upset about Silas. I can't believe the old bugger's dead. It's the end of an era.'

'I can't believe anyone'd go to his funeral,' Mike said. 'Let alone a pretty young thing like that.'

'Life can be very strange. Anyway, how much do I owe you?'

'You don't owe me a bean. I told you, Thaddeus. You fixed our boat, I'll fix your car. So, Silas Summerhill's dead. Wait till I tell the wife.'

Sophie glanced back towards the workshop but Thaddeus had gone inside and she could no longer hear what was being said. She let out a long, meaningful sigh. She shouldn't have snapped at him; there was no call for that. And she was clearly getting paranoid by thinking that he'd followed her. Why would he? She was so worried he might find out what she was really doing here that she'd immediately gone on the defensive. That was stupid. She might need his help at some stage. The plan was to keep him off the scent and avoid him if possible, not make him dislike her intensely.

She'd got to get a grip. She was letting her emotions get the better of her and nothing good ever came of that. Look what happened the last time she did that. But she didn't want to think about Trent Godly – who'd be swanning around New York by now. And she definitely didn't want to think about the fire.

She hauled one of her suitcases from the boot and balanced the box of groceries on the car roof. Why couldn't her life be simple? It seemed to go from one drama to another. It was almost enough to make her believe in the curse of the Summerhills; and what a prospect that was... to either meet an early death or end up miserable and alone.

And here she was again, letting her emotions run away with her.

She slammed the boot shut. Believing in Fate was one thing; believing in silly, ancient curses was a different thing entirely and she'd got to stop that. Right now. Right this second. There was no such thing as the Summerhill curse. They just had more than their fair share of bad luck. But that would change this summer. She was going to make sure of that.

She shoved the car keys in her handbag, extended the pull-handle on her suitcase, balanced the box of groceries under her arm and headed towards the ninety steps to Summerhill.

She'd make it up those steps, no matter what.

Chapter Four

Sophie turned right out of the garage and marched towards the seafront, her mind in a whirl. Her plan had been to arrive at Summerhill this morning and to keep away from prying eyes and awkward questions. To pretend to be a tourist, interested in both the present Beaumonts, because of the trials and the Beaumonts of old, because of the tales of smuggling, piracy and heroism. To feign an interest in all things Tudor, particularly Elizabethan and especially paintings and jewellery. And to somehow find a way to meet the descendants of the Beaumonts, the Suttons and the Pollards in the hope of discovering all she could about the ancient feud between those families. That was her plan.

Instead, she'd met Betty, who was possibly Goldebury Bay's biggest gossip; a good-looking journalist who seemed very interested in her eyes and knew a great deal about the Beaumonts. She'd seen Oliver, a Sutton descendant; been rude to Thaddeus; told Thaddeus and Mike (who both knew Betty, the gossip) that Silas Summerhill was dead and that she was staying at his house. Basically, her plan had been turned upside down and she wondered what would go wrong next.

The wind picked up as she neared the promenade, and the salty smell of the sea mixed with the fetid odour of putrescent seaweed assaulted her nostrils. The sun's reflection in the puddles on the pavements disappeared and she glanced skywards. A massive, gunmetal-grey cloud hovered overhead like some sort of alien spaceship in the movies. Moments later, the heavens opened for the second time and bullets of rain hailed down on Sophie and the rest of Goldebury Bay.

'Fabulous,' she said, as rivulets of water ran down her face and seeped beneath her denim jacket. Her T-shirt seemed to think it was a sponge and her red, cotton skirt flapped around her pale, bare legs like a red rag to a bull. 'That's just bloody fabulous!'

With her head bent, rain squelching between her toes in her open-fronted sandals, and the roar of thunder in her ears, she hurried along the pavement as best she could. She didn't see or hear the car and she stepped off the curb of the narrow road, right in front of it. Luckily for her, it had been slowing down to a stop but she still jumped when she saw how close it was. She expected the driver to shout at her for not looking where she was going.

'Want a lift?' Thaddeus asked, his window down just enough for her to hear.

Without waiting for her response, he switched off the engine and jumped out. Grabbing the box of groceries from her, he ran to the back, tossing the box inside. She stood in stunned silence, dripping from head to toe like a melting ice sculpture; he took the suitcase and did the same with that. It was only when his firm hand gripped hers and he started leading her to the car's passenger side that she reacted.

'What *are* you doing? I'm not going anywhere with you!' Her abrupt halt seemed to surprise him as much as her remarks.

'Are you mad? Do you want to get pneumonia or something? Get in.' He half-dragged, half-lifted her into the passenger seat, shut the door and raced back to the driver's side. A hint of irritation flashed across his eyes as he passed her a towel he'd retrieved from the back seat. 'What is wrong with you, woman?'

She blinked several times clutching the towel to her chest. 'What is wrong with *me*? A complete stranger abducts me and he asks what's wrong with *me*!' She threw the towel back at him, turned towards the door and reached for the handle but his hand came across and caught her wrist, tugging her round to face him.

Adrenaline pumped through her as he stared at her, an odd look in his eyes. But it wasn't fear-induced – and neither was her racing heart.

'I'm not a complete stranger,' he said, dropping the towel back on her lap with his other hand, 'and let's be honest here, you couldn't keep your eyes off me in Betty's Pantry. If you hadn't been with that Timothy Richards guy and also flirting with him, I'd have seriously thought my luck was in. And just now, at Mike's, before you bit my head off, I—'

'What?' She couldn't believe her ears. 'For your information, I wasn't *with* Timothy Richards. I only met him this morning and he just came and sat with me. I wasn't flirting with him – or you – and I have no idea what made you think I was!'

'Then why did you keep looking at me and blushing?'

Sophie gasped. 'Because… because Timothy told me all about you and I've never seen a man who's a member of a crime syndicate and a smuggler, before. I was curious.'

His eyes flashed and his fingers tightened around her wrist. 'I'm not a smuggler and my family is not a crime syndicate. No one's been found guilty of anything yet, despite what Timothy Richards may have told you. What else did he tell you? That I'm penniless and unemployed?' He glanced towards the rain streaming down the windscreen, at the same time lessening his grip on Sophie's wrist.

'And homeless – although he said you'd never have a problem finding a bed for the night.'

'Oh he did, did he?' An odd smile crept onto his lips and when he looked at her again, his eyes sparkled.

'Yes,' she said. 'The only thing he forgot to mention was that you abduct women to do so.'

He grinned. 'I don't need to abduct women, believe me. And I can tell the difference between a woman who is giving me the come-on and one who's wondering whether I'm a criminal or not. You had 'come-hither' written all over your beautiful, blushing cheeks.'

'I *did not*! I have no interest whatsoever in going to bed with you, and if you think I have, you're deluded.'

His laughter affected her almost as much as his voice, his touch and his eyes, and although she glowered at him, she felt the warm flood of attraction course through her veins. She was on dangerous ground here. She needed to get away. Fast.

She took a deep breath and hastily continued: 'And, if you actually think you can pick me up off the street like some prostitute or something, then you really have lost the plot. You're not a criminal, you're insane.'

He shrugged. 'From what I overheard at Mike's, I thought you could use the money.' He didn't try to hide his sarcasm.

'You arrogant bastard!' She grabbed the towel with her left hand and used it as a makeshift whip, catching him on the shoulder. 'If you don't let go of my wrist this minute, you'll live to regret it. You may be much stronger than me but I'll scream my head off till someone comes to my rescue.'

He looked genuinely surprised, both to be struck by the towel and also to see his fingers still clasped around her flesh. He immediately released her.

'I'm sorry! I didn't realise I still... It felt... Sorry. I hope I didn't hurt you.'

'You didn't hurt me,' she said, rubbing her wrist.

He cleared his throat. 'Look, I think we got off to a bad start. You're probably upset about Silas and I've been behaving like a complete moron. I thought we could both do with a bit of cheering up, that's all. I was teasing you. I apologise. Let's start again.'

'I'm not upset about Silas. I'm... I'm upset about being bundled into your car.'

'But it's pouring out there. I thought you'd appreciate a lift.'

'Then you should've asked. Not just grabbed me like... like some caveman.'

Sophie glowered at him but he merely grinned.

'I did ask. I said: "Want a lift?"'

'But you didn't wait for my answer, did you? You just assumed I'd go with you. Just like that.'

'Er...' He frowned but his lips twitched. 'I'm not trying to drag you back to my cave or anything. I'm merely offering you a lift. If you'd rather walk in the pouring rain, please, don't let me stop you. But you're right. I should've waited for your reply.'

She hung her head and tugged at the hem of her saturated skirt. 'Yes. You should.'

Fate certainly did like playing games, she thought. Thaddeus Beaumont was the one person in Goldebury Bay that she hoped to avoid for as long as possible, yet from almost the moment she'd set foot in the place, everywhere she went, Thaddeus wasn't far behind.

'O-kay. Now you're in my car, let me take you to the house. I heard you say you're staying at Summerhill. I promise I won't lay a hand on you and you'll be perfectly safe. I'll even get Poppy, or Cleo and Oliver to come with us if that would make you feel easier. I mean, safer.'

He could put her future happiness in jeopardy in more ways than one and she must try to stay away from him but as the rain drummed out a rhythm on the roof, she reasoned that accepting a lift was better than dragging her things through this weather. Reluctantly, she nodded and reached for the seat belt. Five more minutes in his company couldn't hurt… could it?

'Thank you,' she said. 'D'you know where you're going?'

She patted her face and hair with the towel, grateful now for its soft, dry texture.

'Life's an adventure,' he said with a grin.

She tutted. 'I meant, do you know the way to Summerhill? It's on the cliff called Summer Hill, obviously, but the house is down a private road. Oh, I see you have satnav.'

'I know where it is and how to get there, probably better than the satnav does, but at the risk of being accused of poking my nose in your business again, is there anything else you need from your car? It seemed pretty jam-packed and if there is, I'm happy to get it now. Better one journey than two.'

She threw him a sideways glance. 'You… you'd do that?'

'I'm a sucker for a pretty face. Sorry, I can't help myself. Seriously, it's hardly a big deal, is it?'

'That's… very kind,' she said, avoiding his eyes and dabbing at her jacket.

'My pleasure.' He started the car and turned back towards Mike's Motors. 'You see, I told you I don't need to abduct women. They come of their own free will. And before you jump out of the car, that was a joke. I'll shut up now.'

'That's probably a very good idea.'

Chapter Five

Sophie couldn't help but smile although she turned her face towards the window so that Thaddeus wouldn't see. She could understand why women fell for him. His chat-up lines – if that's what they were – left a lot to be desired... but his charm, undeniable good looks, and his thoughtful, friendly demeanour made up for that.

What she didn't understand was why Fate seemed to be throwing them together. She would have to be very careful. Both she and Thaddeus had had their worlds turned upside down. Both had lost virtually everything. Both had to carve out new futures for themselves. But unlike Thaddeus, she had a chance of finding a fortune; a fortune that possibly didn't belong to her. And if Thaddeus found out, she could lose it.

There was no way she was going to let that happen.

Yet here she was, sitting in his car.

Life was strange indeed.

Just two months ago, she was living with her now ex-fiancé, Trent Godly in his apartment in Chelsea, with no money worries, a well-paid if somewhat tedious job in Trent's art gallery, and a comfortable future ahead of her.

Yesterday, she was living in her friend Amanda's spare room for the third week running, with hardly any money or possessions, no job and very little to look forward to.

Today she was in Goldebury Bay, sitting beside the one man she had planned to avoid and being driven – via

Mike's Motors – to the ancestral home of the Summerhill family, all of whom were dead but her.

And tomorrow – well, probably not tomorrow but sometime very soon – she'd find the Summerhill treasure, sell it and head to the Caymans, to be with her mum and her mum's current boyfriend, Hugh.

And her future would be bright... very bright indeed. All because her great-uncle Silas had just dropped dead.

Well, not all because Silas was dead. The ex-fiancé part had nothing to do with Silas. Unless you believed in the Summerhill curse… which she didn't, of course.

'So what do you need?' Thaddeus said, interrupting her thoughts. 'All of it, I guess.'

She realised they were back at the garage and she nodded. 'Pretty much. If that's okay.'

It was still pouring, but Thaddeus pulled up inside the open-fronted workshop right next to her car.

'How did my car get in here? Did Mike manage to get it started?'

Thaddeus smiled. 'Mike's good but he's not that good. I helped him push it in before I came to pick you up.'

'You… you came to pick me up? Because it started raining?' She wasn't sure which surprised her more. That they'd moved her car in a matter of minutes, or that Thaddeus had specifically come to her rescue.

'No. I was going to pick you up anyway. I came out to offer you a lift but you'd already gone. I told you, I thought my luck was in.' He winked and got out. 'Chuck the towel on the back seat if you've finished with it.'

He opened the tailgate and, as she helped him transfer her belongings from her car to his, Mike appeared, stirring a cup of coffee and offered his assistance.

'You drink your coffee,' Thaddeus said. 'We'll have this done in no time.'

He was right about that. It may have looked a lot in her small car but there were only a couple more suitcases, eight boxes, and a few black sacks. All her worldly goods. Not even she had realised she possessed so little.

Sophie handed Mike her car keys and said she'd see him on Monday afternoon. She even gave him her mobile number in case he needed to contact her, although she hadn't intended to and had no idea why she did.

'Isn't that one of the friends you were with earlier?' Sophie pointed to Oliver who was coming out of a place called Posh Pets, across the road from the garage.

'Yeah. He's collecting Cleover. He'd dropped her off for a quick trim before breakfast.'

He waved but Oliver was busy dragging the black Labrador out of a huge puddle the dog had just leapt into. It happened to be in front of the second bus Sophie had seen in Goldebury Bay, which came squealing to a halt.

'Does that dog have a death wish?' Sophie asked.

'You don't know the half of it,' Thaddeus said. 'Oliver!' he yelled. 'D'you want a lift?'

Having got his dog under control and waved his thanks to the bus driver, Oliver looked across at Thaddeus. He smiled and shouted back: 'No thanks. Cleo went to get the car. She'll be back any second. See you tonight.' He dashed under an overhang to shelter from the rain.

'Okay.' Thaddeus waved and turned to smile at Sophie. 'It's just you and me then.'

'Don't get any ideas,' she said, grinning at him as she clambered back into his car. She glanced towards Oliver. She needed to get an introduction to him at some point in time, or preferably his dad, or possibly his granddad if he was still alive. The older the better for her purposes. 'He seems nice.'

Thaddeus started the car. 'Oliver? He is. He's my best

friend.' He grinned. 'That sounded rather soppy. I mean we've been friends all our lives.'

'And… the girl in the tearoom this morning. The one with jet black hair. She lives with him?'

'Cleo? Yes.' He looked both ways down the narrow street, gave a final wave to Mike and then to Oliver and turned towards the seafront. 'Was that a lucky guess or did Timothy Richards tell you that?'

She lowered her eyes. 'Timothy told me.'

'Hmm. And I suppose he told you that Poppy is my girlfriend.'

'No. Actually he didn't. He said you're friends.'

'We are. And good friends.'

'Yes. That's what Timothy said.' She tugged at the hem of her wet skirt once again. 'He also said that you used to date Cleo.' She saw the look he shot her.

'I bet he did. It's a long and rather complicated story and one I won't bore you with but yes, I dated Cleo. But not for long. It was last summer before the… well, before things went mad. She and Oliver had been in love with one another forever though and we all knew it. They finally got together in September.'

'And you didn't mind?'

'I'm very happy for them. But I bet that's not what Timothy Richards told you, is it?'

Sophie felt she should change the subject. 'Did you say their dog's called Cleover or Clover?'

He stopped at a set of traffic lights and looked at her until the lights turned green. 'She's called Cleover. She was called Cleo but they changed it when they got together. It's a combination of Cleo and Oliver.'

'How quaint.'

Thaddeus gave her an odd look. 'It's romantic.'

'Is it?'

'Well, isn't it?'

'Don't ask me. I don't have a romantic bone in my body,' she lied.

He raised his brows. 'You're not into romance then? Not a 'hearts and flowers' kind of girl?'

'More a 'feet on the ground, love's just a chemical reaction,' kind.'

'I'm surprised.'

'Why? You've only just met me. Have you been making assumptions? Or are you one of those guys who thinks all women are into romance and we're simply all the same?'

Thaddeus burst out laughing and shook his head. 'No. I've learnt from experience that all women are definitely *not* the same.'

'And you've had a lot of experience.'

'Now that sounds like you're making assumptions about me.'

She met his frank look with one of her own. 'No assumptions. Just repeating what I've heard. Are you saying it isn't true?'

'It depends what you've heard. I presume your source is once again, the intrepid reporter of gossip, Timothy Richards. Did the two of you spend the whole time talking about me? I don't know whether to be flattered or annoyed.'

'I can assure you we spent less than five minutes discussing you. But it wasn't just Timothy who said it. You virtually said as much yourself when you picked me up.'

He shrugged. 'I'll admit I've had a lot of girlfriends.'

'Hmm. Are they classed as "girlfriends" if you only spend one night with them? I didn't know that.'

He didn't respond immediately but when he stopped at another set of lights, his eyes held something that made her feel uneasy and she wondered if she'd gone a step too far.

Then his mouth curved into a broad grin.

'Unless you pay them – which I don't – I believe they are. That's what I call them, anyway.'

'But do you ever call them? Afterwards, I mean?'

Why couldn't she stop herself asking him questions? Why couldn't she just sit quietly and take in the scenery as they drove along the seafront and up towards Summer Hill cliff? Why couldn't she stop wondering what it would feel like to spend the night with him?

Thaddeus coughed. 'Are you writing my biography or something? Or are you interested in finding out for yourself?'

Could he read her mind? She turned to face the window.

'Neither, I assure you. Just making polite conversation.'

'If prying into my sex life is your idea of polite conversation, I won't be taking you home for tea with Mother.'

'As your mum's in Spain, I don't think that's likely anyway and I'm hardly prying. You were the one who brought up your sex life originally, remember? Besides, it seems it's public knowledge and you don't appear to try to keep it a secret.'

'How do you know where my mum is? Just how much did that bloody guy tell you? Never mind. Don't answer that. And I don't believe in secrets. They cause nothing but trouble. But you do, don't you, Sophie? You're definitely hiding something… and I'd really like to find out what that is.'

Sophie gasped. 'How do you know—'

'Your name?'

That hadn't occurred to her; she wanted to know why he thought she had a secret but now that he'd said it, how *did* he know her name?

He reached up and brushed the birthmark on her right

cheek with his fingers before continuing. 'You don't remember me at all, do you? This does wonders for my already deflated ego, I can tell you.'

She had no idea what he was talking about. She hadn't set eyes on him until today, and once she'd stop quivering from his touch, she said so.

He shook his head. 'I'd like to think I helped save your life. But perhaps that's just me being dramatic, or wanting to play the hero. It was years ago. I was thirteen and you were about eight or nine. I can't recall exactly. You fell from the cliff beside the steps to Summerhill. You'd climbed over the fence and edged your way along for some reason, but you lost your footing and fell into the sea. I was in a boat just a few yards out with my uncle Theodore. We pulled you from the water and I gave you the kiss of life. You opened your eyes and I don't think I'll ever forget the smile you gave me.' He grinned again. 'I'm even better at it now, if you ever want a repeat performance. Kissing, that is. Not saving lives.'

'That was you!'

She couldn't believe it. It was true; she had been rescued after falling from the cliffs into the sea when she was nine. But she had no recollection of her rescuers and a few days after, she and her mother had left Summerhill and Goldebury Bay, at her great-uncle Silas' request.

'Uh-huh. Do you remember it?'

'I don't remember a thing but Mum told me what happened. Well. It seems I owe you for more than just a lift in the rain. But… are you telling me you recognised me after all these years?'

He laughed. 'You're joking. Although that *would* be very romantic, wouldn't it? Even you'd have to admit that. If I say yes, will you offer me a bed for the night?' He winked. 'No, seriously, I didn't recognise you but I did notice your birthmark and I knew I'd seen it before, I just couldn't think where. It was only when we were at Mike's and I heard you say that Silas had died and you were here for the funeral, that I started putting two and two together. I knew that your dad died when you were young and that Silas didn't have many – if any – other living relatives. His sister – your gran – died a few years back, I heard. So that left you. But it was only a few minutes ago that your name came back to me.'

'This is unbelievable. You, of all people. Fate really does play games, doesn't it?'

'Hey! It could've been worse. Uncle Theo could've kissed you. Now that, you would remember. He ate a lot of garlic in those days. Don't ask me why but he did. Out of interest, d'you remember why you were scaling those cliffs? It seemed like a really dumb thing to do.'

She knew precisely why, but she had no intention of sharing the information. Especially not with the man she'd just discovered had saved her life.

Chapter Six

Summerhill may have been the ancestral home of the Summerhill family for generations but it was certainly no *Downton Abbey*. It was more fitting of the servants' quarters, Sophie thought as she and Thaddeus approached it.

They'd left the tarmacked part of the private road and were now trundling along the old dirt road which, due to the heavy rain resembled a quagmire, not a road. Even in dry weather it was more suitable terrain for horses than for cars and if Thaddeus hadn't had his Land Cruiser they would never have made it past the first few feet. She was thankful that she hadn't wasted money on a cab. She would have been unceremoniously dumped at the spot where the tarmac ended.

'It seems smaller than I remember,' she said, her eyes scanning the whitewashed, rear wall and the leaded-light windows from a distance.

She could picture most of the ten bedrooms, four reception rooms, Great Hall and large kitchen like a slide show in her mind and could recall that there were eight windows at the back and an equal number to the front. Granny Summerhill, her dad's mum had told her once that when the house was built in the mid-15th century, the Summerhills had wanted to see anyone who approached the house from both land and sea. Not that many people probably ever did approach, Sophie thought now. From what she'd discovered after hours of family history research, added to everything her gran had told her, the Summerhills were always a pretty unfriendly bunch – with the exception of Granny Summerhill.

'It's definitely in a worse state of repair than it was the last time you were here,' Thaddeus said.

'I didn't think that was possible.' She noticed the odd look he gave her. 'I never liked this place. It was always cold and damp and I remember the wind howled through the corridors like a banshee. And that was during the summer months. We never visited in winter.'

'Big houses are all the same,' Thaddeus said. 'When you're brought up in one, you get used to all the odd noises they make. Beaumont Hall sounded as if it had its own orchestra sometimes. Very heavy on the *woodwind* section. The floorboards could creak out a symphony of their own, let alone when the panelled walls, doors and window frames joined in.'

Sophie studied his profile. 'Do you… do you miss it? Has it definitely gone?'

He turned and gave her a tight smile. 'The house or the money?' He shrugged. 'It's early days, so I'm not sure I've got used to it all yet. The house has definitely gone. It seems, in his never ending quest to liquidise assets, Dad got his solicitors to find a way to break the trust. Which probably wasn't that difficult, knowing our lot. The Beaumonts were never known for dotting i's and crossing t's. Although Dad dotted lots of i's when he took out all the mortgages and loans. Hundreds of IOUs.'

'Doesn't it bother you that your dad took your inheritance? Something that was rightfully yours?'

He shook his head. 'I'm not bothered about the house. I never wanted it. I'd have given part of it to my sister, Mercedes and the kids to live in. And her husband Turner, of course. And part of it to Mum. Although naturally,' he said with a grin, 'I'd have kept the best part for myself. To impress women. Take them back to the ancestral home and show them the family silver. We didn't stretch to gold, unfortunately. But it's gone, so that's that.'

'Do you make light of everything? Doesn't any of this bother you?' Sophie couldn't believe it. She'd have been furious if she were in his shoes.

'What's the point? There's nothing I can do about it. And it wasn't all bad. The bank screwed up regarding Mum so they had to effectively 'buy her out'. She had rights as far as occupation goes so at least she got some cash. Quite a bit of cash, in fact. To be honest, I miss Beaumont Boats the most. I loved that place. I'd have still been working there on my hundredth birthday if I'd had my way. But that's gone too, so…'

'And there's nothing you can do to get it back?'

'Nope. It was also mortgaged to the hilt. Most of the boats we worked on were other people's and the few we were building, along with the family yacht we owned, were sold. The purchaser closed the business and that was that. When we looked at the books for the rest of the businesses, we discovered that Geoff Hadleigh, our accountant, had done some very impressive, creative accounting. He was also involved in the smuggling although he's done a disappearing act. I think the only things the Beaumont family actually owns now are a few trinkets that Dad had given to Mum and those strangely enough, are covered by another family trust that not even Dad and his snazzy lawyers could break, and a couple of paintings that belong to Uncle Theo. Although he'll probably sell them because he's broke too, thanks to Dad. There were a few pieces of furniture that I wanted to keep and fortunately, I was able to do that.'

'I'm so sorry.'

'That's life. Sometimes we're up. Sometimes we're down. They're only possessions. I'm more upset about what it's done to my family. As you've already heard, Mum's gone back to Spain for a while to get away from all the hoo-ha. Mercedes and the kids went too. Mercedes is pregnant again and Turner's on deployment. He's in the Navy. None of us wanted her to be under any stress. I'm still in shock about Dad, I think, although we'd been drifting apart for a while and I should've known that something peculiar was going on. I'm not sure I can ever forgive him for the pain he's caused Mum and Mercedes and his own brother, Theo, as well as me. But mainly for what he's done to Mum. He had a mistress and…' He shot her an anxious look. 'God! I need to put a cork in it! I don't know why I'm boring you with all this stuff. It just came pouring out.'

'It's not boring but it must be tough to cope with. Perhaps you needed to get it off your chest.'

He looked very worried. 'To a total stranger?'

'I'm not a total stranger. You said that when you picked me up earlier.' She winked and gave him a friendly smile.

'But still. I hardly know you. I honestly don't know why I told you all that. I'd really appreciate it if you didn't tell Timothy Richards what I said. Especially not about Dad's mistress. I don't think he knows about her yet. I shouldn't have told you any of it.' He shook his head as if he had serious regrets.

She could see he was very concerned and she instinctively reached out and touched his hand as he clenched the steering wheel.

'You don't have to worry. I won't tell Timothy Richards any of it. You have my word. I'm glad you told me. I'm just sorry you've had to go through it all. I won't repeat a thing, I promise.'

He seemed to relax slightly as he met her eyes. 'Thanks. I greatly appreciate that.'

'You're welcome. And I told you, I only met the guy this morning when he sat at my table. I'll probably never see him again anyway.'

'I wouldn't bet on that. From the way he was looking at you, I'd say he's more interested in you than he is in my family. And as he's now writing a book about them, he's pretty interested, I can tell you. Which is why I want him to know as little as possible.'

'He's writing a book about your family!' Sophie was horrified by the thought, although probably not, for the same reasons as Thaddeus. She wondered just how much Timothy Richards knew about the Beaumonts. 'Your entire family, past and present?'

Thaddeus shook his head. 'Don't know. I avoid him if at all possible. I've no doubt that great-great-several greats-Grandad, the notorious privateer-cum-pirate, Barnabus, will feature heavily. You know, where the family tradition of rape and plunder all began. Well, kidnapping, smuggling and stealing from the Spanish but legend has it that he was also a bit of a one for the ladies and he didn't always ask… apparently. I'm sure Mr Richards will wangle some connection with Dad and Barnabus and seducing women, especially if he finds out about the mistress.'

'I can promise you he won't find out from me,' she said.

'Thanks.' He smiled again, broader this time. 'And don't believe everything that guy tells you. For example, he told you I'm homeless and I'm not. I can move in with you.' He gave her a playful nudge. 'Don't look so horrified. It was a joke. I've got my own place. It's not quite Beaumont Hall, but it's mine, so I don't know why he said that. And from the looks of your ancestral home, you'd be better off spending the night at my place than you would here. I'd sleep on the sofa,' he added with a wink.

Sophie grinned but as they got closer she spotted the cracks in the walls and the boards at a couple of the windows and thought that she'd probably be more comfortable spending the night anywhere but here.

'I like what Silas has done with it,' she said.

'DIY was never Silas' strong suit. Nor was spending money.'

He pulled up in front of the aged, oak double doors which had clearly taken a pounding from the elements over the centuries.

'At least it's stopped raining.' Sophie glanced skywards as the sun broke through the clouds. 'That's one good thing.'

'I'm poking my nose in here again but… do you inherit the house? Tell me to mind my own business if you'd rather not say.'

Sophie was staring at one of the wrought iron, door knockers. She was sure the lion had winked at her but it was obviously a trick of the light; probably just a glint of sunlight bouncing off its large, otherwise forbidding, face. The other one looked as aggressive as she remembered. She turned to look at Thaddeus.

'Now you *are* joking. He told Mum and me, years ago, that he was leaving everything to charity. And he doesn't have to find a way to breach a trust – there isn't one. Well, not as far as the house goes anyway. As you know, Dad died just after my birth. Silas never liked Mum for some reason and he definitely didn't like me. I always thought it was because I was a girl, not a boy, and, unless I have a child and keep my name, the Summerhill name will die with me. I'm the last of the line because all Dad's lot are dead.'

'Now there's a cheerful thought,' Thaddeus said, getting out of the car. 'I'm not sure Silas liked anyone, did he? He used to shoot at visitors with an air rifle from his bedroom window. Did you know that?'

Sophie smirked. 'He said he'd shoot us if we ever came back. He really was a miserable old sod.'

'He must've been lonely. I don't think he went out much over the last few years and visitors never came twice.' Their eyes met and they both grinned. 'What a way to live.'

'I hope I never get like him,' Sophie said.

'You're almost as grouchy as he was,' Thaddeus teased.

'I know where he kept that rifle. I'd be careful if I were you.'

'Where's the fun in that? Although having seen what you can do with a towel, perhaps I should.'

Their eyes held and Sophie knew she had to get Thaddeus to leave. He already felt like a friend – and she couldn't let that happen. But from the look in his eyes, friendship wasn't all Thaddeus Beaumont had in mind – and that was an absolute, no-no as far as she was concerned.

'Thanks for all your help, Thaddeus,' she said, walking towards the rear of the car. 'If you'll just help me get this stuff out, I can take it from here.'

'I'll help you in with it. You do have a key, I suppose?'

'No, I thought I'd just break in. Of course I have a key. Well, I don't. But the solicitors told me where it is. Great-uncle Silas may not have liked visitors but he did have one of those *Lifeline* alarm things. You know, where you're connected to the emergency services by a push button device and where you leave a key outside in a secure little box. They gave me the code.'

'You might find the old bugger changed it so they couldn't get in.'

Sophie grinned. 'Not even Silas was that stupid. He also had a cleaner apparently, so the solicitors told me. Now I bet that surprises you.'

Thaddeus raised his brows. 'It does. I wonder what she did. Judging by the grime on the windows, she definitely didn't clean those.'

He helped Sophie retrieve her belongings and carried them to the front door. She punched the code into the security box and retrieved the key. The double doors creaked open with a little help from Thaddeus' upper-body strength.

'When did the cleaner last visit?' Thaddeus asked. 'If she could open these doors, I'd like to meet her.'

The pungent smell of damp and something rotting wafted out on an invisible cloud.

'What is that awful smell?' Sophie said, shivering.

'Um. They haven't left Silas here, have they? Sorry, that was in bad taste.'

Sophie gagged. 'So is this. I feel as if I've swallowed whatever it is.' She coughed to clear her throat and immediately screamed as a black streak shot past her legs, knocking her off balance.

Thaddeus reached out to steady her. 'It's only a cat. And there's your culprit, I suspect. You'll probably find a few dismembered bodies scattered about the place.'

She took a deep breath and grinned. 'And those are just the ones Silas left. I wonder if the cat brought any in. Do you think it's been locked in? Oh the poor thing. Did you see where it went?' She searched about her but there was no sign of it.

Thaddeus shook his head. 'No, but I don't think it's been trapped inside. Even if the cleaner hasn't been near, the undertakers would have and besides, not all the broken windows have been boarded up. It could've got in and out of one of those, I'm sure. I noticed at least one of the panes on the ground floor at the rear is missing. These panes of leaded lights aren't large enough for a human to get through but they're plenty big enough for a cat.'

'You're right. Thanks again. I can manage from here.'

He tipped his head to one side. 'Are you trying to get rid of me?'

'No. But I've taken up enough of your time and you must have better things to do.'

He stepped closer and leant forward and she instinctively backed away. He grinned and picked up one of the boxes. 'Just getting this. And no, I can't think of anything better than helping a damsel in distress.'

She felt her face burn; even her toes were tingling. For just one second, she'd thought he was going to kiss her and although she'd backed away, part of her had really hoped he would, even though she knew she mustn't get involved with him.

'You'd better go and look for one then,' she said, trying to ignore her pounding heart.

'Why don't I go and look for the kitchen instead? I'll make some coffee while you change out of those wet clothes. You're soaked. Besides, you never know what else may be lurking in the shadows. I really think I should check the place over, don't you? And what I really mean by that is, I've been dying to see inside this place since I was a kid. Please let me have a look around.'

He pulled a face somewhere between a sulky child and a cute puppy, and Sophie burst out laughing.

'Come on then. Be my knight in shining armour.'

What harm could it do? To turn him away might make him even more curious. He wouldn't find anything just by looking around the house... although that might not be true. She'd found something when she was nine and was looking around the house. She didn't just look though. She poked and prodded and stuck her head in places she probably shouldn't have; places that no one had been for a great many years.

She'd have to go with him and make sure he didn't touch anything.

They walked through the austere hall; the walls, floors and even the ceiling were dust-covered wood. The only hint of embellishment was on the fire surround with its carved, square panels, bearing a variety of ships, ships' rigging, figureheads and other ships' paraphernalia.

'That's a rather grand fireplace,' Thaddeus said.

'This was the Great Hall when the house was originally built. The Summerhills made their money from ships. Of course that was centuries ago, and since then all they've done is spend it or lose it or gamble it… oh I'm sorry. I didn't mean–'

'Don't worry about offending me. You should hear some of the things the press have been saying. But then again, you have… from Timothy Richards. It looks as if the fire's been in use recently. I can almost picture Silas sitting in one of the two high-back chairs here. Although I hadn't seen him for some time, so it's an old image.'

'I think it was probably the cleaner who sat there. It isn't just the windows that're covered in grime.' Sophie lifted her hand from the filthy newel post at the foot of the oak staircase and shook off a gossamer cobweb glove. 'The kitchen's along this corridor.'

She led the way into an astonishingly clean, if somewhat dated, kitchen where Thaddeus made coffee whilst Sophie grabbed a towel, a pair of jeans and a sweater from her suitcase, and nipped into the downstairs cloakroom to change. She came back a few minutes later and unpacked the groceries.

'The fridge works,' she said, 'and it's clean! I take back everything I said. The cleaner did do something.'

'It's good that the power's been left on but I suppose the solicitors knew you'd be staying here. I'll bring in the rest of your things and then can we please go and explore? I'll leave you in peace after that, I promise.'

'Yes,' she said. But alone in the kitchen, she suddenly shivered uncontrollably – as if someone had walked over her grave – and she wasn't sure she wanted Thaddeus to leave, after all.

But how could she ask him to stay? Especially when it might jeopardise her entire plan.

Chapter Seven

Sophie couldn't believe that she was standing in the kitchen of Summerhill. Especially after all these years.

When she'd received the letter from Hardman & Jones solicitors, just the day before, she'd been both astonished and elated. And more than a little guilty for being so. Part of her astonishment was due to the fact that her ex-fiancé, Trent, had obviously arranged for her post to be redirected to the flat where she was staying with her friend, Amanda, but she was equally astonished by the contents of the letter. It informed her that her great-uncle Silas had died and asked if she would please get in touch with them as they had been unable to reach her on the telephone.

Fate had given her the biggest surprise of her life when she needed it the most. Bigger even than discovering, two months earlier, that her then-fiancé, Trent Godly was dumping her and moving to New York.

Bigger than discovering she would be homeless because Trent was selling his flat to fund his move, and jobless. Well, she hadn't been homeless or jobless until after the fire. Trent had initially told her that she could stay on at his flat until it sold and could work at his art gallery in London for as long as she liked, as he wasn't selling that.

'After all, Soph,' he'd said, even though he knew she hated being called 'Soph' – or perhaps because he knew it, 'we'll still be friends. Just because I've fallen in love with someone else and decided to move to New York and open a gallery there so that I can be with her, doesn't mean you and I have to hate one another, does it? And you'll soon find somewhere else to live because, naturally, I need to sell the flat. Money doesn't grow on trees, Soph and I hadn't a clue that New York lofts are so unbelievably expensive.'

For Sophie's part, she had been more than willing to hate him and yet, deep down, she'd known that their relationship had hit a wall, so if having time to find a new home and keeping her job, meant being friends with Trent, she would find a way to be his friend.

That changed after the fire. Suddenly, Trent didn't want a pyromaniac as a friend, a flatmate or an employee. He had told her to leave the flat (what was left of it) and not to bother turning up for work the following day, or ever again for that matter.

No amount of reasoning or explanation would convince Trent that she hadn't intentionally set the kitchen on fire. And she hadn't, however tempting that may have been.

She'd only left the pan for just a second. Her eyes were streaming and her nose was running; every tissue in the flat was gone and the paper kitchen towel had been used up hours earlier, so she'd gone in search of toilet roll. She'd only stayed a moment longer to wash her face... and possibly just one more second to peer at her pathetic, self-pitying reflection.

How the tea towel had fallen onto the hob was as much a mystery to her as it was to Trent… and the Fire Department… and the insurance company. Thank heavens they finally believed it was an accident – a simple twist of Fate. That is apart from Trent, who said he would never speak to her again.

But she wasn't here because her relationship with Trent had gone up in flames… in more ways than one. She was here because Silas was dead. And that meant that she could finally, after more than twenty-one years, resume her search for the fabled, long-lost Summerhill treasure.

Technically, there was a slight possibility that the treasure wasn't actually the Summerhill's. They may have merely… *acquired* it. The fact that they then *misplaced* it was yet another twist of Fate, and one that Great-uncle Silas had flatly refused to discuss with a nine-year-old "brat" or her "trollop of a mother".

Sophie and Julia had later discovered that the treasure had in fact been hidden – and by a Summerhill: Sophie's namesake, Sophia, who had lived and died in Barnabus Beaumont's time and had shared adventures with him that no one but the family seemed to know about.

But now Silas Summerhill was dead. She'd had no idea that he was ill, let alone on his deathbed. How could she? When Silas had asked them to leave all those years ago, he'd told them never to darken his door again. They hadn't seen or heard from him since and that was more than twenty-one years ago.

How his solicitors had known Trent's address and assumed Sophie still lived there was a mystery, and one she would ask them to explain when she met with them next week, but when she had phoned them yesterday after receiving the letter, they informed her that she would benefit from her great-uncle's passing.

'I would rather not discuss such matters on the telephone, Miss Summerhill, but I think you may be pleasantly surprised by Mr Summerhill's will,' Mr Hardman had said. 'The funeral has been arranged, in accordance with his wishes, and will take place next Tuesday. He did not insist that you attend but, of course, you may do so if you wish. However, we do need you to come to our office in Hastings, as soon as conveniently possible, so that we can go over the will, discuss his estate and… explain a few little oddities of which you may not be aware.'

Sophie was surprised by this. Silas had made it clear that he was leaving his estate to charity, so she knew she wouldn't inherit that but she wondered what he'd left her. She also wondered what Mr Hardman meant by "a few little oddities". Was he referring to the Summerhill treasure?

There was no point in speculating and no matter what she'd asked Mr Hardman or how carefully she'd phrased it, he had simply told her they would discuss it when they met.

Sophie knew that under the terms of an ancient and ongoing codicil, the treasure would belong to the person who found it – providing they were a Summerhill.

Unless someone else stepped in and claimed it. And that was her biggest worry. What would she do then? She'd read the pages of the 1996 Treasure Act and the 2003 amendment and that could be a problem.

'Sophie?' Thaddeus said. 'Did you hear me? I asked where you want me to put your stuff. You looked as if you were miles away.'

'Sorry! I was thinking about the past. Um. I think I'll leave everything in here for now. I'm not sure which room I'll be sleeping in until we've had a look around.'

'The offer of my room is still open,' he quipped. 'It feels very cold in here. Does the heating work? Do you know where the boiler is and I'll take a look. Or is the heating run by that *Aga*? If so, we'll need to find some wood or something. It feels more like February than June even though the sun's out now.'

'There's a sort of utility-cum-junk room next door. If I remember rightly, that's where the firewood's kept but there's oil-fired central heating via a separate boiler which is also in there somewhere.'

'I'll take a look.'

He was gone less than ten minutes during which time Sophie tried to put the treasure firmly out of her mind. She rummaged through her belongings and retrieved a silver photo frame containing a picture of her and her mother which she placed in the centre of the large, pine table. Instantly, she felt more at home.

'Found it,' Thaddeus said, returning to the kitchen. 'I've switched it on and it sounds like it's working so you should be feeling some warmth fairly soon. Is that your Mum? She's hardly changed since I last saw her all those years ago. You clearly take after her and not the Summerhill side of the family. Will she be joining you for the funeral?'

'I think the only thing I've inherited from my dad is my hair colour. And possibly my eyes. All the Summerhills seem to have this yellow-gold hair and odd coloured eyes. And no, Mum lives in the Cayman Islands now and it's too far to come – and much too expensive.'

'Oh.' Thaddeus looked thoughtful. 'Sophia Summerhill didn't. Have yellow-gold hair I mean, although her eyes were incredible – just like yours and she also had that crescent-shaped birthmark on her cheek.'

'Sophia! What d'you know about Sophia?'

'Hey. Don't snap my head off. I don't know anything about her. Is there some deep, dark secret then? Sorry. Poking my nose in again. Although as she's been dead for several hundred years, I can't see why you're so worried. I was just saying she doesn't have the Summerhill hair colour, that's all. There's a portrait of her in Ben Sutton's gallery, The Artful Fisher. Ben is Oliver's uncle. I'm not sure why he has the painting but perhaps Silas loaned it to the gallery. You should go and take a look. I can arrange a private viewing if you like,' he said with a wink and a wicked grin.

'What? Do you ever think about anything but sex?'

'I wasn't thinking about sex. I was… Okay. Perhaps I was.' He shrugged. 'Keeps my mind off other things. Can I have that tour now or are you going to throw me out?'

'You can have the tour. So… there's really a portrait of Sophia in… Ben did you say? In Ben Sutton's gallery?'

'Last time I looked, yes.'

'And it's called The Artful Fisher? I must go and take a look.'

'Yep. It's on the seafront, next to a pub called The One That Got Away, which Ben also owns and which I, personally, find far more interesting than the gallery. Now, lead on, Miss Summerhill.'

With her mind racing, Sophie led Thaddeus out of the kitchen, across the hall and into a large sitting room where there were a couple of very old sofas, four small side tables, a less ornate fireplace than the one in the hall, and a few family portraits on the panelled walls. None of which were of Sophia. The heavy curtains at the windows looked as if they hadn't been touched in years.

'Another room the cleaner obviously steered clear of,' Thaddeus said, following Sophie back out.

The dining room and study were the same. In fact, every room seemed to be covered in dust apart from one bedroom, which had obviously been Silas' room.

'Well, it looks like I'll be sleeping in here,' Sophie said almost to herself.

'Are you sure? I hate to point this out but Silas may well have died in that bed. Doesn't that bother you?'

'No. I think that's it for the tour. Have you seen everything you wanted to?'

Thaddeus stood in the doorway, his head cocked to one side, an anxious look on his face. 'Have I upset you in some way?'

'By telling me that I'm going to be sleeping on my great-uncle's deathbed? No.'

He put his arm out to block her exit and she stared up into his face.

'I meant before that. You've hardly said a word other than to tell me which room we were entering next. Is this still about that Sophia thing. I wish I'd never mentioned it.'

Sophie was very glad he'd mentioned it. She thought she'd have a long search for the portrait and to discover it was hanging in a local gallery was more than she could have hoped for. Although to be honest, she had hoped that it would be hanging on a panelled wall in Summerhill and that she'd be able to study it at her leisure. But since Thaddeus had mentioned it, she'd been unable to think of anything else. She must get to Ben Sutton's gallery as soon as she possibly could.

She shook her head. She needed to make him think the portrait wasn't important. He might start asking questions otherwise. And he might start looking at his own ancestor's portrait.

She looked him in the eye. 'No. It's just a little odd being back here, that's all. And from the look of the place, it seems Silas may have been ill for quite some time. I couldn't stand the man but it's pretty depressing to think of him festering away in a dusty old house. Plus, I'm suddenly very tired. It feels as if it's been a long day.'

His eyes held hers for a few moments. He nodded and stepped aside as if her explanation satisfied him.

'I understand. You should go and have a lie down. Or have some lunch. That might make you feel better. And speaking of lunch, I'd better get going.' He glanced at his watch as they headed towards the stairs. 'I'm meeting a man about a boat, at twelve-fifteen and it's just gone twelve. I do the odd repair here and there. So perhaps I'm not really unemployed after all. Hmm. But don't mention that to Timothy Richards either. The less he knows about me and my family, the happier I'll be.'

'I told you. I probably won't see him again and even if I do, I promise you I won't tell him anything you've said.'

'You'll see him all right, you can bet your life on that. And Goldebury Bay is far too small a place to hide, even if you wanted to. Although come to think of it, Silas did a pretty good job. Thanks for the tour.'

'Thank you for everything you've done. I'm not sure how I'd have managed without you.'

'That's what all the women say.' He grinned at her as they stood at the front door. 'But I'm not sure if yours was genuine gratitude or sarcasm. I'll probably find the doors bolted and Silas' rifle pointed at me the next time I visit.'

'It was gratitude.' Sophie smiled, knowing he was joking. 'Will there be a next time?'

'You can count on it. Speaking of the doors. I've got some WD40 in the car. I'll squirt some on the hinges or you'll never get either of them open again and although you're slim, you'll never squeeze through one of those broken window panes.'

'If I'm that desperate to get out, I'll smash the entire window, although I might just try opening it first.'

He laughed. 'The practical approach. I like it. And you never know, there may even be a secret passage in this place. A few of the ancient houses around here have them. Beaumont Hall has three. Have I said something wrong again? You've gone as white as a ghost!'

Chapter Eight

Sophie called her mother from her mobile a few minutes after Thaddeus left.

'Did I wake you, Mum?'

'No, darling,' Julia Summerhill said. 'We're always up early, you know that, although this morning we were … well, you probably don't want to know that your mother was having sex at seven in the morning, do you?'

'Eww! But you had to tell me anyway. I suppose it's another gorgeous day on Grand Cayman?'

'It is. You can always count on the Caymans for hot weather, darling. That's one of the things I love about it, and you will too, when you get here. And I'm being positive, you see. I'm certain you'll solve the mystery, find the treasure and be flying here first class before the month's out.'

'I hope so, Mum. I miss you. And apart from anything else, I could do with some sun. It's absolutely freezing here and it's been pouring with rain nearly all morning, although it's stopped now. I'm at the house, you'll be pleased to hear and the place is just as depressing as I remember, but it's a lot dustier and more dilapidated than it was twenty-one years ago.'

'Aren't we all, darling? And I miss you, too. I wish I could be there with you. Does the heating work?'

'So do I and yes, the heating works.' Sophie switched the kettle on to make some more coffee. 'The roof seems to be intact but I could be wrong, I haven't ventured into the attic yet. There're some broken windows. I suspect local kids have been daring each other to come up here and throw stones at scary old Silas Summerhill's creepy house.' She giggled at the thought of that. 'It's been a very strange morning actually. You'll never guess who I've just spent the last couple of hours with.'

'Tell me.'

'Thaddeus Beaumont.'

'The son? Already? Was that wise? I know you, darling, once you set your mind on something you go all out to get it but I thought we agreed it would be best not to involve the Beaumonts unless it was an absolute necessity?'

'It was pure coincidence… or Fate, or a little of both perhaps.'

'I think they're one and the same thing. So what happened?'

'My car broke down and—'

'Oh Sophie! Is it okay? Can you afford to get it repaired? D'you have enough money to pay for somewhere to stay if the solicitors say you have to leave the house after the funeral?'

'I never thought they'd agree to let me stay in the first place but as I told you, they seemed perfectly happy about it. I'm hoping that once I tell them about my car, they'll take pity on me and let me stay for a week or two. I'll ask them on Monday when I meet them. The car's going to cost a couple of hundred at least but I may be able to sell it as is, so that should tide me over. Anyway, I was saying, whilst Mike at the local garage had a look at it, I waited in a tearoom called Betty's Pantry.'

'Is that still there? I remember Betty. Does she still run it? She must be in her seventies by now. She was an old waggle-tongue, as I recall.'

Sophie laughed. 'She still is. She told me all about the trial and the Beaumonts within five minutes of my arrival. I must remember to steer clear of her, if possible. But I met a journalist in there. He could be both useful and a problem.'

'A journalist? Oh, reporting on the trials, you mean?'

'That's what I thought – and I suppose he is – but he's also writing a book about the Beaumonts. He might've discovered things we don't know. I want to find a way to have a chat with him without alerting him to the fact that I'm also researching the Beaumont's history.'

'Invite him to dinner and flirt with him, darling. You're a beautiful, young woman. You know what to do.'

'He's rather good-looking and not much older than me.'

'I said flirt, darling, not take him to bed. Although… you may as well have some fun whilst you're there. And now that idiot, Trent… well, let's not talk about him. Have you heard from him?'

Sophie took her coffee to the table and sat. 'Not one word. But I told you that he's had my mail redirected – which is how I got the letter from the solicitors, so he doesn't completely hate me.'

'You should hate him for what he did. Men. Honestly. Some of them don't have the sense they were born with. I should've made you come out here with us in January. If I'd known that idiot Trent was… anyway, if things go to plan, you'll be out here soon and if not, we'll find the money to pay for a ticket for you. Three of us can live as cheaply as two and once the dive business takes off, we'll have a reasonably good income. We'll make it work. So what's Thaddeus Beaumont like? You said you spent the last few hours with him. He's not the journalist, is he? No, of course he isn't. Sorry, darling, I'm running away with my excitement.'

Sophie giggled. 'He's… not what I was expecting.

Which reminds me. He told me he was the one who saved my life all those years ago. Did you know it was him?'

'Oh yes. I'd forgotten that. Not you falling, obviously, but that it was Thaddeus and his uncle, whose name I can't remember, who rescued you. So you told him who you are? I thought you were going to try to keep that quiet for as long as possible?'

'I was. But as usual it seems Fate had other plans. That's what I was telling you. When I was in Betty's Pantry talking to Timothy, the journalist, Thaddeus came in with some friends. One of them is Oliver Sutton, so that means I can get Thaddeus to introduce us. Anyway, when I went back to the garage, Thaddeus came to pick up his car and – I won't bore you with the details – but he ended up giving me a lift here because it was pouring with rain. He's just left. He told me there's a portrait of Sophia in a local gallery which is owned by another member of the Sutton family. Isn't that great? And it seems that even after hundreds of years, our families are all still connected in some way or other. Life really is strange, isn't it?'

'You can say that again, darling. So the portrait does exist? How exciting. But is it definitely Sophia? And does it show the Girdle brooch? And the rest of the jewels? Will you send me a photo of it when you go to see it? Did you tell Thaddeus you were looking for it?'

'I'll send you a photo. Until I see it I don't know if it's definitely her but Thaddeus says it is and no, I didn't tell him. We were talking about the colour of the Summerhill hair, oddly enough, and how all Summerhills have yellow-gold hair and odd-coloured eyes. That's when he told me about the painting. I couldn't believe my ears! Until I see it, I won't know for sure but everything seems to be falling into place rather nicely… although not at all as I'd planned. Not that that matters. If things carry on like this, I'll solve the mystery and find the treasure before dear old, Great-uncle Silas is long in the ground.'

'God rest his soul. And then promise me one thing, darling. You'll go and spit on the old bastard's grave.'

'I'll dance on it. I'm going to go to the gallery the minute I've finished my coffee but I just had to call and tell you. There may be a portrait of Barnabus Beaumont there too. I'll call you later and let you know. I love you, Mum.'

'Love you too, darling. I've got everything crossed for you out here but you be careful. And don't go climbing any cliffs without making sure you're securely tied in.'

Sophie laughed. 'I honestly don't think the treasure's hidden in a cave in the cliff now Mum, you know that. And I have the strangest feeling it's going to be in the last place we'd ever think of looking for it. It could even be somewhere in this house. Don't ask me how or why I think that, but somehow I just do.'

Chapter Nine

'I think the sign says, "No photography".'

Sophie spun round, her phone camera still hovering in front of the portrait of Sophia Summerhill, and came face to face with Timothy Richards.

'Bloody hell! You almost gave me a heart attack,' she said. 'What're you doing here?'

'I've been looking at the paintings and photographs of the Beaumonts, although there aren't as many as I'd have liked. It does seem to be the most popular section for the tourists though and there's a rather grand portrait of Barnabus. I even bought the postcard.' He pulled it out of his jeans' pocket to show her. 'Striking resemblance to Thaddeus, don't you think?' He was smiling but his eyes held the curiosity of a reporter.

She smiled back, glancing briefly at the postcard and nodding. She'd already seen the original and taken photos when there had been a brief lull in other viewers. She too had been struck by the resemblance and she'd had to force herself to walk away and go in search of her ancestor.

'So, what're you doing here *Just Sophie*?'

It was time to get Timothy Richards on her side. 'I've got a confession to make but first, I need to take a couple of photos. You won't tell on me, will you?'

He cocked his head to one side. 'Not if you let me buy you lunch.'

'You're on.' She quickly took some photos, picked the

best one and sent a photo message to her mum. She then turned her attention to Timothy. 'All done. Okay. My name's Sophie Summerhill and this woman,' she said, pointing to the portrait, 'is an ancestor of mine. My namesake, in fact. I'd never seen a picture of her before. My great-uncle's just died and I'm in Goldebury Bay for the funeral next week. That's why I was… a little unfriendly earlier. Well... and because my car had broken down.'

'I'm so sorry,' he said. 'If I'd known I wouldn't have behaved like such a Neanderthal. Were you close?'

'Not at all. I hadn't seen him in years, but… he was family, you know.'

'I know what you mean.' He nodded towards the painting. 'You don't look much like her, although she does have your eyes and… is that a birthmark on her cheek? You have it too!'

'I take after my mum. She lives in the Caymans now and I wanted to send her a photo of Sophia … who was my dad's ancestor, not my mum's. And yes, it's a birthmark. Sophia's very beautiful though, don't you think?'

'Yes. She's got a dark, sultry look about her. Those jewels she's wearing are pretty stunning as well. They'd be worth a fortune today. Are they still in the family? That girdle is particularly beautiful and the brooch. Shit. That alone would keep you in style for many years. Will you inherit any of them? I'm sorry, that's really none of my business, is it? I can't forget I used to be an investigative reporter.'

'Used to be?'

'Yeah. I chucked it in. I'm doing some freelance stuff on the Beaumont trial but I'm writing a book now. About the Beaumonts. The more I delved into that family, the more interested I became. There's a lot more to them than just class B drugs and tobacco smuggling, you know. It almost seems a shame that Jeremiah and Hermione will go down for something so … mundane. And they will go down for it. It should've at least been heroine, or diamonds or something. Even human trafficking would've been sexier than sodding drugs and tobacco.'

'And you like your reporting to be… sexy, do you?'

He grinned. 'I like everything in my life to be sexy. Shall we go to lunch?'

He held out his hand and Sophie hesitated for just one second. It was almost as if by taking it she'd sealed some sort of deal. She dismissed the feeling and slipped her hand in his.

'Summerhill?' Timothy said deep in thought as he led her out through the gallery's double front doors, which were shaped like half a fishing boat. He looked along the coast towards the west. 'You can't see it from here but isn't that the name of that old house set back from the cliff, just past The Mound? Did your great-uncle live there? Weren't the Summerhills once connected to the Beaumonts in some way? Or am I getting confused?'

Sophie needed to think on her feet. 'Yes. To all of it... apart from the confused bit. Once you start looking into the past though, it seems everyone was somehow connected in a place like this. I don't really know much about the Summerhill history, so if you've come across anything interesting I'd love to hear about it. The only thing I do know is that Sophia Summerhill never married and she died when she was twenty-three. Where're we going for lunch?'

'An old maid then,' Timothy said with a grin. 'Let's go to Sutton's. It's only two doors away and the food's superb.'

'Sutton's? Is it owned by the same guy who owns this gallery?'

'No. His nephew, Oliver. Ben Sutton owns the gallery and the pub next door, The One That Got Away. Oliver Sutton owns the restaurant on the other side of the pub. I mentioned it earlier when we were in Betty's Pantry this morning and Oliver came in with Thaddeus. He also owns a cookery school just a bit further along the seafront.'

As they left The Artful Fisher and strolled past the mock Tudor pub towards the restaurant, Sophie slipped her hand from Timothy's in the pretence of tidying her hair.

'If I'd known we were going somewhere as posh as this restaurant looks, I'd have nipped to the loo and done something with my appearance. That rain this morning's made me look like a drowned rat and these jeans and T-shirt are a bit scruffy.'

'You look lovely,' he said. 'This place may look posh but it's got a really laid-back, relaxed atmosphere.'

Compared to the mock Tudor pub next door, Sophie thought that Sutton's looked very trendy. It had a large, outdoor terrace encircled by sheeted blue canvas strung on thick, white ropes at waist height. *Sutton's* was written on the canvas in white rope-like letters. Matching blue umbrellas stood ready to shade the wooden tables, which were covered with pristine white tablecloths, but as the sun only appeared intermittently between a long line of cloud, none of the diners seemed yet to require a shield from its rays.

Set between the tables, stood large, pale terracotta pots filled with a variety of herbs. The glorious scent of lavender, rosemary, mint and coriander was enough to tempt Sophie's palate, particularly as the toast she'd had for breakfast seemed but a distant memory.

'The Suttons are quite well off then?' Sophie asked as they waited to be seated.

Timothy nodded. 'I don't know if you already know this

but there's an ancient feud between the Suttons and the Beaumonts – or at least there was, until Oliver and Thaddeus became best buddies. The Beaumonts were rich in those days and the Suttons, poor. It's almost ironic how much things have changed.'

'Family feuds,' Sophie said, shaking her head. 'Another thing all these sort of places seem to have in common. I suppose when people live in such close-knit communities, arguments are bound to happen.'

'From what I've read and heard, it was rather more than an argument. The Beaumonts accused the Suttons of taking a precious treasure. The Suttons accused the Beaumonts of murder, and another local family, the Pollards, of helping to cover it up. It was in Barnabus Beaumont's time and rumour has it that they've been accusing each other of the same things ever since. Every time anything went missing, they blamed one another, and whenever there was a mysterious or sudden death, well, you get the picture. It started to go quiet by the time Jeremiah Beaumont came along but there was still enmity between him and the Sutton brothers. That's Christopher Sutton – Oliver's father – and Christopher's brothers, Jed and Ben. It's the most recent generation, that's Thaddeus and Oliver who seem to have finally put an end to it all. The Pollards…' His voice trailed off.

Sophie glanced in the direction Timothy was looking and saw a couple wandering towards them, hand in hand. The woman wore a purple, flowing, maxi dress and colourful scarf, and her jet black hair and striking looks reminded Sophie of Oliver's girlfriend, Cleo Merrifield. There was a definite resemblance. The man had thick, curly, fair hair and a youthful look about him although as they got closer, Sophie could see he was probably in his forties or possibly a little older. He wore plain black trousers and a yellow T-shirt with the words: 'The Golde Boys Rock Band' emblazoned across the front.

'Who are they?' Sophie leant in close and whispered just as Cleo Merrifield appeared from inside the restaurant.

'Hi, Mum!' Cleo called to the woman and waved. 'Hello, Paul. D'you want to sit inside or out? Oliver says it won't rain again until this evening and he's always right about the weather.'

'We'll follow you, sweetheart,' the woman said.

Cleo glanced towards Sophie and Timothy. 'A table for two? Oh, it's you! Sit where you want but make sure it's nowhere near us.' She glowered at Timothy and as she flounced off, she called to her mother and Paul: 'We'll sit inside, Mum.'

Sophie blinked in astonishment but Timothy shook his head and grinned. 'It's a good thing I'm not a restaurant critic, isn't it? Where d'you want to sit?'

'You want to eat here? After that? Aren't you worried they'll spit in your food?'

He chuckled and, with his hand on the small of her back, led her to a table closest to the building, in the corner of the outside terrace.

'I wouldn't put it past Cleo,' he said, 'but Oliver loves food too much to do anything so gross or allow anyone else to. He has a reputation to maintain, after all. Trust me, it'll be fine and anyway, it's only me they hate, not you. Unless you think you may be tarnished by association? If you'd rather go elsewhere, we can.'

'No, it's fine. If you're happy to stay then so am I.' She sat on the chair he pulled out for her. 'So that's Cleo's mum? I assume the guy isn't her dad.'

Timothy shook his head. 'Now there's another story I'd quite like to write about. Honestly, for such a small place this little town has more going on than any TV soap. I don't know all the details but I do know that Cleo only found out last summer that Clara – whom she thought was her aunt – is actually her mum. Clara had an affair with her own sister's husband and gave birth to Cleo. The husband and the sister adopted Cleo and it's only because the sister died a couple of years ago, that it's all come to light. Are you still with me?'

Sophie nodded but she wasn't absolutely certain that she'd grasped it. And she thought her family history was complicated! There must be something in the water in Goldebury Bay to make all the locals go a bit mad, she thought.

'So the man with… Clara? Is he Clara's husband… but not Cleo's dad?'

'No. He's the local vicar.' Timothy grinned. 'Actually, that bit's rather romantic. Clara never married. I'm not sure why not because she must've been pretty stunning when she was younger. She still looks good and she must be getting on for fifty now. Anyway, The Reverend Paul Temple who only came here a few years ago, and Clara, became friends because she helps out at the church. When it all came out about the affair and the fact that Clara had an illegitimate daughter, he stuck by her and they've been dating ever since. You won't believe this, but she apparently wrote a letter admitting her past and had it delivered with the local papers. They're all a bit mad here, I think,' he said.

Which was exactly what Sophie was thinking.

'And... here's another interesting little titbit,' he added. 'You remember I told you just now about the Pollards? Well, Cleo Merrifield, who lives with Oliver Sutton, is actually a Pollard descendant. Her mum Clara, is Clara Pollard. So the Beaumonts, the Suttons and the Pollards are now all the best of friends… after several hundred years of feuding.'

Sophie couldn't believe what she was hearing.

'Although,' Timothy added, 'as I also told you earlier, Cleo Merrifield slash Pollard dumped Thaddeus Beaumont for Oliver Sutton, so who knows, it may all blow up again.'

It may very well all blow up again, Sophie thought, but it will be because of a Summerhill, not a Pollard or a Sutton, or even a Beaumont.

Chapter Ten

Sophie rarely answered calls on her mobile if 'unknown caller' appeared, but it could be Mike from the garage, even though it was five-thirty on Saturday. Or possibly Trent, calling from New York just to see how she was and to bury the hatchet.

'Hello,' she said.

To her surprise it was Thaddeus. 'Sophie? Hi. I'm glad I got the number right.'

'How did you get it?' She wasn't sure whether she was annoyed that he had, or pleased, as the prospect of her first evening alone in Silas' creepy, old house loomed ahead of her.

'I overheard it when you gave it to Mike. I've got an excellent memory for numbers, although I'm rubbish at maths, strangely enough, but until I heard your voice I wasn't certain I'd got it right. How're you settling in?'

'Hmm. Fine thanks. I'm a bit anxious about my first night but…' She stopped herself. Was she really going to tell him she felt scared? 'Um. In a strange bed, I mean.'

'I rather like strange beds.'

She could hear the laughter in his voice and it made her smile. 'It's always about sex, with you, isn't it? Are you calling to see if I've changed my mind and want to take you up on your offer of a bed for the night?'

'No. But the offer's still there if you have.'

'I haven't, but thanks.'

‘Another time then. And before you bite my head off, that was a joke. I’m actually calling to ask if you’d like to go out tonight. I know you’re probably tired but as you said yourself, it’s your first night in a strange bed. An evening out and a few drinks might make it a bit easier for you.’

‘Are you… are you asking me out on a date?’

‘God no! Sorry. I didn’t mean it to sound like that. I meant this isn’t how I’d ask a girl out on a date. If I was asking you on a date you’d know it because…’ He let out a long sigh. ‘Because when I ask a girl out on a date, I make an even bigger fool of myself than I am now, except I wasn’t asking you… Let’s start again. I’m meeting Oliver and the others for a drink this evening and I wondered if you’d like to join us, instead of spending your first evening alone. There. That’s what I meant. I really need to brush up on my telephone conversational skills. You may find this hard to believe but I can chat up any girl I want, providing I don’t know her but let me loose on the phone with a woman I know and I fall apart completely.’

She burst out laughing but she couldn’t deny feeling a touch of disappointment that it wasn’t a date, even though if it had been, she would have had to refuse. At least, she hoped she would have done so.

‘Won’t your friends mind?’

‘Nope. I’ve already asked them and they’re fine with it. Oliver may not stay long as it’s Saturday and his restaurant’s fully booked tonight but he’ll pop in and out. Cleo and Poppy are looking forward to meeting you.’

Sophie remembered the look Poppy had given her that morning and the one Cleo had given her at lunch, and she somehow doubted that, but this was her opportunity to meet a Sutton and a Pollard and she couldn’t pass it up, no matter what. She’d asked Timothy at lunch what else he knew about the feud between the families but to her surprise, he didn't know as much as she did.

'Then I'd love to, thanks. Where shall I meet you?'

'I'll come and pick you up. Can you be ready by seven-thirty? It's just casual so you don't have to dress up or anything.'

'The inference being that I'd need more than two hours to get dressed up?' She grinned, wishing she could see his face; see the sparkle of laughter in his deep brown eyes; the twitch of his perfect lips…

What was she thinking? She had to stop this right now.

'If you're anything like Poppy or Cleo, you'll need about four hours,' he said. 'See you at seven-thirty.'

She was about to say she'd changed her mind and that she needed an early night but he'd hung up. Should she call him back? No matter what happened, she must not fall for Thaddeus Beaumont.

She had lied when she'd told him she wasn't a 'heart and flowers' kind of girl and that she was more of the practical kind. She was a 'hearts and flowers with bows on, a cherry on top and stardust sprinkled liberally all over' kind of girl.

Not with Trent, oddly enough and she wondered, not for the first time, why she'd planned to marry him. Trent was good-looking, successful and rich and when they met she'd been attracted to him but... since then, they'd become more like brother and sister than lovers. She couldn't really blame him for finding passion somewhere else.

But with Thaddeus it was different. Every time he looked at her, something flipped inside. If she wasn't careful, she knew that she could fall for him in a big way. She was already beginning to see him as her knight in shining armour… and a whole lot more besides.

Then again, when she'd been with Timothy at lunch, hadn't she felt something similar about him? With his tousled dark hair, intense blue eyes, long, lean frame and his determination to get to the heart of the matter at all costs, she found him more than a little appealing.

It was just a pity Timothy felt he had the right, no, the duty, to share his 'news' with the world. Sophie believed people had a right to privacy. Timothy believed people had a right to know what their neighbour was doing, even if it meant destroying that neighbour's reputation and ruining their lives.

'I've got nothing to hide,' he had told her. 'If other people have, that's not my fault. You should never do anything you wouldn't be happy to have made public, that's what I believe. That goes for affairs of the heart, business and financial dealings, family, friendship – the lot.'

'That's a rather simplistic and idealistic attitude,' she had replied. 'No one is perfect. We all make mistakes. Do things we're not proud of. Things we'd rather no one found out about. That doesn't necessarily make us bad people. It just makes us human and I, for one, wouldn't want my mistakes printed in black and white for all to see, not to mention flying around in cyberspace for all eternity.'

He had studied her face for several seconds. 'And what mistakes have you made, Miss Sophie Summerhill? What are you hoping no one will find out?'

That had been too close for comfort and she'd hastily changed the subject back to the Suttons, the Pollards and the Beaumonts.

And thinking of the Beaumonts, she realised she had better get a move on or she wouldn't be ready when Thaddeus came to pick her up at seven-thirty. And she could just imagine how much fun he'd have teasing her for that.

Chapter Eleven

Not only was Sophie ready when Thaddeus arrived, she was standing at the door waiting for him.

'You're keen!' Thaddeus said, his eyes sparkling with amusement as he pulled up in front of her and got out to open the passenger door. 'It's just as well this isn't a date or I'd definitely think I had a bed for the night.'

'If this was a date, I'd have kept you waiting for at least ten minutes… and it's even possible that I may have cared what I looked like. Then again, I wouldn't have said yes, if this was a date, so I guess that's a moot point.'

He laughed as he closed the door behind her and got into the driver's seat. 'Well, for someone who doesn't care what she looks like, you look pretty good to me. That's a very nice dress. Turquoise suits you.'

'This old thing?' She hated herself for saying that the moment it left her lips. What a cliché? 'It's the only thing I had that didn't need ironing,' she added hastily. 'The skirt and T-shirt I wore earlier are still not dry and the jeans and sweater I changed into are now covered in as much dust as the rest of this place.'

'Didn't Silas own an iron?'

'I didn't look for one. I didn't know I'd be going out. I've spent the last two hours cleaning and thought I'd be spending the evening doing the same. When I speak to Silas' solicitors I'm going to tell them to sack the cleaner and employ me instead. The place is filthy. Oh, and you may be interested to know, I had second thoughts about sleeping in Silas' bed. I've cleaned the room I slept in when I was here as a child. It's much smaller – and cosier – than Silas' room and with my own sheets and pillows, I think I'll sleep a lot better.'

'If you're worried about ghosts, or about being alone here, I'm more than willing to spend the night,' he said as he turned left out of the private road and headed towards the seafront. 'No funny stuff. Just so that you've got someone else in the house. Someone who's still living, that is.'

'You never give up, do you?'

'Only when I know I'm beaten. I don't believe in wasting energy on a hopeless cause.'

'Especially when there's another woman just around the corner. One's as good as another, as far as you're concerned.'

She laughed but was surprised to see a serious look in his eyes when he glanced at her. It was gone in a second and the light-heartedness was back.

'I wish that were true. But some have been much better than others. I keep a scoresheet, so I know that's the case.'

'You do *not*!' Even she knew that was a joke. 'But I bet you wouldn't like it if you discovered they kept one on you.'

'I wouldn't mind at all. I have no doubt I'd score a perfect ten every time. Possibly even an eleven if I really make an effort.'

She burst out laughing. 'You're terrible, Thaddeus. I pity any girl who falls for you. She'll have no idea what she's getting into or that she'll just be another in a very long line of broken-hearted women.'

She saw the look he gave her and waited for his reply. He drove down the hill and turned onto the seafront in less than a minute and passed through two sets of green lights before he answered.

'I'll tell you something that not many people know about me. I don't pretend to be something or someone I'm not. I may be a bit of a Jack the Lad but women know exactly what they're getting into. I just want to have fun, no strings and no regrets. But when I fall for a girl, all that goes out the window. And my heart breaks as easily as anyone else's, I can assure you of that.' Their eyes held for just a second before he turned away.

'Oh. Are we having drinks here?'

He'd pulled into the private car park of Sutton's restaurant.

'No, I'm just parking here. We're going next door to The One That Got Away. Now let's go and have some fun. There's Oliver, Cleo and Poppy.' He almost leapt out of the car.

'Hi Thaddeus,' Poppy said. She pulled her sunglasses down the bridge of her nose with the tip of her finger and gave Sophie a decidedly cool look. 'So you're Sophie. I thought you were with that Timothy Richards guy when I saw you two having breakfast this morning, but Thaddeus tells us you're not.'

'You're friends though, aren't you?' Cleo said. 'You had lunch with him too.'

'Did you?' Thaddeus was clearly surprised. 'I didn't know that.'

Sophie felt the warm evening air growing colder by the second. She needed to defend herself but not from the elements; from the increasingly cool stares of those around her.

She shook her head rapidly. 'We're not exactly friends. I'd never met him until this morning but he's been nothing but polite to me. I have no reason to dislike him, so when I bumped into him again at The Artful Fisher and he invited me for lunch, I went. Just as I've come here this evening because all of you have very kindly invited me to join you. But if you've changed your minds…' She let her voice trail off.

'Of course we haven't,' Oliver said. 'Have we, Thaddeus?'

Sophie wasn't sure if that was a statement or a question and she couldn't help but notice the odd look Thaddeus was giving her; as if he was actually considering the matter. After what was merely a moment but felt like an eternity to Sophie, Thaddeus shook his head.

'Of course not. We're not the type of people who tell others who they can and can't have breakfast and lunch with. Although speaking for myself, I draw the line at dinner. Have dinner with the man and you're off my Christmas card list.'

'I hadn't realised I was on it,' Sophie said with a smile, although she felt the smile he had given her wasn't quite as bright or as genuine as his previous ones had been. 'But I'll make sure dinner's off the table, if you'll excuse the pun.'

'It's nice to meet you, Sophie,' Oliver said. 'I'm Oliver and this is my girlfriend, Cleo. This is Poppy, Cleo's best friend. And ours, of course.'

'Yes,' Poppy said, still with a hint of ice. 'Oliver, Cleo, Thaddeus and I are all best friends. Welcome to our little group, Sophie.'

Sophie gave her the biggest, friendliest smile she could muster. 'Thank you, Poppy. And thank you all for letting me join you tonight. I don't know anyone in Goldebury Bay and although my great-uncle Silas and I were definitely *not* close, not by any stretch of the imagination, it's still unsettling to be at his house… alone. My mum and her boyfriend sailed to the Cayman Islands earlier this year.

They live there now and it's far too far, not to mention, far too expensive, to come back for the funeral. It's good to feel I have the chance of getting to know some friendly people, even if only for the short time I'll be here.'

She knew her speech had worked because she saw the looks on Poppy and Cleo's faces and when Cleo spoke again, there was a warmth in her voice.

'We're sorry to hear about your great-uncle. I never met him but I know Thaddeus and Oliver knew him. And my great-aunt and great-uncle, even my mum visited him a few times.'

'That surprises me!' Sophie said, thinking she must get to know all of Cleo's relatives. 'Not that your relatives would visit him but that he would allow it. Thaddeus and I were only talking about the fact that he was known to shoot at visitors with his air rifle, weren't we, Thaddeus?' She turned to look at him but he seemed deep in thought. 'He wasn't the friendliest of men,' she added.

'How long will you be here?' Poppy asked as they headed towards the rear of The One That Got Away. 'Just for the funeral, or will you be staying for a while? Where do you live?'

Poppy still had some thawing out to do; that was evident.

'I'm honestly not sure,' Sophie said. 'I've been staying with a friend in her flat in London but I'm hoping to stay in Goldebury Bay for at least a few weeks.'

She wondered just how much she should give away. Perhaps it would be good to seem as if she were open and friendly and had nothing to hide.

Perhaps telling them about her ex-fiancé would make her seem less of a threat to Poppy for Thaddeus' attention. If what Timothy had told her was true: that Poppy wanted to be Thaddeus' girlfriend, Poppy wouldn't be happy that

Thaddeus had invited her tonight.

It might also make her less of an attraction to Thaddeus. She could say she was still in love with Trent. That might make Thaddeus back off a bit and that wouldn't be a bad thing. She mustn't get too close to him. She really mustn't.

And saying she still loved Trent wouldn't be a complete lie. Would it? She did still care about him even if he had dumped her, sacked her, made her homeless and told her he never wanted to speak to her again.

Of course, there was always a chance that telling Thaddeus she'd just been dumped and was therefore vulnerable, might make her more of an attraction to a man who liked a one- night stand. Although from what he'd told her in the car just now, he wasn't quite the Jack the Lad he wanted people to think he was. And he'd shown he had a sensitive side more than once since they'd first met this morning.

'You're quiet, Thaddeus,' Cleo said, linking an arm through his, her other arm linked through Oliver's.

Sophie saw the way Thaddeus smiled at Cleo and noticed that he reached across with his other hand and clasped hers.

'Am I?' he said. 'I'm trying to decide whether I want fish and chips later, or a curry.'

He smiled but it didn't reach his eyes and Sophie felt that at least one thing Timothy had told her about Thaddeus was true. He still had a thing for Cleo Merrifield and unless she was very much mistaken, Cleo had broken Thaddeus' heart.

Chapter Twelve

The rear of The One That Got Away had a large, paved terrace, similar to the one at the front of Sutton's restaurant, Sophie noticed. There were tables shaded with multi-coloured umbrellas; some still open even though the sun was slowly disappearing below the horizon. The terrace was surrounded by a white picket fence, in front of which sat hand-painted pots of all shapes and sizes brimming over with lobelia, geraniums, fuchsias, pelargoniums, violas and, like the pots at Sutton's restaurant, lavender and rosemary.

Sophie inhaled the heady concoction and could almost see herself with a man she loved, sitting on this terrace on a balmy summer's night, cooled only by the occasional breeze wafting in from the sea just a few hundred metres away. It disturbed her that the image of the man seemed to be a combination of Thaddeus, Timothy and Trent.

'Coo-ey,' an effeminate voice called from a window overhead and as she glanced up, she saw a man leaning out and waving at them.

'Hi Ben,' Oliver called back. 'We're coming up.' He turned to Sophie and smiled. 'That's Ben, my uncle. He owns this place but I should warn you, he's prone to strange moods and he's a little sensitive right now. He's just been dumped by his boyfriend.'

'I know the feeling,' Sophie said and she saw the keen look Poppy gave her.

The pub's interior had the same mock Tudor look as it

did at the front, which Sophie had seen when she'd walked past it with Timothy at lunchtime. It was jam-packed and she felt as if she were back on the London underground as she squeezed through the deafening cacophony of voices and the clashing colognes emitting from warm bodies pressed elbow to elbow.

She followed Oliver and Cleo towards a door and once or twice, felt Thaddeus' hand as if he were trying to shield her from the prod of an elbow or the nudge of a shoulder. She was relieved when she reached the door and saw a flight of stairs leading away from the crowd.

At the top of the stairs, another door led into a room with just a few tables and chairs. What stood out were the walls, which were full of shelves crammed with books. Only one wall was without shelves and that featured a large, marble fireplace with an ornate mirror above. Sprigs of lavender and rosemary, sprinkled with rose petals adorned the iron fire basket in the grate and in her mind's eye, Sophie could imagine this room in the winter. With the fire lit, the doors and windows closed and the wind and rain bombarding it straight from the sea like a war ship with full guns blazing, it would feel a safe and cosy harbour.

'Welcome to my library, *darling*,' Ben Sutton said, taking her hand in one of his and giving her air kisses beside both cheeks. 'I'm Ben, but of course, you already know that. My dear nephew has no doubt told you all about me. And if he hasn't, I want to know why not.'

Clearly he'd been told about her even if she hadn't known she'd be meeting him.

'Thank you, Ben,' she said. 'It's a lovely room. You obviously have an eye for design. I believe you designed the gallery too, The Artful Fisher. It's beautiful. I was there today. You have some wonderful pieces. You've even got a portrait of an ancestor of mine, Sophia Summerhill. I'd heard there might be a portrait but I'd never seen it. Thaddeus told me it was there. I'd love to have a chat with you about it when you've got a spare moment, and any other similar portraits. I've always been interested in art from the Tudor period, particularly the Elizabethan era. I worked in an art gallery in Chelsea, owned by my fiancé... ex-fiancé, I should say. He dumped me a few weeks ago.'

Ben's eyes lit up. She'd clearly got his interest.

'Oh, you poor darling!' He patted her hand. 'I know exactly how you feel. I've just been dumped by the love of my life. Well, the most recent love of my life and I do hope, not my last. It doesn't make the pain any less though does it, darling? Even though you know in your heart, they were clearly not *'the one'*. After all, if they were, they'd still be with us, wouldn't they? And not out throwing themselves at someone else. I'm speaking about my ex there, darling. He was throwing himself at someone else before he told me a dickie bird.'

'So was mine,' Sophie said. 'I hadn't got a clue. I was sitting at home, planning our wedding in the Cayman Islands next year and he was out screwing someone he'd met at the gallery. She came in to sell a painting of some famous, dead actor from the fifties, apparently, and walked out with my fiancé. They're now in New York.'

'No! We definitely need bubbles at a time like this,' Ben said. 'Oliver, are those drinks coming any time soon?'

'Give me a chance, will you?' Oliver said, heaving a tray with bottles of chilled champagne from the dumb waiter. 'Why didn't you bring this stuff up earlier?'

'Because I like it chilled and I still don't have the heart to put a chill cabinet in here. It'll ruin the entire ambience. Sit down, darling,' Ben said to Sophie, 'and have some champagne… when my delightful nephew finally gets around to pouring it.'

She turned towards a red club chair and as she did so, she noticed a glint of sympathy in both Poppy and Cleo's eyes but Thaddeus looked as if she'd slapped his face. He was positively glaring daggers at her.

'Well,' he said. 'I've discovered more about you in five minutes this evening than I did in the two hours I spent with you this morning. You're full of surprises, Sophie Summerhill.'

Ben glanced from Sophie to Thaddeus. 'You seem a tad peeved, darling, and that's not a good look on you, but as you've been going through the mill yourself lately, we all understand. Sit down, you hunk of a man and if you'd rather have beer, call down to Dom and get him to bring some up. Honestly, must I do everything myself?'

Thaddeus scowled at Ben momentarily before his expression changed to a large, if somewhat fake-looking smile.

'Tell us more about your… ex-fiancé, your wedding plans and your life in London, Sophie. We'd all love to hear about it.'

She knew he was being sarcastic and wondered why.

'I think everyone's heard quite enough about me for one evening,' she said. 'Sorry, I do tend to go on a bit once I get started.'

'Nonsense,' Poppy said. 'Had you been together long?'

'And did you live together?' Cleo asked.

'And is that the reason you've brought most of your belongings with you to Goldebury Bay?' Thaddeus said, sitting in a chair opposite Sophie. 'Are you planning on staying here, following him to New York in the hope of a reunion, or moving to the Caribbean to be with your mum and try to mend your broken heart?' He closed his eyes, crossed his legs at his ankles and placed his linked hands behind his head as if he couldn't be bothered listening to the answer.

Sophie stared at him. 'It all depends,' she said but he didn't reopen his eyes. 'But the Cayman Islands are my first choice.

'Ooh!' Ben said. 'I simply adore the Caymans, darling. And what a wonderful venue for a wedding! No wonder you're heartbroken. Oliver! This lovely creature needs a drink. *Are you pressing those grapes*?'

'I'll hit you over the head with this bottle if you don't stop carrying on,' Oliver said. 'You're clearly in one of your moods but don't take it out on me, okay? Here.' A cork popped and he passed Sophie and Ben each a glass of champagne.

Ben raised his brows and rolled his eyes. 'Sometimes darling,' he whispered to Sophie. 'It's hard to believe we're family. Now, you were saying…'

She took a large gulp of champagne and twisted in her seat so that she wasn't looking directly at Thaddeus' long, athletic-looking body. For some absurd reason, she had an almost overwhelming urge to jump on it, rip off his black casual trousers and navy crewneck T-shirt and wipe that sanctimonious look right off his gorgeous face.

'There's not much more to tell,' she said after several, calming gulps of champagne. 'We met about three years ago, at a friend's party, dated for about two and then decided I should move in with him – mainly because I couldn't afford to keep paying the rent on my flat. As his was just a stone's throw from the gallery he owned in Chelsea, it made sense. It was either that or me move further out of London.'

'How romantic,' Thaddeus said, eyes still closed. 'But I remember you telling me you're more of a practical kind of girl and not the romantic type.'

Sophie sucked in a breath. She was very tempted to

throw the contents of her glass over him.

'I think living in a flat in Chelsea is pretty bloody romantic,' Poppy said. 'So you moved in, Sophie. Then what? Did you get engaged at the same time or did that come later? Was it a romantic proposal at least?'

Sophie shook her head. 'Not really. We were going through some things his aunt had left him and there was this fabulous ring. It was a sapphire and diamond and it went on easily enough but when I went to take it off, it was stuck. Trent… that's his name, Trent Godly. Trent said that I may as well leave it where it was. So I did.'

A snicker of laughter escaped from Thaddeus' lips and even Ben and Oliver looked amused.

'The old, "I can't get it off" ploy,' Thaddeus said, finally opening his eyes and looking at Sophie. 'So that really works?'

'I don't suppose it's a sentence that's ever passed your lips,' Sophie said. 'You're adept at getting things off, aren't you?'

'What?' Poppy said, glancing from one to the other.

Thaddeus grinned and his eyes held Sophie's for a couple of seconds before glancing up at Poppy. 'Timothy Richards has been telling Sophie that I'm a bit of a bastard where women are concerned.'

'Oh,' Poppy said. 'Well, I suppose he had to get at least one thing half right.'

'Thanks,' said Thaddeus.

'Don't mention it,' replied Poppy.

'So when did you find out Trent was cheating on you?' Cleo asked.

'When he told me two months ago that he was moving to New York to be with Bettina – I'm sorry, but that's a bloody silly name. It sounds more like a cocktail than a woman. She came into the gallery about four months ago but whether that was the first time they met, I have no idea. She was over here on an extended break or something.'

'And he told you you'd got to leave the flat? Immediately?' Poppy queried.

'Not immediately. And he said I could keep my job at the gallery but… there was an accident. A fire at his flat and… he blamed me for it. I swear I didn't do it on purpose. It was truly an accident, but he was understandably furious and he told me he never wanted to see me or speak to me again. So I moved in with a friend.'

The silence that followed was almost deafening.

'Oh darling,' Ben eventually said. 'You're not one of those awful 'bunny boilers', are you? I'm usually a very good judge of character and I certainly didn't have you down as one of those!'

Thaddeus let out a peel of laughter.

'No!' Sophie shrieked, not meaning to. 'Honestly, it really was an accident. But I don't see what's so funny about me setting my fiancé's flat on fire, Thaddeus Beaumont.'

'Ex-fiancé,' he said, still laughing. 'Open some more champagne, please Oliver. I think we should raise a glass to Sophie… and to Trent and Bettina's future happiness.'

'Now that's just cruel, darling,' Ben said. 'But I do agree about opening more champagne. I'll do it though. We'll wait all night if we leave it to Oliver.'

'Sod off,' Oliver said. 'And who the hell's Bettina? Did I miss something?'

'I'll tell you later,' Cleo said, smiling at him. 'Ignore your cantankerous old uncle. You know he loves you really. Although not half as much as I do.' She leant over and kissed Oliver firmly on the lips.

'*Old*!' Ben shrieked. 'Cantankerous I'll give you... but *old*! Really, darling. You know how to cut a person to the quick. And if you're going to do that, please get a room. Voyeurism is not one of my little fetishes.'

Sophie glanced at Thaddeus. As she had half expected, he was looking at Cleo and Oliver but to her surprise, he smiled and then his eyes met hers and the smile vanished completely.

Chapter Thirteen

'You don't have to take me home,' Sophie said to Thaddeus when they left the pub at a little after eleven. 'I can walk. It's not far.'

'Don't be bloody ridiculous! Goldebury Bay might be small but it doesn't mean it's safe to walk the streets alone at night and especially not to walk along the beach, up a flight of steps and over a deserted cliff.'

'If it's deserted, it won't be an issue, will it? Have I done something to upset you? You seem in a really bad mood.'

He glared at her. 'Get in the car. It feels as if it's going to rain again.'

'How can you tell that?'

'Because I know the weather. I've spent most of my life outdoors, in, on or around boats and the sea. Trust me. It's going to rain.'

'Of course it is. But you didn't answer my question.' She got in and slammed the door. 'Why are you in such a bad mood?'

'Apart from the fact that you're trying to wreck my car, you mean? Perhaps it's because I thought we… I thought we got on well this morning. I told you things I haven't told anyone apart from my very best friends.'

She waited for him to continue but instead he drove towards Summerhill in silence.

'I know you did, Thaddeus and if you're worried I'll repeat any of it, I've already told you, I won't.'

'You also told me you wouldn't be seeing Timothy Richards again but the moment I left, you ran off to have lunch with him.'

'I didn't! And even if I had, I don't see why that should upset you. Unless you think I've been reporting back to him or something?'

'Have you?'

'No! How many more times do I have to say it? I only met him today. I went to the gallery to see the portrait – which may I remind you, I didn't know was there until you told me. He came in and asked me to lunch. I was hungry so I went. End of story. And believe me, we didn't spend our time talking about you.'

Okay, she thought, so that was a lie but there was no way she was going to tell him what they'd discussed. Besides, he was cross enough already.

'I bet you didn't.'

He didn't slow down when they reached the dirt road and Sophie was tossed back and forth like a rag doll.

'Do you want me to throw up?' she asked. 'I haven't had anything to eat since lunch but I have drunk rather a lot of champagne.'

'I noticed,' he said, but he slowed down and pressed the button to open the passenger window. 'Lean that way if you do.'

She didn't feel in the least bit queasy; she just wanted to have a few more minutes in his company. Although she had no idea why. The guy was acting like a complete jerk.

'Can we call a truce?' Sophie took a quick glance at his firm jaw and the tight line of his lips. 'I swear, Thaddeus, I haven't repeated a word you told me – and I won't. Not to Timothy or to anyone. Oh! That's not entirely true. I did tell my mum you'd told me about the portrait of Sophia but I didn't think you'd mind that.'

She saw him relax a little. 'I'm sorry,' he said. 'I know I'm behaving like a moron and I know I said the guy doesn't bother me but… sometimes he does.'

'I can understand that but please, please trust me. I may let you down in other ways but I won't breach your confidence by repeating things you say.'

He glanced across at her and there was an odd look in his eyes. 'I'm not sure I find that very reassuring. What do you mean, "let me down in other ways"?'

'Nothing, I…' She grinned at him and fluttered her eyelashes. 'I mean, in never offering you a bed for the night.'

He grinned in return. 'We'll see about that. But… it's not just that you had lunch with him. I've got no right to tell you who you can and can't have lunch with, as I said. It's… that I was surprised by what you said tonight. I had no idea you'd been engaged, or dumped or any of it. And I suddenly realised, I didn't really know anything about you.'

'Well, it didn't really come up, did it? I think we spent this morning talking about you and your sex life, not me and mine.' Sophie picked at the hem of her shift dress. 'Are you and Poppy more than just friends? I only ask because she didn't seem too happy to see me at first. She seems lovely, as does Cleo, but I felt a distinct coolness in the air when I arrived with you.'

He pulled up at the house, switched off the ignition and turned to face her. 'No. She's just a bit protective of her friends, that's all.'

'She's beautiful.'

'She's very beautiful,' he agreed.

'And… she's got a fantastic figure.'

He nodded. 'I can't argue with that. She's definitely hot.'

'So why…?' She had no right to ask him this and she

wasn't sure why she wanted to know the answer.

'Why…? Why haven't we had sex, you mean?'

Sophie nodded and Thaddeus shrugged.

'I thought about it once. I think we both did. We even kissed a couple of times but it just didn't feel right. She's Cleo's best friend and just as Cleo and I finished, this whole thing with my dad blew up. Poppy helped me and my family go through our books and accounts. She's brilliant with financial stuff. Then she went travelling with some friends for three months. She came back at Christmas and Cleo tried to get us together –which is when I thought about it, but she wasn't sure whether or not she was going back to Gibraltar. That's where she and Cleo both lived before last summer. She had to go back – they both did – to pack up their things and when she came back, I thought about it again but the trial was about to start and what with the press and one thing and another… I think we both knew it would be a mistake. Sometimes friendship and sex just don't go together.'

'And sometimes they do?'

'Definitely. I'd never marry someone I wasn't friends with. What's that look for? I'm serious.'

'I'm sure you are. I was just surprised to hear you use the 'm' word. I got the impression marriage wasn't on your agenda.'

'It isn't. But only because I haven't met anyone I'd want to marry.'

'Apart from Cleo.'

He frowned. 'What makes you think I'd want to marry Cleo? Oh, don't tell me. Timothy Richards said I'm holding a flame for her.'

'I think the exact words were, "carrying a torch", so yes.'

'Well, there's another thing he's wrong about. I love

Cleo very much, but only as a friend now, and yes, we dated last year and if she hadn't been nuts about Oliver, perhaps it would've gone somewhere. But it may surprise you to know two other things about me. First, I was the one who told Cleo we should be honest and accept she was in love with Oliver, not me. And second, I didn't have sex with her either. Coming from a man who's supposedly a bit of a bastard where women are concerned, I expect you'll find that hard to believe. But it's true, I assure you.'

Sophie stared at him in disbelief. 'What? Never? But... you dated for the whole summer, didn't you?'

'Most of it, not all,' he said with an odd little smile.

'And you never had sex? Not once?'

He took a deep breath, let it out and with a serious look in his eyes, said: 'I'll tell you something I may very well live to regret. The one time I thought we would, I was very drunk and I... couldn't.'

'You couldn't? You mean...?'

He nodded. 'Yep. Now wouldn't that be a scoop for Timothy Richards? There was a second time, when I didn't have that problem. In fact I had quite the opposite problem, but that was the night I told her it wasn't really me she wanted and I had to make her see that sex was out of the question. We spent the entire night talking instead. And believe me, that was the hardest thing I've ever had to do – and that was neither a euphemism nor a pun. It was bloody difficult because I wanted her more than I'd ever wanted anyone, but I knew that she loved Oliver and that Oliver loved her and if she and I'd had sex, it could've ruined everything.'

Sophie couldn't believe the things he was telling her. 'Wow. You really are a knight in shining armour, aren't you? Do you always put other people's happiness before your own?'

'Only if I really care about them. I'm no saint, believe me. And I'm sure I don't have to tell you that I'd appreciate it if you didn't repeat a word of what I've just said, to anyone. Not even your mum.'

Sophie grinned at him. 'Cross my heart.'

'Thanks. Speaking of hearts. Why didn't your ex-fiancé, Trent Godly, believe the fire was an accident?'

'Oh. Because I've been known to do stupid things when I let my emotions get out of control. Nothing bad, just stupid. Not that I can think of any as it happens but I know I do them.'

'I'll bear that in mind. Now, are you going to invite me in for coffee or are we going to sit in this car all night?'

'Neither. I think it's time we went to bed. And before you get any ideas, I meant separately. You in your bed, me in mine.'

'Fine,' he said grudgingly. 'I'll just walk you to the door?'

She giggled. 'It's two feet away, if that.' But stepping out of the car, she screamed. She nearly trod on the black cat from earlier. 'Oh my God! That's the second time that cat's almost given me a heart attack. Where the hell did it go this time?'

'It does seem to keep appearing, then disappearing every time we arrive at this door.'

He grabbed a torch from the car and shone the beam in all directions.

A sudden and rather frightening thought occurred to Sophie. She was with Thaddeus Beaumont each time the cat appeared. When she'd come home alone this afternoon there had been no sign of it. She shivered uncontrollably.

'You don't think it's… it's…'

'A ghost? A sign?' He laughed and turned to face her, holding the cat in his arms. 'He seems very much alive to me and from the sound of his purr, very friendly. I'd say the only sign here is the sign that's someone's been feeding him. He may even have belonged to Silas. He's probably hungry. Open the door and I'll come in with you. We'll find something for him and see what happens. Okay?'

'Okay,' she said but her heart was still thumping and her skin felt cold with fear. A rumble of thunder echoed through the still night air and a drop of rain landed on her cheek. 'Thaddeus, please don't take this the wrong way but would it be too much to ask you to stay the night?'

She expected him to make some flippant remark but instead he set the cat down gently on the ground, took the key from her shaking hand and with his arm around her shoulder, opened the door and led her inside. The cat followed close at their heels as the heavens opened for a third time in one day.

'I told you it would rain,' he said. 'I'll sleep in the room next door to you. And don't worry about a thing. I'm a light sleeper and the slightest sound will have me by your side in seconds. Okay? Now let's sort this cat out and see if Silas left any brandy in this place. I know that was his favourite tipple, so there's bound to be some somewhere. Unless the cleaner's drunk it all.'

Chapter Fourteen

Sophie slept far better than she'd expected. In fact, she slept so soundly that it wasn't until her nose caught the whiff of bacon, eggs and toast that she knew Thaddeus must be up and making breakfast.

The heavy curtains blocked out the light but the fluorescent luminous dial on her watch showed her that it was eight-thirty and she threw off the covers, wrapped her dressing gown around her and ran downstairs.

Thaddeus was standing in front of the cooker, flipping bacon and the cat was sitting at his feet, staring hopefully up at him whilst basking in one of several beams of lemon-yellow sunlight streaming through the leaded panes of the kitchen window.

'Morning sleepyhead,' Thaddeus said. 'I was just going to send Silas up to wake you. Oh sorry, I've named the cat, Silas. You don't mind, do you?'

Sophie scratched her head and yawned. 'It suits him. Silas used to frighten me to death half the time too. I can't believe I slept so late. I'm usually an early riser.'

'It's the sea air. Even I slept well and I've lived by the sea all my life but never in a house on a cliff with nothing but fresh air around it. Apart from the trees at the back that is. Sit down. I hope you don't mind me making breakfast. I seem to have made myself at home. Sorry about that.'

'Please don't apologise. I'm very glad you're here. And thanks so much for last night.'

He grinned. 'That's what all the girls say. Coffee?'

She nodded and smiled as he served her breakfast. 'Please, Thaddeus, I'm too sleepy to talk about sex.'

'I don't know what your plans are,' he said, handing her a mug of coffee and sitting opposite her. 'But next Saturday is the Midsummer Parade and Sunday is The Summer Fete. There's a parade, surprisingly enough given the name, and the seafront is lined with stalls selling everything from cakes to books and tea to wine. There's music in the streets and everyone dresses up. Well, not everyone but most people. We used to help organise some of it but now…' he shrugged. 'It'll be fun though. We'll all be going, so you're welcome to join us but Oliver has a stall at the Midsummer Parade, so he'll be working there that day. And so will Cleo, possibly, I suppose. She's a school teacher. I'm not sure if she mentioned that last night, but she helps Oliver at the restaurant and his cookery school quite a bit. Come to think of it, so may Poppy. She works part-time for Oliver and part-time at Ben's pub.'

'So… I'd just be going with you then?'

He grinned and nodded. 'Yes. But it won't be a date.'

'I'm hoping I'll still be here. I'm seeing Silas's solicitors tomorrow and I'm going to ask them if they'll let me stay on at this place for a couple of weeks. I won't know what's happening until then. Can I let you know after that?'

'Of course,' he said. 'I told you. It's not a date. Just two friends hanging out together. I'll give you my mobile number and you can let me know.'

'I've got it,' she said. 'I saved it when you called me yesterday.'

A forkful of bacon hovered inches from his mouth. 'So that you could call me and ask me round for dinner tonight?'

'No. So that I could avoid your calls asking for a bed for

the night.' She laughed. 'I just like to know who's calling me, that's all.'

'So… can I come to dinner tonight? I'll bring the wine. I'll even cook. And if you require my protection services again, that's okay with me.' He popped the forkful in his mouth and grinned.

She cradled her mug of coffee and met his eyes. 'Thanks, but I think Silas and I are good now.' She nodded towards the cat who was busy washing after devouring a piece of bacon, Thaddeus had tossed him. 'As for dinner, why don't I return last night's favour and invite not just you, but also your friends? Nothing fancy, just pasta and a salad. I'm sure Silas' solicitors won't mind if I pinch a couple of bottles of wine from the cupboard where you found the brandy.'

'That sounds like a plan. I'll call the others and ask as soon as we've finished breakfast. Did you mean Ben, too?'

She nodded. 'The more the merrier. Although will it be a problem for Oliver? With the restaurant, and Ben, of course runs the pub so… Perhaps that's not such a good idea, after all.'

'No, it's cool. Ben does practically nothing as far as running the pub goes, these days. He just likes swanning around and giving orders – as you may've noticed last night, and Oliver has Sunday evenings off, so I'm sure it'll be fine.'

She watched him eat and couldn't help feeling a stab of guilt. Was she using him? Was this fair?

She wanted to spend more time with Oliver, Ben and Cleo in the hope of finding out if they knew anything about the feud or about the past in general, and she also wanted to find out who their living relatives were in the hope of meeting them.

She needed to solve the mystery as quickly as possible

so that she could find the treasure and get out of here. She had to leave Goldebury Bay far behind her. And as soon as she possibly could.

Thaddeus suddenly frowned at her. 'Where will you go if the solicitors won't let you stay here? Back to London? You said the Caymans were your first choice. Do you have the money to go there?'

'Not at the moment, no. But I'm fairly sure they'll let me stay. I don't know why I am, I just am.'

She really hoped she was right. And suddenly, the thought of living thousands of miles away from here on an island paradise didn't seem quite as idyllic as it had done only yesterday.

Finishing his breakfast and pushing the plate to one side, he smiled across at her. 'I'll call the others now, about tonight.' He pulled his mobile from his trouser pocket, leant back in the chair and tapped the screen.

Sophie gathered the plates and mugs – and tried to gather her thoughts at the same time.

'You cooked, I'll wash up,' she said, heading for the sink. As she let it fill with water and Thaddeus chatted on the phone, she stared out the window towards the horizon.

The view was spectacular, especially on a day like this. The sun had gone from lemon-yellow to buttercup and was spreading its petal-like rays across a gleaming, sapphire sea to the cliffs and onwards to the house.

Summerhill, the house, was perched on the brow of Summer Hill, the cliff and had views of The Mound and Golde Cliff to the east, and smaller hills, scattered with a few houses, to the west. It looked out across the open expanse of the English Channel and on clear days, one could see the promontory of Eastbourne and Beachy Head, just as she could today.

Below, was Summer Hill cove and its sandy beach, to

the east of which was the derelict building of the Goldebury Bay Yachting and Sailing Club and further east, the town of Goldebury Bay, cradled in a valley between The Mound and Golde Cliff.

To the west, more beach and small coves like the one below Summer Hill, and further on, the much larger town of Hastings, where Sophie must go on Monday in order to visit Silas' solicitors. Onwards from Hastings, lay Eastbourne.

As a child, she'd wondered which had come first: Summer Hill, the cliff or the Summerhill family name. She'd thought of it as a 'chicken or the egg' conundrum. When she'd asked Silas, he'd told her in no uncertain terms that the family had come first.

'The Summerhill family always comes first,' he'd said. 'You're a Summerhill, so don't you ever forget that. Nothing, and no one, is more important than that. The Summerhills came here, saw this cliff and took it. Whatever it was called before that, if it was called anything, is irrelevant. It's been Summerhill, the house on Summer Hill since before the Norman Conquest. And so it will remain, long after we're all dead.'

And Summer Hill cliff probably wasn't the only thing the Summerhills had seen and taken throughout their history, Sophie thought.

'We'll be here at seven,' Thaddeus said, coming up and standing right behind her. 'This is an incredible view. I didn't really notice it yesterday.'

She could feel his breath on her neck and for one brief moment, could imagine his strong arms slipping around her and pulling her into him. She shook the image from her mind.

'It certainly is,' she said. 'Although as you're at least six inches taller than me, your view is slightly different to mine.'

She'd said that to try to make a joke; to stop herself from thinking things she shouldn't, but it backfired.

'We can remedy that,' he said, and before she knew what was happening, he'd put his hands on her hips and lifted her in the air.

She screamed in surprise, wobbled in his hold and, in an attempt to stop herself from falling, twisted sideways and flung her arms around his shoulders.

It was like a scene from a film as she slid slowly, sensuously, down the length of his body, his arms now around her, their eyes locked, their breathing in unison. When their lips were level, she was certain he would kiss her. His head moved closer, she was sure of that.

Silas jumped onto the draining board with a loud meow and the spell was broken. Thaddeus loosened his hold on her and her feet were on the floor a split second later.

He glanced at the cat, then back at Sophie. 'I think it's time I went,' he said, a strange, gravelly note in his voice. 'We'll see you at seven. Do you want me to bring anything other than some wine?'

Sophie swallowed whatever it was that seemed to be stuck in her throat and managed a grin. 'A tin of cat food might be good so that Silas doesn't get too used to eating 'human' food. And I said I'd pinch some of Great-uncle Silas' wine, so there's no need to bring that.'

'You haven't seen how much Cleo and Poppy can drink. We'll all bring wine. I'll bring cat food. And unless you object, I'll ask Oliver to bring some of the salad he grows. It's organic and he's got varieties you've probably never even heard of.'

'I don't object in the least. In fact, I'd be really pleased.'

'I'll see you at seven then.'

To her surprise, he leant forward, kissed her lightly on

her cheek, gave Silas a quick stroke and was gone before she had let out the breath she hadn’t even realised she was holding.

Chapter Fifteen

Sophie cleaned the dining room, the sitting room and the hall. She even gave the kitchen a quick wipe over. Guests were coming for dinner and although this wasn't her house, she had to make it as welcoming as possible. She wished she could afford some flowers to brighten up the place but her funds were tight and now that she would be feeding five other people they would be even tighter. Why on earth had she suggested this?

At twelve, she phoned Julia and although she told her mum almost every detail of what she'd done since they'd spoken the previous day, she didn't tell her that Thaddeus had stayed the night.

After hanging up, she wondered why not. They'd talked about her spending the evening with Thaddeus and his friends; about her having lunch with Timothy and his news regarding Cleo Merrifield and Clara Pollard; about the portrait of Sophia Summerhill and how beautiful the jewels were; about the portrait of Barnabus Beaumont and his likeness to Thaddeus; every single thing in fact, except that Thaddeus had stayed.

Sophie even told her about the cat; that he had been named Silas and that for one terrifying moment she'd thought Sophia had sent it from the spirit world to warn Sophie to keep away from Thaddeus. They'd both laughed about that.

But Sophie didn't tell her mum that she'd spent last

night having lurid dreams of the man who was occupying the bed next door – or that she'd dreamt that she was in that bed with him. And she definitely hadn't said what she had dreamt they'd been doing together. Or that when she woke up, alone in her bed, she'd wanted nothing more than to make those dreams come true.

Nothing.

Not even the Summerhill treasure.

Sophie blushed just thinking about her dreams and she remembered how she'd felt in his arms this morning. She'd never felt like that with Trent. She wasn't sure she'd felt like that with anyone. What was happening to her? Was she simply getting caught up in the moment? Was she letting her emotions run away with her?

Her life had changed so much over such a short period of time and that was bound to have an effect. She was feeling vulnerable and lonely; she was feeling guilty and stressed. She was worried about the future and dealing with issues from the past. It was all taking its toll.

And last night, having spent most of the day thinking about Sophia and Barnabus; about passion and power; love and betrayal; treasure and treachery, her mind was in a whirl. Add to that, several glasses of champagne, a creepy house, a scary cat and a handsome hero, and thoughts of rampant sex weren't going to be too far behind.

She needed to go and take a shower; preferably a cold one.

The knock on the front door stopped her in her tracks and a vision of her opening it and Thaddeus sweeping her up in his arms, teased her addled brain. She wondered whether to ignore it and pretend she wasn't in. She had just decided that was the best thing to do when she heard Timothy Richards call her name.

'Sophie! It's Timothy. Are you in there?'

'Just coming,' she called back.

'Hi,' he said when she yanked open one of the heavy doors. 'I hope I'm not disturbing you.'

'No. But you'll have to excuse the way I look. I've been cleaning and this place is filthy. I was just going upstairs to take a shower.'

'Need a hand?'

She blushed; not because of his words or the saucy grin on his lips but because of her thoughts prior to his arrival.

'I think I can manage, thanks.'

'Your eyes are truly incredible. They're like little galaxies exploding right now.'

She looked away. 'Don't start that again,' she said, but she laughed and stepped aside to let him in. 'Would you like a cup of tea? Or is this a flying visit? Have you come to ask if you can look around the house? You said at lunch yesterday that you'd like to.'

His eyes seemed to be taking in his surroundings and he didn't answer immediately.

'Timothy?' Sophie prompted. 'Is there something I can do for you?'

'What? Yes. Actually no. It's more something I can do for you, I think.'

'Oh?'

'You said you'd be interested if I stumbled on anything about your ancestors. Well, I did some poking around and I think I have.'

His smile was at first triumphal, turning to apologetic and finally almost sympathetic, and she had a worrying feeling that not only would this be something she would rather he hadn't found out but that it would have peeked his interest in the Summerhill family. And that would be a very bad thing.

'Oh! I didn't mean I wanted you to… to waste your time

researching them. What've you discovered?'

'Have you eaten?'

'What?'

'Have you had lunch?' He held up a rucksack and pulled out a bottle of wine. 'I've got pizza, too. Let's talk and eat. Unless you had other plans?'

'No. No plans.' She thanked her lucky stars he'd come for lunch, not dinner. 'Follow me.'

She led him to the kitchen and got glasses and plates. Silas was curled up on one of the chairs and he raised his head, yawned and stretched. He could clearly smell pizza.

'Is this yours or did it come with the house?' Timothy asked.

'I assume he belonged to my great-uncle. That's why we've called him Silas.'

'We?'

Trust Timothy to pick up on that. 'Me and the cat,' she said.

He offered Silas some chicken from the pizza and the cat woofed it down. 'He likes that.'

'Yes, and he had bacon this morning. Somehow I have a feeling that cat food is not going to be seen as a treat tonight. So what've you discovered?'

Timothy opened the wine, poured it and took a large swig of his. 'I think we should eat first.'

Sophie had a feeling he had done a lot more than just a bit of "poking around". He must have spent the rest of yesterday and all this morning researching because by the look on his face, he was about to tell her something he thought she would find unsettling.

If it was what she expected, he must be one heck of a good investigator because if she and her mum hadn't been told the story by Sophie's, Granny Summerhill, they probably would never have found out. Granted, Timothy no doubt had access to things they didn't and he also undoubtedly knew exactly where to look, but even so. The Summerhills, the Beaumonts and the Pollards had done everything they could to remove all record of it. If it had taken him less than twenty-four hours to discover, what else would he find out that Sophie would much rather he didn't?

Then again, if he was that good at uncovering secrets, perhaps he could solve the mystery of the feud in just a matters of days when it might take her weeks to do so herself. Could she trust Timothy Richards? And did she really want him as her ally?

'Okay,' she said. 'I hope it's not something unpleasant. I almost wish I hadn't asked.'

'I think I would've stumbled on it anyway during my ongoing research into the Beaumonts. I just found it sooner because I went at it from a totally different angle and I was looking for mention of a Summerhill. And I have you to thank for that. You're not eating. Aren't you hungry?'

'Not very and I'm really keen to hear your news. Please don't keep me in suspense.'

'Okay,' he said, taking another swig of wine. He looked her directly in the eye, his face, serious. 'But first I should tell you that, if what I think I've discovered is correct, it will add an entirely new dimension to my book. Although… you might not like what it's going to say and I'm very sorry about that. It's something I'll need to talk to you about… to talk to everyone about… when I know for sure.'

Oh great, Sophie thought. I really am crap at this.

Not only had her plan gone wrong from the very start but now the present Beaumonts, Suttons and Pollards would find out because Timothy was bound to tell them – whether they wanted to hear it or not.

Then Sophie may not be quite so welcome in their friendly little group. Her only hope was to find the treasure and get out of Goldebury Bay before they all discovered the rest of the story and the truth about why she was really here.

Of course, there was a chance that they already knew the story. Which was something else she hoped to find out tonight. Just how much of their own family history did the current generation know?

Sophie took a deep breath and met Timothy's slightly apologetic look.

'You mean you're going to write something about Sophia Summerhill in your book? The book you're writing about the Beaumonts? Is that what you're telling me? And it's something unpleasant?'

He nodded.

'Okay. So what is it?'

He looked her in the eye. 'I believe Sophia Summerhill was accused of being a witch.'

Tell me something I don't know, Sophie thought but she feigned an air of surprise. 'A witch? What makes you think that?'

'That's not all.' He took another swig, larger this time. 'I'm not absolutely certain about this either, yet, but… I have a feeling that Sophia and Barnabus Beaumont were lovers.'

Without thinking, hunger got the better of her and she took a bite of pizza. This wasn't exactly earth-shattering news and if he wasn't sure, then perhaps he didn't know as much as she thought he might. It would still be a problem if he started asking questions of course, and if he continued poking around, he could discover more. Much, much more. She'd have to find a way to stop him or at the very least, to slow him down. Either that, or take him into her confidence, tell him only what she wanted him to hear and get his help instead.

'Doesn't that surprise you?' Timothy asked.

She swallowed her mouthful and nodded. 'Uh-huh. I mean, yes. Yes, of course it does. But you said you're not sure so…' She shrugged but realised he wasn't convinced.

'Are you sure you don't know anything about Sophia? I thought you'd be astonished by both pieces of information.'

'Hmm. Perhaps it takes a lot more to astonish me than you think. I was surprised about the lovers bit but to be honest, I always thought there was something between Sophia and Barnabus, just from something my gran once told me. As for the witch part, well, she actually *looks* like a witch, don't you think? So it doesn't surprise me that people might accuse her of being one. Especially with the crescent moon birthmark on her cheek. But it may not be the case.'

He frowned. 'Well, it surprised me. Sophia was from a wealthy family. It was usually the poor who were accused of witchcraft, not the rich.'

'Wasn't Anne Boleyn accused of 'bewitching' Henry VIII? And she was Queen of England. Admittedly, Henry wanted to be rid of her but even so. I know she was beheaded for treason for her alleged affairs and not because of the witch thing but it shows that status didn't necessarily matter.'

'No, that's true. Although there's some debate about whether the witchcraft allegation was romantic licence and didn't actually come into it at all, but in any event, it was unusual for the wealthy to be connected with such things. I did a quick bit of research and The Witchcraft Act of the 1560s reinstated the punishment of death. It was usually by hanging, not burning in those days – in England at least. But I don't think many women from good families were ever tried, let alone found guilty and executed. By Sophia's time, the trials were heard by Assize Judges, not by the Church and that's where I found mention of Sophia's name but the odd thing is, there's no record of the trial or what happened after. You said that you knew she died at twenty-three. Do you know how?'

'No.' Sophie hoped he couldn't tell by her eyes that she was lying and she quickly turned away. There was no way she was going to tell him that, or about Barnabus Beaumont's involvement. And she hoped he wouldn't find out. Not just for her sake but for Thaddeus and all the Beaumont family. 'But I know she wasn't hanged. I think she had an accident. At least, that's what I seem to remember hearing. Would you like a cup of coffee? I think that wine's going straight to my head.'

'No thanks. I have to say, you've taken the wind out of my sails. I thought you'd be shocked – and possibly even a little impressed by what I've told you.'

She turned back and touched his hand. 'I am, Timothy. You found it out so quickly, too. I am impressed. You're clearly very good. But you're not really certain and although I'm sure you could dig deeper and find out more, I'm beginning to think I'd rather not know.' She smiled at him and their eyes met. 'Are you really going to put it in your book? To say that they were lovers and that Sophia was a witch? Is that really necessary to your story?'

She stared into his eyes, allowing them to slowly travel down to the top button of his shirt. She watched his Adam's apple rise and fall.

'Sophia and you may not look alike but your eyes are just like hers. They seem to mesmerise me. I went back and looked at her portrait today and I couldn't stop staring at her. It was as if her eyes were pulling me into the picture. And your eyes...' He swallowed hard, licked his lips and reached out, lightly brushing her right cheek with his fingers. 'And this little crescent moon... Do all the Summerhills have it, or just you and Sophia?'

Sophie shook her head. 'I think it only passes down to the women for some bizarre reason. Granny Summerhill had it but I don't think Dad did. It doesn't show up on any photos of him. He died when I was a baby so I don't remember him but Gran lived with me and Mum after his death and she told me lots of stories from the past. She was Silas' sister but they didn't get on. I… I can tell you some of the stories, if you like. She would've told me if Sophia was a witch and that Barnabus was Sophia's lover.' Sophie tried to put him off the scent but even she was surprised when a tear rolled down her cheek. 'Sorry. She died a few years ago and I still miss her.'

Timothy got to his feet and pulled her into his arms. His kiss was sudden but it wasn't completely unexpected.

She didn't expect it to be as soft and gentle as it was. Or as warm and comforting.

And she definitely didn't expect to enjoy it.

Chapter Sixteen

Sophie cursed loudly as she stubbed her toe on the edge of the kitchen unit. It was her own fault for running and she cursed herself for that. Why was she rushing to open the front door anyway? Her guests could wait a few seconds, couldn't they? It wasn't raining or anything. In fact, they'd be basking in the evening sunshine whilst standing at the door.

She needed to calm down and get a grip. It wasn't as if she hadn't had people to dinner before. She'd hosted hundreds of dinner parties with gourmet menus, making every course from scratch when she'd been with Trent. Tonight was pasta and salad; hardly anything to get worked up about.

But it wasn't dinner she was worrying about. She'd been dashing around like a dragon with its tail on fire ever since Timothy had left this afternoon. Ever since that kiss. Well, two kisses. Three, if you counted the goodbye kiss at the door, which wasn't so much a 'goodbye' kiss as an 'I'll see you very soon and I'm looking forward to it' kiss. And she was feeling guilty. Very guilty. She was feeling like a traitor, not to put too fine a point on it. Worse than a traitor. Although she couldn't think of what was worse than a traitor as she limped towards the door.

But why was she feeling guilty about kissing Timothy? She was young, free and single. Just because Thaddeus and the others didn't like him, didn't mean she had to follow suit. Although if he did as he said he might and wrote something unpleasant and unflattering about her ancestor, Sophia, she may very well hitch her horse to the 'anti-Timothy wagon'.

Kissing someone was hardly a crime. And that's all she'd done this afternoon. She'd been sorely tempted to take things further but some inner voice had told her to back away, so she had. She'd made an excuse. Said it was too soon after Great-uncle Silas' death. Said that she had dinner plans. Said she needed time.

She didn't need time, she thought as she tugged the front door open. She needed to get a grip and stop letting her emotions run away with her but as a smile curved on Thaddeus' perfect lips and the light from the hall danced in his chocolate-brown eyes and made his inky blue-black hair gleam, she realised there wasn't much chance of that. Less than no chance, in fact.

'We come bearing gifts,' he said, holding two bottles of wine aloft with one hand and a wicker basket brimming over with salad leaves in every shade of green, in the other.

Her voice seemed to have deserted her; instead she smiled and stepped aside.

'Hello Sophie,' Oliver said. 'Ben's running late but he should be here in half an hour. He told me there's something he needed to look for. I hope that doesn't mess up your schedule.' He was carrying a blue canvas bag bearing the Sutton's logo, and Sophie could see at least three different types of bread sticking out of the top. In his other hand, she saw a duplicate bag with bottled water, by the looks of it.

'No. That's fine,' she croaked, noticing that Cleo and Poppy carried bags too. 'You all look laden down. I thought I was making *you* dinner, not that you'd bring your own provisions.'

She wondered if Thaddeus had told them what he'd overheard at Mike's Motors about her funds being tight and instantly felt a little embarrassed.

'We always do this,' Cleo said with a friendly smile. 'I've brought chocolate fudge cake and Poppy's got Amaretto ice cream.'

'This place is like something out of a horror movie,' Poppy said. 'Did you spend last night here on your own? You're a braver woman than I am.'

'No, Thaddeus stayed.'

The words had tumbled out of Sophie's mouth before she realised she'd said them, until Thaddeus added: 'In a separate room, before you lot get any ideas.'

'Really,' Poppy said, giving both Sophie and Thaddeus distinctly cool looks over the rim of her sunglasses. 'That was… nice of you, Thaddeus.'

Hastily trying to recover the situation, Sophie said: 'I was terrified. I almost trod on Silas… oh, not Great-uncle Silas… Silas the cat.' She shook her head. 'It's a long story but he gave me the fright of my life. The cat, that is. And then the thunder started and, well, I virtually begged Thaddeus not to leave me.'

'Yeah,' said Poppy. 'I hear lots of women do that. Join the club. Where's the kitchen? This ice cream needs to go in the freezer before it runs down my dress.'

'Oh. Um. Follow me.'

Well, that's a really good start to the evening, Sophie thought as she led Poppy and the others along the corridor to the kitchen. Now Poppy hates me, and they all think Thaddeus and I slept together. This is just great.

'You should've seen this place yesterday,' Thaddeus was saying from somewhere behind her. 'Silas was supposed to have had a cleaner but we can't figure out what she did because it wasn't housework. There were cobwebs as thick as blankets along here. No spiders though, strangely enough, but I suspect Silas ate them all. And I don't mean Silas the cat.'

Cleo giggled. 'Was he really that bad, Sophie? Your great-uncle, I mean. From what Mum tells me, some people were terrified of him but she said he was okay once you got to know him, although, he did have a bit of a temper on him.'

They'd reached the kitchen and Sophie turned to face her. 'I hadn't seen him since I was nine so I don't really know what he was like. He definitely frightened me though. Mum says he was probably a lonely, bitter old man from the day he was born. He didn't like her, and she wasn't the only one. He never seemed to have a kind word to say to anybody. But he did love my dad, so Mum says and he took Dad's death very badly.'

'It must have been hard for him,' Oliver said as he began unpacking the bags he'd brought. 'Being the only one left.'

'But he wasn't the only one left,' Sophie said, grabbing some glasses for the wine. 'There was me. And there was Gran, his sister – although she died a few years ago. But it was as if we didn't exist. Silas really hated women.'

'That's probably because he was jilted at the altar,' Cleo said, placing the chocolate fudge cake on a plate.

'What?' the rest of them said in unison, immediately stopping what they were doing.

'Oh.' Cleo glanced around her. 'I assumed you all knew. Except Poppy, of course.'

'Of course,' Poppy said, picking up a wine glass and holding it out to Thaddeus like an orphan asking for a bowl of gruel. 'I'm always the last to know anything in this place.'

'Sorry,' Cleo added. 'Great-aunt Miff told me this afternoon when I had tea with her and Mum and Mary. Um.

Mary is Oliver's mum, Sophie. She knew Silas too.'

'Well, come on then,' Thaddeus said as he opened a bottle of wine and filled Poppy's glass and then the other glasses on the table. 'Don't keep us in suspense. Who was the lucky lady? And I mean 'lucky' because she got away, not 'lucky' because Silas loved her.'

'Er... Do you honestly not know, Thaddeus?' Cleo sounded hesitant as he passed her a glass.

He tilted his head to one side and raised one dark brow. 'I wouldn't be asking if I did, Cleo.'

'That's probably Ben,' Oliver said as the single, piercing ring of the doorbell broke the moment's silence. 'He's earlier than I expected. Shall I go? Don't say another word until I get back, Cleo.'

He kissed her on the cheek and as he ran to the door, no one made a sound. It was almost as if time had stopped for them all. Apart from Silas, who was sticking his head into one of the empty canvas bags, followed by the rest of his body.

A second or two later, Sophie could hear Ben's dulcet tones.

'Well hello to you too, Oliver! I'll shut the door then, shall I? What on earth's the hurry, darling? Shall I follow you? Am I talking to myself here?'

'Hurry up, Ben. Cleo was just about to tell us something and you interrupted it.'

'Well, why didn't you say so? Get a move on, Oliver. I've seen tortoises go faster. Cooey! I'm here, darlings.' Ben burst into the kitchen, pushing Oliver out of his way. 'What have I missed?'

'Nothing yet,' Thaddeus said, his gaze fixed on Cleo. 'We were just about to discover who jilted Silas at the altar.'

'Oh.' Ben sounded disappointed as he dumped a crate of

champagne on the table. 'Make yourself useful and open one of these will you, Oliver? I thought it was something exciting. Everyone knows that *darling* Serenity Beaumont broke the old bugger's heart. And not just his, of course. That's probably where you get it from, Thaddeus. Your great-aunt was the female equivalent of you. That woman clearly knew the meaning of the words: Young, Free and Single.'

A loud thud made them all jump, followed instantly by an even louder, caterwauling Silas who shot across the kitchen floor after both he and the bag had toppled from the kitchen worktop.

'Well,' Poppy said a moment later, one hand resting over her heart. 'That's let the cat out of the bag in more ways than one.'

And from the look of surprise on everyone's face except Cleo's and Ben's, she was right.

Sophie was astonished. Silas Summerhill had been jilted by Serenity Beaumont! Did Fate ever stop playing games? And why hadn't Granny Summerhill told her about that? She'd told her virtually everything else. Or had she? Perhaps Granny Summerhill had known even more than she'd told Sophie or Julia.

Honestly, she thought, these people needed to get out more. There were other people in the world besides Beaumonts, Suttons, Pollards and Summerhills. Did they have to keep repeating history, by falling in love with one or other members of the same families over and over again?

'Serenity?' Thaddeus queried. 'Are you sure? Great-aunt Serenity and Silas Summerhill? I don't see that at all. They're like chalk and cheese.'

'Great-aunt Miff told me that Serenity was the love of Silas' life,' Cleo said. 'She said that he never looked at another woman again and that he put a single red rose on

Serenity's grave every day of his life.'

'Ahh,' Poppy sighed. 'That's so romantic.'

Thaddeus let out a snort of laughter. 'That's bloody nonsense. If Silas could get out of bed during the last few weeks, the first thing he would've done was beat his so-called cleaner around the head for not doing what she was paid for. He clearly didn't do that, and from the state of this place, I'd say he'd been in bed for some time, so there was no way he would've made it to St Peter's-in-the-Cliff churchyard. And I find it hard to believe he'd spend that much money on roses anyway, especially when he didn't even replace a broken pane of glass in this place.'

'I find it impossible to believe Silas was ever in love!' Sophie said. 'Or that any woman would've been in love with him. I know he wasn't bad-looking when he was younger. I've seen photos of him and some people would probably call him handsome but he was… well… him! A smile would crack his face. The thought of him actually kissing someone.' She shuddered. 'Yuk. I can't even think about it.'

'Well, he wasn't just handsome, darling,' Ben said. 'He was rich. And money is very, very attractive to some people.'

Thaddeus glared at him. 'Are you saying Great-aunt Serenity was after his money, Ben? Why? She had money of her own. And I know that, because she left most of it to Dad – who's spent the lot of course. But she had piles of it and she never married.'

Ben tutted. 'I said no such thing! Money attracts money. That's what I meant. He was rich. She was rich. Together, they'd be richer. But she changed her mind. Did Miff tell you why, Cleo darling? That bit of the story I don't recall. I just remember people talking about it when I was a boy, even though it happened years before. People have long memories in Goldebury Bay.'

'Clearly you don't,' Poppy said, 'or you'd remember, wouldn't you?'

Ben pursed his lips and scowled, as the beep of the oven timer announced that Sophie's home-made lasagne was ready.

Chapter Seventeen

'So what exactly did your Great-aunt Miff tell you then?' Sophie asked when they were all seated and eating dinner. 'I'd love to meet her and see if she has any other stories to tell about Silas.'

'Oh, she has lots of stories,' Cleo said. 'Her and GJ. He's my Great-uncle Jim. Mum does too. Although whenever she goes on about the feud between the Beaumonts, the Suttons and the Pollards, I usually tell her to stop. There's no point in raking over old ground, is there? And that's all in the past now. Oliver, Thaddeus and I have ended it once and for all.'

'The Three Musketeers. Yay!' Poppy said.

Ben said: 'Sarcasm's not an attractive quality, darling.'

Poppy stuck out her tongue. 'And you would know.'

'Stop it, you two,' Oliver said. 'You seem very interested in the past, Sophie. I thought it was just the Tudor and Elizabethan era but it's clearly history in general, isn't it?'

Sophie coughed. 'Um. Well it's only that I don't know much about my family. I never knew my dad and although Granny Summerhill told me a lot, there're things she didn't know. For example, I hadn't a clue that Silas was ever in love, so she didn't tell me anything about her own brother. Probably because they didn't get on.' She shrugged. 'I simply feel as if I'm missing something sometimes.'

'I feel like that all the time,' Poppy said. 'Perhaps we

should have a big get-together where everyone tells tales of old. Of course, I'll just be a bystander because I have no connection to any of this. It all makes my family seem pretty normal.'

Ben raised his brows. 'Normal! You? Hardly, darling. But that's not a bad idea. And I've got a little piece of news for you, Sophie darling. That's why I was late this evening. When you mentioned the portrait of Sophia yesterday it reminded me that it wasn't the only item Silas had given to the gallery. Well, when I say 'given' I don't actually mean given, obviously. I mean, lent.'

'Oh? What else?'

'A particularly beautiful rapier and a matching double-edged dagger. They're superbly crafted and both have a curved row of small rubies on the hilts. They're in the *Pirates – Heroes or Villains?* Exhibition. The one with Barnabus Beaumont's portrait in. They date from around that time and they just seemed to fit in nicely. Exactly the sort of thing a dashing young pirate would own. They're rather valuable, I would think. Who inherits Silas' estate? Is it you, darling? If so, I'd be very interested in discussing a price. Sophie? Sophie, darling? I said I'd be—'

'Yes. Yes, I heard you. But it's not me. I mean, I don't inherit. He said he'd leave everything to charity. I'll give you his solicitors' details and you can contact them if you like.'

The rapier and the dagger. So they existed too, Sophie thought. And Silas had them all along. Together with the portrait.

Why hadn't he been able to find the missing Summerhill treasure then? He had nearly all the clues and if anyone knew the history of the feud between the Beaumonts, the Suttons and the Pollards, it was Silas.

Although… perhaps there was even more to that than

she knew. He'd been engaged to a Beaumont and she'd jilted him. Why wasn't the Summerhill name ever linked with the feud? Especially as the Summerhills had played such a big part in the cause of it.

'Planet Earth to Sophie,' Cleo said. 'You didn't hear a word I just said, did you?'

'Sorry.' Sophie shook her head. 'No, I didn't. I'm still trying to get my head around Silas and Serenity Beaumont.'

'You and me both,' said Thaddeus, giving her an odd look.

Cleo continued: 'I suggested you come round to Mum's for supper one day next week. I'll get GJ and Great-aunt Miff to come and Mary and Christopher Sutton. That's Oliver's mum and dad. We can have a good old natter and you can hear all their tales.'

'Can I come?' Poppy asked. 'I want to hear them too.'

'That goes without saying,' Cleo said.

'I'd also rather like to be there,' Thaddeus said.

Ben glanced around the table. 'Well, I'm not being left out of this little party. Make room for me too, darling. In fact, why don't you all come to me? We can have a little 'do' in the library.'

'You're kidding, right?' Poppy said. 'Have you seen GJ, and Cleo's great-aunt Miff lately? They couldn't make it up those stairs.'

'Poppy's right,' Cleo agreed. 'Oliver? Couldn't we all have dinner at the restaurant?'

Oliver shrugged. 'I don't see why not. I'll check the bookings and see which night is best. We don't really want a packed restaurant to hear all about our family skeletons, do we?'

'Why don't you all come here?' Sophie offered, immediately wondering why she'd become such a willing hostess. She had very little money to feed herself, let alone everyone else.

'Excellent!' Ben pronounced. 'Now where's that chocolate fudge cake, Cleo darling? I should be watching my figure but a teensy mouthful won't hurt, will it? And Oliver, grab the champagne whilst you're up, will you? Champagne and chocolate are a must.'

'It may have escaped your notice, Ben, but I'm not actually "up". I'm sitting down,' Oliver said.

'I'll get it,' Thaddeus said. 'Have you ever considered employing a personal servant, Ben? One who would follow you around and pander to your every whim.'

'That's what partners are for, darling. But the bastard just left me.'

'And you wonder why!' Thaddeus said as he headed for the kitchen.

'I'll get the cake,' Sophie said, following him.

'Well,' Thaddeus said when he and Sophie were alone in the kitchen. 'It seems that one of your relatives offered one of my relatives a bed for a lot longer than one night. That was a bit of a surprise, wasn't it?'

He was leaning against the worktop with his arms crossed, a sparkle in his eyes and the most seductive grin she'd ever seen; she immediately crossed to the other side of the room to avoid him.

'And your relative dumped him and humiliated him.'

He eased himself away from the worktop and moved round to her side of the table. 'That's not a mistake I'd make. I'm pretty sure I can promise you that.'

She met his eyes and saw a look in them that troubled her. He knew nothing of the history between Sophia and Barnabus obviously, but coupled with that and what she'd just learnt about Silas and Serenity, she knew she must stay away from him.

'Well,' she said, unwittingly stepping closer to him. 'It's

one I want no part of, thanks all the same.'

'Are you sure about that?' He reached out for her and pulled her to him, wrapping his arms around her waist. 'Because from where I'm standing, it feels as if you want me almost as much as I want you. And I want you a lot.'

'Y... you do?'

'I do.'

Her brain told her to walk away – to run – but her feet didn't want to move, couldn't move. His lips brushed hers and—

'Oh!' Poppy shrieked. 'Shit! Um. Don't mind me. I just came for the ice cream. I'll be gone before you can say the word, 'sex'. Shall I tell the others you'll be a while?'

Sophie pushed Thaddeus away and gripped the edge of the kitchen table. She was finding it hard to breathe.

'No! No,' she said. 'We'll be right there.'

She grabbed the cake and fled from the kitchen without as much as a backward glance.

'Everything all right?' Cleo asked when Sophie dashed into the dining room.

'Fine. Absolutely fine,' Sophie replied.

'They were starting dessert without us,' Poppy quipped, carrying the ice cream and dessert bowls, and plonking them unceremoniously on the table. 'If you know what I mean'.

'We were discussing our ancestor's... mistakes,' Thaddeus said, returning to the dining room with a gleam in his eyes.

'Is that what it's called?' Poppy teased. 'It's been so long since I've had any 'mistakes' that I can't remember.'

'Really, darlings, is the dinner table the place to discuss sex?' Ben said.

Poppy sighed. 'Yeah. And not just discuss it but have it. Not that I can remember that either. Make mine a large one,' she said, slumping down on her chair. 'And I wish I wasn't just talking about a slice of chocolate fudge cake.'

'So,' Oliver said, grinning and wrapping his arms around Cleo. 'When do you want to have this big get-together? I'll be pretty busy at the restaurant most evenings but Wednesday would be good for me. That's usually a fairly quiet night.'

'And me,' Cleo added.

'Wednesday's good for me, too,' Thaddeus said, eyeing Sophie as if he were mentally undressing her.

'And isn't Wednesday Hump Day?' Ben queried.

'No sex at the dinner table!' Poppy jokingly snapped.

'It means, it's the middle of the week, darling. It's got nothing to do with sex.'

'I know what it means, Ben.' Poppy sighed again. 'I'm very sorry to say that any day's good for me. My social calendar's depressingly empty these days.' She glanced towards Thaddeus. 'And I have a feeling it's about to get even emptier.'

'Wednesday it is then,' Sophie said, desperately trying to avoid looking in Thaddeus' direction. 'Um. Shall we have a buffet supper?'

'We could have a BBQ if the weather's okay,' Oliver suggested. 'I'll bring steaks, burgers and sausages. Oh and salad. You girls organise the dessert.'

Sophie could feel the relief sweeping over her. She could make a summer pudding. It was cheap – and given the fact that she was a Summerhill in Summerhill on Summer Hill, quite apt. She just hoped it would be summer weather too.

Chapter Eighteen

One hour later, Sophie closed the heavy, right-hand front door and drew the bolt across the left and then leant back against them, letting out a long, deep breath.

She had enjoyed the evening but for the last hour all she could think of was Thaddeus and the fact that for a second time in only two days, they'd almost kissed. Timothy's kisses were now completely forgotten – overshadowed by the mere thought of kissing Thaddeus.

This was very troubling and just remembering the feeling of his arms around her did more than worry her: it made her ache for his touch; made her long for his kiss. How could Fate do this to her? Hadn't it done quite enough already?

She ambled to the kitchen and tried to find something to occupy her mind but as her guests had helped her tidy up, there was nothing left to do and everywhere she looked, she saw his face. Those deep brown eyes, more appealing than the chocolate fudge cake she'd savoured for dessert; that olive skin over his firm jaw and angled cheek bones; those perfect lips. She longed to run her fingers through the inky blackness of his hair and feel it brush against her skin.

She ran from the kitchen to the dining room but saw him sitting at the table, his eyes devouring every inch of her body.

She fled to the sitting room but saw him standing before the mantelpiece, a fire roaring in the hearth as they sunk to the floor in each other's arms.

'Okay! That's enough!' She shouted at herself. Now she was having hallucinations of him. Or was it wishful thinking? Either way, it must stop.

She went back to the door and sighed. She'd already locked it, she remembered.

The thud on the solid wood made her heart leap to her mouth. It was eleven o'clock at night. Who would be calling at this hour? It didn't even occur to her that she shouldn't open the door. Did she know in her heart of hearts who it would be?

'Thaddeus!'

'Sophie!'

She flung herself into his arms and his lips met hers in a kiss so deep and passionate that it made her head swim. His arms tightened around her as if he would never let her go and she could feel how much he wanted her as her body moulded into his.

Her arms locked around him in a vice-like grip as if she were terrified he might slip away, and her passion matched, if not surpassed his. She forgot where they were. Forgot the door was open. Forgot that she was supposed to be keeping her distance from him. Forgot everything except how much she wanted to feel his hands on her bare skin, on her breasts, between her legs, everywhere and anywhere possible. To caress, to possess, to enrapture. She knew she was about to experience the sort of pleasure most women dream of but rarely have. So exhilarating and all-consuming that she would never have enough of it. His lips made her feel things she'd never felt before, as if parts of her body had been sleeping like some fairy tale princess awakened by his kiss.

He pushed the door shut with his back and they tumbled against it, still locked in each other's arms. She felt tiny explosions in her head as if her neurons couldn't take the pressure of the amount of stimuli they were transmitting. Her heartbeat increased so fast that a cardiac surgeon would have an arrest just monitoring it and if she didn't catch her breath soon, she was sure she would expire. But she didn't care. She couldn't stop.

But suddenly, he did.

'Sophie. Sophie, wait!' he gasped. 'I need to say this now.' He cupped her face between his hands and stared into her eyes, his chest rising and falling like an oxygen pump. 'I don't know what this is but one thing I do know, I don't want just a one-night stand. I want more than that. I… I need to know if you feel the same.'

She couldn't speak at first and she wasn't quite sure she understood what he was saying; all she knew was that she wanted him to kiss her again; to hold her; to make love to her and frankly she would have said the moon was made of Swiss cheese if that was what he wanted to hear.

'So do I,' she moaned. 'Much, much more.'

His eyes flickered towards the stairs and then to the sitting room.

'Bed!' Sophie said decisively, reading his mind.

He smiled like a man who'd just been told he was a god and without a word, he swept her up and carried her upstairs, banging his elbow on the newel post but not seeming to care... even stumbling on the treads and laughing with her. Kissing her at every opportunity and finally, laying her gently on her bed and throwing himself beside her.

Chapter Nineteen

'Sex,' Julia Summerhill had told a teenaged Sophie more than once, 'is like a pair of shoes. There'll be good pairs and bad. Pairs that hurt and leave blisters. Pairs that need some time to break in. Pairs that make you walk as if you're ten feet tall and pairs that make you feel as if your heels are scraping the ground. Pairs that cost a fortune, most of which aren't worth the price you paid. Pairs that you get for a snip but are worth their weight in gold. Pairs that look sensational but fall apart after just a few outings. Pairs that you can't wear outside on a rainy day. Pairs that feel more like comfy slippers than shoes. But... when you find the right pair, the pair that fit you like a glove, that make you taller without the unsteadiness of a heel, that don't feel like shoes at all but merely an extension of your own feet, that make you smile every time you look at them, that you know you'll want to keep for a lifetime even if they may not look as good as they did when you first took them from the box – that's when you know you've got something special. And when you find that pair, make sure you wear them every day because shoes like that only come along once in a lifetime.'

Sophie wasn't sure she understood at the time but when she'd looked inside her mother's cupboards there were always lots of shoes, so her mum clearly knew what she was talking about.

This morning as the first pale beams of sunlight peered

in through the windows where the curtains hung wide, Sophie smiled at Thaddeus and understood. This pair of shoes seemed to have been made especially for her. They fit her so perfectly they were like a second skin and just looking at them made her feel that she could take on the world and anything it threw at her, providing she was wearing these shoes.

'Morning, gorgeous.' Thaddeus opened his dark eyes and smiled so brightly that he made the sun redundant. 'Did you sleep well?' He reached over and pulled her into his arms, kissing her softly on her lips.

She could feel herself blushing although after everything they'd done last night, it was a bit late for modesty. She grinned and nodded. 'For the whole five minutes that you actually let me sleep, yes thank you.'

A mischievous look flashed into his eyes. 'Did we waste five minutes? We'd better make up for that right now.'

She shrieked with laughter as he rolled her on top of him.

'No… Thaddeus…we…can't,' she said between kisses. 'I…have to…go and… see the… solicitors… this morning.'

He ran his hands through her hair. 'Tell them your watch stopped.'

'You stop!' Sophie rolled away from him and clambered out of bed, laughing. Realising she was naked, she tugged at a sheet.

'That's a bit like shutting the stable door after the horse has bolted,' he said with a wicked grin.

'Thanks. So much for a knight in shining armour. Has gallantry gone out the window now you've unlocked the chastity belt?'

'Was it locked?' He placed his linked hands behind his head with a self-satisfied smile until the cushion she threw at him hit him squarely on the jaw.

'It will be. And you'll never find the key.'

'Ooh. Nothing inspires a knight more than a quest – especially for the Holy Grail. I'd better start out on that right away.'

She fled, laughing and screaming to the bathroom with Thaddeus close behind her.

Chapter Twenty

The offices of Hardman & Jones, solicitors weren't at all what she was expecting, Sophie thought as she sat in reception, yawning. She'd been expecting something out of a Charles Dickens' novel complete with tall, wooden desks and rickety chairs, dusty papers piled high and sallow-faced clerks hunched over in silence, save for the scratching of quill pen nibs on parchment. Well, perhaps not quite that bad but the image seemed appropriate for Great-uncle Silas' solicitors.

What she saw was more like something out of *The Good Wife*. Slick glass offices enclosed by tinted full length windows, filled with beautiful-looking people who wouldn't seem out of place between the pages of *Vogue,* using gadgetry that looked as if it had just beamed down from some futuristic planet, light years away.

Even the transparent, polycarbonate chair on which she sat, felt as if it had come from another world. It was definitely uncomfortable and although she was sure it was sturdy and wouldn't collapse any second – a firm of solicitors being the last people who would be likely to invest in flimsy, law suit-courting furniture – she perched on the edge just in case.

Ludicrously, she was already missing Thaddeus. He'd only left her five minutes ago after insisting on dropping her at the door, in good time, surprisingly, despite them having spent at least half an hour in the shower together.

She quivered at the memory and the air-conditioned offices suddenly felt very warm.

But during those five minutes, she had come to a decision – a life-changing one. It was far too soon to know if she and Thaddeus had a future together but there was one thing she was certain of: she wanted a future with him, if that were at all possible. And you couldn't build a future on a lie. She would have to tell him everything. About Sophia. About Barnabus. About the treasure. All of it. Every last detail. And she'd have to tell him today.

But she'd have to talk to her mother first. Her mum had a right to know. After all, the plan had been for Sophie and her mum to share the treasure. Now Julia would have to share just Sophie's half because the other half would be going to Thaddeus Beaumont.

'Good morning, Miss Summerhill. I'm Tony Hardman. It's good to finally meet you.'

Mr Hardman extended his right hand, mentally dragging Sophie from her thoughts.

He wasn't what she'd expected either. He wasn't old; he wasn't short; he wasn't dressed in black and he didn't wear glasses. In fact, he was bloody gorgeous and for a split second, Sophie even forgot about Thaddeus. But only for briefest of moments.

'It's good to meet you too. And please, call me Sophie.'

'Oh. Thank you, Sophie. Please call me Mr Hardman. Sorry. That was a joke. Best not give up the day job, eh? Call me, Tony, please. This way.'

He led her to his office: more shiny glass. Obviously, his cleaner was far superior to Silas', she thought. She sat in the chair he indicated she should; a normal-looking chair, even if it was covered in a purple and lime-green, dogtooth patterned, twill.

'Coffee or tea?' Tony asked and before she could

respond, a model-like assistant appeared, carrying a tray with a plate piled high with biscuits, two gigantic cups and trendy pots of both tea and coffee, plus jugs of milk and cream.

Sophie wondered what the firm's hourly rate was and in her case, who would be paying it. She didn't think her funds would cover even the designer-looking biscuits.

'Coffee please, with milk.' She realised she hadn't eaten and helped herself to a biscuit. Bloody hell that's good, she thought as she bit into the crumbly texture. I definitely can't afford this place. 'I'm going to the funeral tomorrow,' she said when she'd finished it and then helped herself to another.

'That's good. I'll have a car collect you from the house. Shall we say two p.m.? The funeral starts at two-thirty. I'll be there, of course but it'll be a small service as per Mr Summerhill's wishes. It's a cremation and as you know, your great-uncle wasn't religious so it'll all be over fairly quickly. No flowers, again as per his wishes but he did request that his ashes be buried in a plot he purchased many years ago. That'll be done at a later stage, of course.'

'Um. I didn't know, actually. We hadn't been in touch for… several years. Speaking of which, how did you know where to find me?'

Tony Hardman coughed and fidgeted in his seat. 'Well – and I can fully appreciate this may not be pleasant news – but Mr Summerhill wanted us to… keep track of you, shall we say?'

'Keep track of me? You mean… have me followed?'

'Dear me, no. No, no. Nothing quite so crass. Just… follow the paper trail so to speak. And everyone has one – unless they're trying to hide – and even then, there are ways and means. He just wanted to be sure that we knew where you were in the case of his… departure.'

'Death?'

'Yes. How are you finding things at the house, Miss… I mean, Sophie? Is there anything you need? Does the heating work? If I'd known the weather was going to be so cold over the weekend I'd have had the boiler checked.'

'It's fine,' she said. 'Everything's fine.'

'I know some windows have been broken. Mrs Phelps, the cleaner notified me and they're due to be repaired today. The firm we use is excellent and there shouldn't be a problem.'

'Um. I don't want to speak out of turn, and obviously it's none of my business but, the house was very… dusty. When did… Mrs Phelps last visit?'

Tony frowned. 'Are you saying her work isn't up to scratch? Please tell me if that's the case. I won't tolerate poor standards.'

'Um. Honestly? The only rooms she seems to have touched were the kitchen and Silas'… I mean Great-uncle Silas' room.'

'You are joking?'

Sophie thought his face might explode. 'No. Sorry, I'm not.'

He pressed a button on the phone on his desk. 'Veronique. Sack Mrs Phelps. Organise a firm to give Summerhill a thorough clean. Top to toe. As a matter of urgency, please. But co-ordinate with Miss Summerhill.' He turned to Sophie. 'There's a rather nice hotel just outside Goldebury Bay if you're happy to stay there whilst the house is cleaned. I can't apologise enough. Mr Summerhill would've been livid. I'm so sorry, really I am. I've clearly dropped a ball on this. I assure you this doesn't usually happen – and it won't happen again.'

Sophie managed a smile. 'Thank you but… um… I can't afford a hotel and… I know it's a bit of a cheek but I was…

well, I was really hoping I could stay at the house for a few weeks. A few days even. You see my car's just broken down and my fiancé and I have just broken up and I was staying with a friend and… It would only be for a little while. Please?'

He blinked several times and confusion filled his eyes. Suddenly, he said: 'Oh I see. Oh dear. Miss… sorry, Sophie. I think this may also come as a shock but a pleasant one, I hope. You may stay at Summerhill for as long as you like.'

'Thank you! Sorry. I didn't mean to shriek like that.'

'Please don't apologise, Sophie. But you didn't let me finish. You may stay at Summerhill for as long as you like... because – other than the ten per cent of his estate that he left to charity, and after payment of inheritance tax and once probate is granted, which is merely a formality – you own Summerhill.'

'What! I… I own Summerhill? How?'

'Your great-uncle left it to you.'

'All of it?'

'Yes. As I said, apart from the ten per cent that goes to charity, the rest of his estate is yours. That means the house and everything in it, under it and around it. Although there are legal stipulations as to exactly how far under a property a person can own, as well as above it of course, but I digress. You are the main beneficiary of his estate which means you own the house and its contents, the land, the money in all of his accounts, the stocks and shares, the property investments. Well, there's a portfolio listing the details and I'm happy to go over that with you line by line when you're ready to do so. Sophie? Are you feeling unwell? You've gone as white as a sheet of paper and your eyes look… glazed. Veronique!' he yelled. 'Tell Claudia we need her first-aider skills right this second. Here Sophie.

Drink this water.'

The last thing Sophie remembered was Tony Hardman standing beside her with one hand resting against her back and a glass of water in the other.

Chapter Twenty-One

Thaddeus couldn't remember the last time he'd been this happy. Was it when Cleo had come back to Goldebury Bay last year and they'd started dating? No. Even if it had lasted, he hadn't felt this kind of euphoria at just the thought of her.

Was it the first time he'd gone sailing... with the wind in his hair and the expanse of the English Channel in front of him; just him and the elements? No. That had been a wonderful experience – exhilarating, thrilling, but it hadn't felt like this.

Was it when…? Oh what was the point? He knew the answer so why waste time doubting it; questioning it. He'd never, ever felt this good and it was all because he'd spent the night in the arms of Sophie Summerhill.

He had to laugh at himself. He was behaving like a love-sick puppy. He'd only dropped her at the solicitors about ten minutes ago and he was missing her so much that he could actually feel the pain in the pit of his stomach.

Or was he just hungry? They'd skipped breakfast, after all. He felt a surge of testosterone rush through him at the thought of what they'd done instead. He grinned and had to stop the car because the feeling overwhelmed him.

Shit! This was serious. He'd only met the girl on Saturday. How could he feel like this in such a short space of time? Is this… is this what love felt like? Real love. Not just lust or passion but real unadulterated love. He'd have to ask Oliver because Oliver was nuts about Cleo so if anyone knew what love felt like it would be him. Thaddeus had definitely never, ever felt like this about anyone. And no, not even Cleo.

His mobile rang and in his agitated state he answered it without checking who was calling. He didn't say a word. He couldn't find his voice. He was still thinking how wonderful it felt just to be alive. Just to be him. Just knowing that he'd see Sophie again in an hour or so. Just to be in love.

'Hey sexy,' a man's voice said. A voice he thought he recognised. Was it a friend playing a joke on him? 'I can't wait to hold you in my arms again and kiss you all over your wonderful, gorgeous, body. How about I take you to dinner tonight? Or I could just come up to Summerhill. Maybe spend the night? Sophie? Sophie, it's Timothy. Can you hear me? Shit phone. Shit technology. I'll call you back.'

Thaddeus was still holding the phone to his ear when it rang again.

'Hey babe, it's Timothy. I can't seem to stop thinking about you. I—'

Thaddeus ended the call and stared at the phone. Only then did he realise it wasn't his. It looked like this. It didn't have a screen lock on; neither did his. It was set to answer by lifting it to the ear, as was his. But now that he took the time to look at it, the screen had a picture of a tropical beach, not the sandy beach of Goldebury Bay as his did.

Even though he now knew whose phone it was, he scrolled through the list of numbers and saw: *Amanda; Bank; Hardman sols; Mum; Thaddeus; Timothy; Trent.* That was it. That was the extent of the phonebook. He didn't know whether to laugh or cry. This was definitely Sophie's phone, not his. He must've picked up hers this morning and she'd picked up his. Did she only know seven people? Two of the numbers were a bank and a firm of solicitors so that left five. And one of those was him.

And one of those was Timothy.

The same Timothy who had just called her.

Twice.

And not just called her, but called her… "*sexy*" and "*babe*".

And she'd told him that she and Timothy weren't friends. That she'd only met him on Saturday. That she probably wouldn't ever see him again.

But she'd had breakfast with him. And lunch. And clearly a lot more if he was calling her sexy. And they'd kissed at the very least. And they obviously had plans to do so again. And was that all they'd done?

Thaddeus gripped the steering wheel until his knuckles turned white.

If this is what love felt like, it stank. And not only that, it hurt like hell. His heart was disintegrating in his chest. Breaking into little bits like a melting glacier crumbling into the sea.

Why hadn't he listened to his instinct? He'd known from the moment he saw her that she was hiding something. He'd thought it was her birthmark. He knew how self-conscious women were about such things. But something had told him there was more to it than that. And even after he'd poured his heart out to her, he'd only found out things about her when she'd told him and the others in The One That Got Away on Saturday night.

Shit! *He'd poured his heart out to her*. He'd told her things he hadn't told anyone. Why? Why had he done that?

Was she working with Timothy? Was that her secret? Was he paying her? Was she going to repeat it all to that shit? Was he sleeping with her? Were they lovers pretending to be strangers?

How could he have been so stupid? And last night he'd opened up to her in ways he'd never opened up to anyone.

And he'd given her his heart.

And she'd stomped on it and ground it to dust.

And she and Timothy Richards would probably be having a good laugh about that.

In between kisses.

In between the sheets.

The sound of the blaring car horn as he banged his head against it made several people jump. But Thaddeus didn't care. He didn't care about anything anymore.

Chapter Twenty-Two

Shortly after Sophie came to, on the sofa in Tony Hardman's office, she realised she'd picked up Thaddeus' phone by mistake.

Tony, Claudia and Veronique had all insisted she lie still for a while and she'd done so whilst they clucked around her like a flock of anxious hens. But she couldn't rest or relax. As Tony's words finally began to sink in, she wanted to tell someone. And the first person she wanted to call was Thaddeus. This surprised her almost as much as Tony's words had.

Not her mum, who was usually the first person she told anything and everything. But Thaddeus, a man she'd only met on Saturday; a man she hardly knew, but a man who had suddenly become the person she wanted to speak to first.

How on earth had that happened?

She'd decided earlier that she'd share her secret with him – and acknowledged that she'd like to share her life, but how had he become as important to her as her mum?

More so perhaps, if she thought of calling him first.

Maybe it was partly because she knew her mum would be asleep in bed due to the time difference.

Did that matter though? News like this was worth waking someone up for.

But still, she wanted to speak to Thaddeus.

It was when she pulled out her phone and scrolled

through the phonebook that she realised this wasn't her phonebook. And then she realised it was Thaddeus' phonebook. It was easy to scroll through because, just like her phone, it didn't need a personal pin to unlock it. She smiled at the thought that neither of them protected their phones, although it wasn't really something to smile about.

She was amazed at the number of people he knew. The list was endless. She thought of her own phonebook and smiled again, albeit somewhat half-heartedly.

Eventually, she found her name listed simply under *Sophie.* At least she was the only Sophie. She should be thankful for that. She pressed the button and called her own phone.

'Thaddeus? It's me. We got our phones mixed up this morning. Where are you? Did you stay in Hastings as you said you probably would? I need to tell you something and you'll never believe this but—'

'Actually Sophie,' came Thaddeus' reply in a tone as cold and disinterested as a frozen chicken. 'I'm on my way back to Goldebury Bay. Something's come up. I'll drop your phone in to Oliver at the restaurant. You can collect it from there. Give him mine, will you? Oh, and thanks for last night. It was fun. We should do it again sometime.'

The line went dead.

'Hello! Thaddeus? Thaddeus? Hello!' She cast her eyes around an empty office and burst into tears, Tony and the others having left her in private so that she could make her call. But Veronique and Claudia ran back in the moment they heard her distressed voice. They handed her a box of tissues and some more water. And Tony asked if there was anything he could do.

'I… I don't understand it,' Sophie sobbed into her third tissue. 'What's happened? What could possibly have happened? Everything was perfect when he dropped me off. He kept pulling me back every time I tried to get out of the car. "One more kiss", he kept saying. "Just one more, then I'll let you go. But I'll be picking you up the minute you step out the door and I'll be kissing you for at least ten minutes, so be prepared." That's what he said. Was it all a lie? Why? Why would he lie? Why would he do that? Surely, if I was just a one-night stand he wouldn't have insisted on giving me a lift here. Wouldn't have said he wanted to spend as much time with me as possible. Would he?'

Tony cleared his throat. 'Erm. This is a little out of my area of expertise, Miss Summerhill. Sophie. I… I think I'd better let Veronique and Claudia advise you on this subject. But if there's anything else I can do, please let me know. I'll… I'll be just outside. Stay here for as long as you wish. My office is at your disposal.'

'Thank you, Tony!' Sophie screeched. 'I just want to die.'

'There, there. Don't talk like that,' Veronique said, wrapping a comforting arm around her shoulder.

'No indeed,' Tony said. 'You have to survive for twenty-eight days after Mr Summerhill's passing in order to inherit. So let's not be hasty.'

'That's not funny, Tony,' Veronique said. 'I suggest you break open the brandy. Nothing like a tot of brandy to ease a broken heart. Now you let it all out, Sophie. May I call you, Sophie?'

Sophie nodded and sobbed: 'He'll never call me, will he? I'm just another in a long list of one-night stands, aren't I?'

'At least you're a wealthy woman now, Sophie,' Tony said, clearly trying to comfort her but failing miserably. He handed her a large glass of brandy. 'Money may not buy happiness but it can make misery look a damn sight better.

Especially from the deck of a luxury yacht or the balcony of a ski chalet, or whatever takes your fancy.'

Sophie's head shot up. 'Mum! I want to see my mum.'

'Well,' Tony said with an audible sigh of relief. 'That I can arrange. No problem at all. Just give her a call and I'll get the ball rolling.'

Chapter Twenty-Three

After two glasses of brandy, or possibly three, she wasn't sure, Sophie called her mum. Tony kindly let her use the office phone although she'd been sorely tempted to use Thaddeus' and speak for as long as possible. That would show him she wasn't the kind of girl he could spend one night with and then toss aside. She'd make him pay for that. And a call to the Caymans from his mobile would cost a fortune. A fortune he didn't have. And wouldn't have. She'd see to that. There was no way she was going to share the treasure with him now.

But she decided a landline would be clearer and there'd be no risk of being disconnected by the vagaries of mobile technology, so revenge on Thaddeus would have to wait.

'Hello,' Julia said, clearly wondering who the unknown caller was.

'Hi Mum, it's me.' Sophie had finally pulled herself together and it had only taken her two hours. That wasn't bad, she thought. Perhaps Thaddeus didn't mean that much to her, after all. She rubbed her eyes to stop more tears from falling.

'Darling, is everything okay? Your voice sounds… odd. Are you all right? Tell me, Sophie. Tell me now. What's happened? Please darling!'

Sophie bit her wobbling lip and took a very long, deep breath. 'I'm at the solicitors, Mum. You'll never guess what Great-uncle Silas has done.'

'Dear God. What? Don't tell me he's strictly forbidden you to stay at the house. That wouldn't surprise me one bit.'

'No, Mum, he hasn't. He's left me the house. He's left me everything. Well, he has given ten per cent to charity but the rest he's left to me. And it's not just the house and land, Mum. It's everything. It seems he was rich. Very, very rich. We're loaded, Mum. For the first time in our lives, we don't have to worry about money. And we'll never, ever, have to worry about it again.'

There was silence.

A long silence.

Then Julia Summerhill screamed.

And then she fainted.

At least, that's what Hugh, her boyfriend told Sophie after a couple of minutes.

'Is Mum okay?' Sophie asked.

'Yeah, she's fine,' Hugh assured her. 'She landed on the sofa, so no harm done and she's come to. I've just given her a brandy and she—'

'Darling! I'm fine,' Julia said. She'd clearly snatched the phone back from Hugh. 'Did you really just say what I think you said? That the old bastard left you the lot.'

'Except the ten per cent to charity, yes. It's… it's unbelievable, isn't it?'

'It certainly is. But what I'm finding more unbelievable is that you don't seem very excited. Why is that? I suppose you must be in shock, just as I am, but still. My Sophie would be laughing and dancing and singing. What's wrong, darling? You usually tell me everything. Please tell me why you're not yourself today.'

Sophie couldn't go through it again. 'I want to come and see you, Mum. Is that okay? Tony says he can arrange everything.'

'Of course it is! You know you don't have to ask. But how… oh silly, silly me, you're rich now, and there was me wondering how you'd afford to get here. Who's Tony?'

'Oh. The solicitor. Tony Hardman. He's… very nice.'

'That's good, darling. Well, when will you be here? Are you leaving today? Oh Sophie, darling. I can't wait to see you again.'

And that was too much for Sophie because that was almost exactly what Thaddeus had said when he'd finally let her get out of his car just a few short, miserable hours ago.

'Sophie! Sophie, why are you crying, darling? What's wrong? Oh Hugh, my baby's crying. Sophie, darling!'

'I'm okay, Mum. It's… it's been an emotional day, that's all. I'll come out on Wednesday, if that's okay. It's Silas' funeral tomorrow and I really have to go to that. It's the least I can do for him and… I need to cancel something I'd arranged for Wednesday.' Sophie swallowed hard to stop her voice from cracking up.

'Of course, darling. Hugh, sweetie, Sophie's coming out! Isn't that wonderful…? She can afford it because the old goat has left her the lot… I'll tell you later. Sorry darling, just telling Hugh the wonderful news. Oh, how I wish I were there with you. Even I wouldn't mind saying goodbye to the old sod now. What sweetie? Hold on, darling, Hugh's trying to tell me something. Yes… yes… Oh, yes! That's an excellent idea. I love you sweetie. Darling, darling! Hugh's just had a wonderful idea. He says there's a flight from here today at twenty past two our time, which will get me to Heathrow tomorrow at nine-fifteen. Don't ask me how he knows these things but he does!'

'Oh, Mum! That would be fabulous!'

'What? Oh yes. He says it's because he helps our friend Barry with airport runs sometimes. Anyway, what do you think, darling? Would you like me to come over for the funeral?'

Sophie giggled, despite her misery. 'Oh, Mum. I just said yes. That'd be great. I'll ask Tony to arrange it. He can do it, I'm sure. Will you have enough time though? It's seven a.m. there now, isn't it?'

'Yes, but the airport's not far. Nothing's far on Grand Cayman, darling. And it only takes me ten minutes to pack. Don't snort, Hugh, it does only take me ten minutes. You're the one who takes an eternity. Sorry, darling, Hugh again.'

'Will Hugh come too?'

'I'll ask. Hugh, d'you want to come too? He's shaking his head. He says, "as much as he'd love to see you again, funerals aren't his thing." As if they're anyone's darling, but no, he'll stay here and mind the fort. Well, the yacht, but it's one and the same thing. So, how shall we leave this? Shall I book the ticket or will you see if your Tony can do it?'

'I'll get Tony to, Mum. I just said that. Are you listening to me at all?' Sophie laughed, happy at the prospect of seeing her Mum very, very soon.

'Yes, darling. It's Hugh though. He keeps talking and I may be able to do many, many things but I can't listen to two people talking at once. Hugh! Do shut up sweetie, for just one second. I'm trying to have a conversation with my baby, here. Men. Honestly. They're adorable, but they want your constant attention. It's exhausting, it really is. Call me back with the flight details, will you, darling? Sophie? Did you—'

'Sorry. Yes, Mum. I'll call you back as soon as I've spoken to Tony.' Sophie was thinking of Thaddeus and wishing he still wanted her constant attention. Just as he had last night. And as he'd seemed to this morning. 'Bye for now, Mum.' She hung up the phone and burst into tears.

Chapter Twenty-Four

Tony Harman, it seemed, could arrange anything in the wink of an eye. By the time Veronique had made Sophie more coffee and given her a new box of tissues – and a little womanly advice about what Sophie should do the next time she laid eyes on the shithead known as Thaddeus Beaumont – Julia Summerhill was booked on the two-twenty flight from Owen Roberts International airport on Grand Cayman.

'Your mother will be flying to Miami,' Tony informed Sophie, 'where she'll change planes and fly overnight, landing in Heathrow at nine-fifteen tomorrow. First class, of course. There'll be a car at Heathrow to collect her and take her directly to Summerhill. If there's anything else you need, please don't hesitate to ask. Either myself or Veronique are happy to assist you in any way we can.'

'Thank you, Tony. You've been so wonderful. I am so, so grateful for everything you've done.'

'My pleasure. Now, I'm not sure if you're up to this today or whether you'd like to wait until after the funeral – and have your mother here, which is perfectly acceptable if that's what you'd like – but I did mention there are a few little oddities in your great-uncle's will that we need to discuss.'

'Um. May we leave that until after the funeral, please? I don't think it would sink in today. Unless it's something very important that I need to know right away.'

'No, no. Nothing terribly important. It doesn't affect Mr Summerhill's legacy. It's about an ancient codicil that passes down with every will from that of your ancestor, Sophia Summerhill. It's rather odd but each will from that day to this includes a codicil, setting out the terms as laid down by Sophia's original. She was a wealthy woman and being single and over the age of consent, could dispose of her property as she saw fit. It's unusual but from what I know about Sophia Summerhill, she was a most unusual woman.'

'You can say that again,' Sophie said. 'How much do you know about Sophia, Tony?'

He smiled. 'Quite a bit actually. But don't worry, all the Summerhill secrets are safe with me. This firm has been acting for the Summerhills for generations. But we can talk about that when you come in to discuss the codicil and the rest of the estate.'

Surprisingly, as much as she wanted to hear about Sophia, the codicil and the treasure, she just didn't have the heart for it today.

She thanked Tony for his help. Phoned her mum to give her details of the flight, confirmed with Veronique that the cleaners could go to the house today and finally, climbed into the executive car that Tony had arranged to take her back to Goldebury Bay. She had to go to Sutton's restaurant to collect her phone and leave Thaddeus' phone with Oliver.

Where she'd also leave her broken heart.

But the odd thing was, as she nestled into the luxurious leather, back seat of the car which whisked her away from Hastings and headed east towards Goldebury Bay, a plan formed in her head. A plan that would show Thaddeus Beaumont he had messed with the wrong girl – Sophie was a Summerhill and the Summerhills came first.

The Summerhills *always* came first.
Great-uncle Silas had told her that.

Chapter Twenty-Five

Sophie had a lot to do and it required nerves of steel. She knew she didn't have those but the brandy Tony had given her, did help a little. First stop was Sutton's and when the car pulled up outside, she stepped out as if she were a Hollywood star and this was her red carpet.

She sashayed into the restaurant and spotted Oliver and Cleo in the kitchen.

'Hello-o!' She forced herself to smile, and waved the mobile phone in her hand. 'You've got mine and I've got his,' she said, depositing Thaddeus' phone on a worktop in front of them. 'And in case he didn't tell you, yes, he stayed the night, and no, not in a separate room.' She winked and poked her tongue out of the corner of her mouth. 'And I've got to give it to him. I can see why women are so keen to offer him a bed. Phew. That's the best workout I've had in a long time. Anyway, must dash. Things to do. If I can have my phone, please, I'll get out of your hair.'

Cleo and Oliver were looking at one another and at Sophie as if they had just been visited by an alien life form, unsure whether to befriend it or shoot it.

Oliver reached up to a shelf above his head and retrieved the phone. He handed it to Cleo who handed it to Sophie.

'Thanks,' she said. 'Oh! And before I forget, as you may recall, it's my great-uncle's funeral tomorrow. I don't expect you to come, of course but I am having a few drinks at the house afterwards if you or any of your relatives would like to pop round and pay their respects. From three o'clock onwards.'

'Are you okay, Sophie?' Cleo asked, looking doubtful.

'Yes! I'm absolutely fine, thanks. Better than fine. In fact, I couldn't be happier. See you tomorrow perhaps. Oh! And we're still on for Wednesday, aren't we? I'm really looking forward to it. Thanks for this.' She waved her phone in the air as she turned on her heel to leave, not caring if they replied but she glanced back over her shoulder. 'And please say 'Hi' to Thaddeus for me. See you!'

With that final comment, she sashayed back out, exactly as she had come in: with her head held high, a fake smile on her quivering lips and willing the tears to stay put and not start pouring down her face.

Back in the car, she reached for the complimentary brandy decanter. Dutch courage, she told herself.

Next stop was Mike's Motors and the expression on his face was similar to the ones on Oliver's and Cleo's.

'Blimey, love,' he exclaimed. 'You've gone up in the world since Saturday morning. Nice wheels.'

'They're not mine. My great-uncle's solicitors were kind enough to arrange it for me. They're doing everything they can to make my stay here more comfortable.'

'That's nice of them,' he said, scratching his balding head. 'We've had no luck with the part but my brother thinks he may be able to get his hands on—'

'May I stop you there please, Mike? It turns out my funds are not as tight as I'd thought. You can go ahead and get the new part. Do you want me to pay you a deposit?' She had her credit card in her hand.

Mike looked uncertain but he shook his head. 'No need for that, love. When do you need it by? I can probably get the part and have it fitted by Wednesday. Thursday at the latest.'

'Whenever. There's no rush.' Sophie threw her hand in the air and the credit card flew out of her fingers and shot across the forecourt. 'Oh!'

'Seems like you're throwing your money away now,' Mike said.

He stepped forward, about to retrieve it for her but Timothy Richards, who it seemed, happened to be walking past the garage forecourt, got there first.

'I believe this is yours,' Timothy said, handing her the card and grinning. 'Are you okay? You seem to be swaying.' He reached out his hand to steady her and looked into her eyes. 'Actually, you don't look too good. I was joking but… have you been drinking?'

Sophie nodded.

'And… and crying? Your eyes look very red.'

'You're always talking about my eyes, aren't you, Timothy? Isn't there anything else about me that you find interesting?'

Mike coughed, turned round and hurried back into his workshop; Timothy blinked as if he didn't understand the question.

'I find everything about you interesting. Didn't you hear me this morning?'

'This morning? When this morning? What?'

'When I called you. I heard you answer the phone but I couldn't hear your voice. I didn't know if you could hear mine or not. I called you twice.'

'This morning?'

'Yes.'

'*This* morning?'

'Yes.'

'As in: This. Morning?'

'Yes, Sophie. As in this morning. Just a few hours ago. I

didn't look at the time so I can't be precise but it was somewhere around ten or possibly eleven.'

'And I answered?'

'Yes. Well, it sounded as if the call had connected and I thought I could hear you breathing but you didn't say a word so it may have been a dodgy line.'

'Oh shit! What did you say?'

'It doesn't matter now. I can tell you in person.' He grinned and winked at her.

'It *does* matter. Tell me. What did you say when you called me?'

He furrowed his brows. 'Why?'

'Bloody hell, Timothy! Just tell me, will you?'

'Okay! Okay. I can't remember exactly but something along the lines of, "I can't wait to hold you in my arms again and kiss you. Kiss you all over," I think I said. Or something like that. "Or kiss you all over your gorgeous, sexy body" perhaps.' He winked again. 'Which is true by the way. I can't wait to do that.'

He stepped forward and took her in his arms and as he did so, Sophie buried her head in his shoulder and burst into tears.

'Hey! What's wrong? There's no need for tears. I'm here.'

'Yes!' Sophie sobbed. 'That's just the point… You're here… He's not.'

'Er… Who's not? Your great-uncle? Is this about him?'

'No! Of course it's not.'

She pushed him away and wiped her nose with the back of her hand. She saw the expression on his face as he reached into his pocket and pulled out a handkerchief.

'Use this,' he said.

She pushed that away too. 'I've got my own… tissues, thank you… very much!'

He grimaced. 'Well… may I suggest you use one?'

'No!' But she yanked one from her handbag and blew her nose.

'So… if you're not upset about your great-uncle, who are you upset about?'

She glowered at him through tearful eyes. 'Thaddeus, of course. And… you've just ruined everything. At least… I think it was you.' She blew her nose, louder this time.

Timothy frowned. 'Thaddeus! What…? Oh, I see. So you were attracted to him, after all. Why am I even surprised?'

'I wasn't. But I am now.'

He shook his head. 'I thought you were different, Sophie. But it seems you're just like all the rest. Out of interest, was this 'attraction' before or after you kissed me?'

'You kissed me! But it was after.' She wiped her eyes. 'Well, maybe it was before. I liked him before. I didn't realise how much until after. Not that it's really any of your business. And all you and I did was kiss. That's nothing.'

He stared into her eyes. 'Whereas… the implication being that you and Thaddeus have done a lot more than kiss. Oh, Sophie. He just uses women, you know.'

'And… and you don't! That's rich. You use everyone to get your story. You even want to use my… Never mind. I'm sorry. I shouldn't be taking this out on you. It's… it's been a strange day.'

He screwed up his eyes. 'Hmm. For your information, Sophie, if you and I had… well, if anything had happened between us, I would've given serious thought to seeing if it was possible to leave Sophia's name out of my book. If you'd asked me to. Now though…' He shrugged.

Sophie gasped. 'That's blackmail!'

'Hardly. I would've done that for you because I liked

you.'

Sophie took a deep breath, blew her nose one last time and looked him straight in the eye.

'You know what, Timothy? They were right about you. Write your damn book. But you'd better check your facts because I know exactly what Sophia was and the whole story about her life and how she died. Perhaps I should write a book of my own. How would that make you look when the things you say are proved wrong? Good luck, Timothy. I don't expect I'll be seeing you again.'

'Sophie. Sophie! Come back.'

Sophie hurried to the waiting car, slammed the door and told the driver to: 'Get me out of here, please. And as quickly as possible.'

Heading to the house, Sophie went over what had just happened. She hadn't meant to have a go at Timothy but suddenly Thaddeus' behaviour made sense. Well, about as much sense as jealousy ever can.

Thaddeus had answered the call, thinking it was his phone and he'd heard what Timothy had said. He was jealous. He was possibly cross. And he'd reacted in the only way he knew how to – like a Jack the Lad and pretending he didn't care.

But if this were true, it meant he *did* care and the realisation of that brightened Sophie's day far more than Tony Hardman telling her she was now a wealthy woman.

That was rather ironic given the circumstances. She'd come to Goldebury Bay hoping to find the treasure and keep it a secret from Thaddeus so that she wouldn't have to share it with him – which was a possibility. Now she had money beyond her wildest dreams – and all she wanted was Thaddeus.

Fate really did like playing games, she thought.

Chapter Twenty-Six

'She said *what*?' Thaddeus was livid.

Cleo cringed and repeated once again what Sophie had said in the restaurant. 'Hey! Don't shoot the messenger, Thaddeus. I'm simply telling you what she said. She was acting really weird, if you ask me. Her eyes were red and she looked as if she'd had a few too many drinks. We both thought so, didn't we Oliver?'

'Don't bring me into this. All I'll say is that she'd definitely been drinking. Her voice had that edge. You know, when you think you sound sober but to everyone else, you're slurring. I didn't notice her eyes.'

Thaddeus watched him as he poured coffee for the three of them and then continued prepping the vegetables he'd been washing just before Thaddeus' arrival.

'She'd definitely been crying too. I'm a woman. I can tell,' Cleo said, offering Thaddeus a chocolate brownie.

'What does she have to cry about?' Thaddeus said, shaking his head at the brownie offer. 'If I gave her the best workout she's had in a long time, she should be bloody happy. She even said so. You just told me that. She said she "couldn't be happier".'

'Oh Thaddeus,' Cleo tutted. 'That means she's never been so miserable in her life. You men really don't get us women at all, do you?'

Oliver and Thaddeus exchanged glances. 'No,' they said in unison.

'Then why pretend she's so fucking happy?' Thaddeus said, fiddling with the handle of his cup.

'You pillock,' Poppy's voice echoed from behind him.

'What?' Thaddeus spun round on his chair and glared at her.

'Cleo phoned and told me. I've come to give you my advice.'

'Oh great. Thanks. But I don't want it.'

'I didn't ask if you did. I said I've come to give it, not ask if you'd like to hear it. Now shut up and listen, you plonker. But... tell me exactly what happened first. All I know is that you came in here in a right strop earlier, threw Sophie's phone across the worktop, accused her of shagging both you and that git, Timothy Richards and said: "Tell the bitch I never want to see her again." Then Sophie came in later and acted like a bunny who'd been drinking battery fluid and promptly announced you were a good lay... or words to that effect. So why is she a bitch? Did she give you a taste of your own medicine? Did she use you as a sex toy and cast you aside?'

Thaddeus could feel his temper rising. 'Poppy. You're my friend and I love you. Let's keep it that way, shall we?'

Poppy sighed. 'Thaddeus. You're my friend and I love you. Friends give one another advice. Friends listen. Friends talk. Friends try to lighten the mood. You've got a lot to learn about friendship. And about women from the sounds of this. So what's this all about? It goes without saying that after we all left last night, you went back for… second helpings, shall we say?'

'I went back because… It doesn't matter why.'

'Actually, it does,' Cleo said. 'If you went back just to get laid, that's one thing but if you went back because you actually like her and wanted to be with her, well, that's a whole different bucket of crabs, as GJ would say.'

'Would GJ say that?' Poppy queried. 'I thought it was "putting crabs in a pot of custard".'

Cleo shook her head. 'No. That's what Great-aunt Miff says. And that means stirring things up and causing trouble. A "bucket of–'

'Girls!' Oliver piped up, nodding towards Thaddeus. 'I don't think anyone cares about crabs.'

Poppy helped herself to a chocolate brownie. 'You would if you got them. I know someone who did and it took weeks for the creams and tablets to work. You can never be too careful.'

'How the hell did we go from talking about crabs in a bucket to crabs, the sexually transmitted disease?' Thaddeus demanded. 'And why are we talking about crabs anyway?'

'Don't blow a fuse,' Poppy said. 'We're talking about you and Sophie having sex.'

'Well neither of us has crabs, I can assure you of that.'

'I didn't say you did. Bloody hell Thaddeus, what is up with you?' She nodded at Cleo. 'Sounds like love to me. These brownies are fab. Can I take some home?'

'Sure. Help yourself,' Cleo said.

'I thought you came here to give me advice,' Thaddeus snapped.

'I thought you didn't want it.'

'I don't. I just want to go next door to The One That Got Away and get completely rat-arsed.'

'Sounds to me like Sophie's "the one that got away",' Poppy added.

'Dear God, give me strength.' Thaddeus buried his head in his hands. 'Can we please just get this over with?'

'Certainly.' Poppy sat beside him, tapped him on the arm and offered him a brownie. 'Tell us what happened and we'll see what we can do.'

He raised his head and arched his brows. 'I don't want a brownie, thank you.'

'Thaddeus Beaumont,' Poppy said. 'For once, will you just do what's good for you! Take a sodding brownie before I shove it down your throat. You'll thank me later, believe me.'

Cleo nodded. 'Chocolate makes you happy. Everyone knows that.'

'The way I feel at the moment,' Thaddeus said. 'Poison's the only thing that would make me happy.'

But he took a chocolate brownie and he had to reluctantly admit, it did make him feel slightly better. So much so, that he told his friends the entire story.

'So what do you think?' Thaddeus asked when he'd finished.

'Hmm,' Poppy said. 'I think we should all go to the after-funeral party or whatever it's called.'

'That's it? That's your advice?'

'Actually,' Oliver said. 'I think she may be right.'

'So do I,' Cleo added. 'Think about it, Thaddeus. If Sophie is 'with Timothy' then he'll be there tomorrow and we can all see what they do. You know, how they behave.'

'Yeah. And I can ask her outright,' Poppy said.

'You wouldn't?' Cleo sounded surprised.

'She would,' Thaddeus said. Even he knew she was capable of doing just that. 'But I'd appreciate it if you didn't, Poppy.'

'Why not?' Oliver asked. 'Surely it's better to know for sure. Sometimes it's better to just come right out and say it.'

'Hmm,' Thaddeus said. 'For a man who spent the whole of last summer trying to convince himself that he was in love with someone he wasn't, and that he wasn't in love with someone he was, and wouldn't talk to anyone about it,

I'm not sure if that's good advice or bad.'

Poppy said: 'If you look in someone's eyes and ask them a direct question, you can often tell if they're lying.'

'Says the girl who was shagging a criminal without the faintest idea that something wasn't quite right.'

'Don't be mean, Thaddeus,' Cleo said. 'Oliver didn't know about Hermione either. Some people are very good at telling lies and keeping secrets.'

'Yes. And you'd know all about that, wouldn't you? Sorry. I didn't mean it to sound like that. I just mean that people will only tell you what they want you to hear. That doesn't mean it's the truth and it doesn't mean they're not hiding something.'

'That's true,' Oliver said.

'But I still think we should go to the party thing and I also think we should go on Wednesday – and that means you too, Thaddeus.'

He stared into his empty coffee cup. 'I'm not sure I can face it, Poppy. Face her, I mean.'

'We'll be there with you,' Poppy said, getting to her feet. 'That's what friends are for. Now let's go with your other plan and head to The One That Got Away for a drink. All this talking's made me thirsty.'

'I think that's more likely to be the five chocolate brownies you've just eaten,' Thaddeus said, but he followed her anyway.

Chapter Twenty-Seven

Sophie was feeling – if not quite herself – at least a lot happier than she'd felt yesterday. She'd spent the night in the hotel Tony Hardman had recommended, having collected Silas from the house and taken him to a cattery that Veronique had booked so that the cleaners could give Summerhill a thorough 'going over'.

After her little contretemps with Timothy yesterday, and once Silas was settled at the cattery, Sophie had gone back into Goldebury Bay and told as many people as possible about the funeral reception at the house. She didn't expect them to go to the funeral itself, having told them all that it was a private, family service. She knew her great-uncle wasn't well-liked and besides, he'd wanted a quiet affair; Tony had told her those were his wishes. But she was sure free food and drink, together with a chance to see inside Summerhill, would entice many of the locals to pop in to the funeral reception. Veronique was helping her to organise a buffet fit for royalty. Great-uncle Silas was going to have a good send-off, Sophie had decided, whether he wanted one or not. It was the least she could do, especially bearing in mind that he would be indirectly paying for it.

She'd told Mike, at Mike's Motors and Betty in Betty's Pantry, thereby ensuring that at least half of Goldebury Bay would know about it. She'd told the Reverend Paul Temple, even though Silas wasn't religious. She'd told the friendly couple called Phyllis and Trevor Franks, who ran the Post Office Stores, and asked them if they would please tell all the locals who came into the store.

After that, she'd spent a very pleasant evening being pampered in the hotel spa, followed by a superb dinner of freshly caught turbot washed down with a delicious bottle of Pouilly-Fumé and, slept like a princess in the comfiest bed she'd ever lain on.

Feeling refreshed and invigorated, this morning, she'd spent fifteen minutes in Got My Eyes On You, having her eyebrows threaded by a rather sour-looking girl called Sara, followed by an hour in the hairdressers, Carolyn's Cuts, Colours and Curls having her yellow-gold hair, cut, blow-dried and twisted into a long, loose plait down one side. She was very pleased with the result – which was a surprise in itself. Usually, when she left the hairdressers, it was with a feeling of disappointment and she'd washed and blow-dried her hair again the moment she'd got home. This time, she'd smiled at her reflection and inwardly oohed and aahed. And when she'd tried on the clingy, black, fitted dress and bolero jacket she'd spotted in a shop window in the High Street, she'd purchased it immediately.

Now, Sophie was heading back to the house and she was looking forward to seeing what difference a 'proper' clean had made. Veronique had texted her to let her know that she'd collected Silas from the cattery and that they were both back at the house. She was showing the caterers where everything should go and Silas was investigating every item they brought in. There was nothing for Sophie to do but relax, she'd told her.

From the back seat of the car as Sophie was driven down the private road leading to the house, she could already see a great improvement. All the broken windows had been replaced and every pane in the eight windows at the rear was glistening in the dappled sunshine. The sun was shining directly on the windows at the entrance to the house and they positively sparkled as the car drew up in front of the double, oak doors. Sophie was amazed to see they too were pristine and the lion-head door knockers gleamed as they basked in the sunlight like big, sleeping cats.

Inside, the house was almost unrecognisable. Even the rooms Sophie had cleaned, were far brighter and neater than they'd been yesterday and Summerhill wouldn't look amiss in the pages of a magazine stuffed full of pictures of palatial, country homes, Sophie thought. Well, perhaps that was taking things a bit too far but as she walked across the polished wood floor of the hall, saw the plump cushions on the two high back chairs and the colourful floral display in the hearth of the fireplace, she had tears in her eyes. And they were tears of pride and joy, not tears of sorrow.

'Oh Veronique!' Sophie enthused. 'It looks beautiful. Truly, beautiful. Thank you so, so much.'

'I'm glad you're pleased with it,' Veronique said. 'It really was in an appalling state, wasn't it? Tony would've been beside himself with anger if he'd popped his head in and seen it like that. Mrs Phelps won't be getting a reference from us, you can count on that. Now, the caterers are in the kitchen and everything's running to schedule so why don't you just relax and wait for your mum to arrive. The driver called ten minutes ago and they'll be here in half an hour or so. There were slight delays due to road works but it's not yet eleven-thirty so there's still plenty of time. I'll arrange a spot of lunch for you and Mrs Summerhill at, shall we say, twelve-thirty?'

'I don't know how you've done all this, Veronique but I hope Tony appreciates how valuable you are, and please, call my mum, Julia.'

Veronique smiled. 'Thanks, Sophie. I make sure Tony

appreciates me, don't you worry about that. I tell him how wonderful I am every evening before I leave the office.' She winked, checked her iPad and dashed off into the kitchen adding: 'Excuse me, Sophie but it seems Silas has taken a liking to the salmon mousse. I'll bring you a coffee in a sec.'

Sophie considered offering to help but Veronique had it all under control, she was sure of that. She strolled into the sitting room and marvelled at the spruced-up curtains and the revitalised sofas; at the family portraits that no longer looked dim and dusty but as dapper as if the subjects had just posed for them today. Vases of flowers stood on shiny tables and rays of sunlight danced around them, bouncing off every polished surface.

Sophie smiled and dropped onto a sofa in awe of what a cloth and a can of polish could do. She knew, of course, that it had taken more than that to turn Summerhill from the ugly duckling it was yesterday into the stunning swan it was today but she felt that not even her great-uncle would begrudge the money this transformation had cost. Now all she had to do was have the outside repaired and repainted and the roof and chimney…

She sat bolt upright. What was she thinking? She had no plans to stay at Summerhill; no intention of refurbishing the place. She was going to the Cayman Islands to live a life of luxury on a sun-soaked beach with her mum, not live a life of loneliness in a rain-soaked seaside resort.

Of course, that was before she knew that she'd inherited the house. But even so. What difference did that make? She'd never lived in Goldebury Bay. She'd never wanted to live here. The longest she'd ever stayed was for two or three weeks during her summer visits as a child and those had ended when she was nine. And it had often rained during those weeks too.

Not that Goldebury Bay was rain-soaked today. Far from it, in fact. The sky was clear and the softest blue imaginable. The sea was flat like sheer blue glass and it sparkled beneath a white-hot sun. Even the gulls sounded melodious today rather than the usual piercing caw they gave as they hovered in the thermals at the head of Summer Hill cliff.

Silas wandered in and mewed. He sauntered over to Sophie and jumped up on the sofa, curling up beside her and purring with contentment. What would happen to him if she sold the house? She couldn't take him to the Caymans and she couldn't just leave him here to fend for himself, obviously. She'd have to find a home for him. Veronique would know how to go about that. Sophie had never owned a pet before so she had no idea where to start.

She reached out and stroked him and the level of his purr increased. He was a very friendly cat even though he'd frightened the life out of her at first. She'd have to make sure he had a good home, not just any old place.

'Here's your coffee, Sophie.' Veronique appeared at the sitting room door carrying a tray. 'He's a gorgeous boy,' she added, nodding towards Silas.

'Yes. I was just thinking the same thing. I assumed he belonged to my great-uncle as he seems quite at home here but I wouldn't have thought Silas was the type of man to own a pet. Do you know anything about him?'

Veronique shook her head. 'No. I never heard Tony mention Mr Summerhill owning a cat. I can ask him.'

'No. It doesn't matter.'

'Perhaps he was lost and lonely and needed a place to live. Perhaps he's a recent resident. He certainly seems at home.'

'Yes,' Sophie said. 'He certainly does.' And he wasn't the only one, she thought.

And then she thought of Thaddeus and she had to stop herself from crying.

Chapter Twenty-Eight

Sophie felt oddly emotional as she and her mum returned to Summerhill after Silas' short funeral service. As expected, only the two of them and Tony Hardman had attended but now Sophie was wondering if anyone would actually turn up for the reception.

The house seemed eerily quiet as she opened the front door and her heels clopped across the hall floor, echoing in the silence.

'Well that's that then,' Julia said, tossing her black hat onto one of the high-backed chairs. 'I never liked the man, as you well know, darling but it was rather depressing to see just the three of us at his funeral.'

'He wanted it that way,' Sophie said. 'Those were his wishes, weren't they, Tony?'

Tony nodded. 'Yes. He didn't want a fuss.'

'I don't suppose he'd be happy about this reception,' Sophie said. 'But after he left me the estate I felt I owed him this. I know it's silly.'

'It isn't silly at all, darling. I just hope someone comes.'

Veronique appeared from the kitchen. 'Everything's ready. And I believe I can hear a car. Shall I?' She nodded towards the front door.

'Yes please,' Sophie said.

The four of them couldn't believe their eyes. It wasn't just one car coming down the road; it was a stream of cars and in between the cars were people on foot. They were coming over the cliff too, up the ninety steps from the beach.

'Bloody hell!' Julia said. 'Do we have enough food and drink?'

Veronique nodded. 'Yes,' she said. 'And if not, I can send out for more.'

Sophie grabbed her mother's arm.

'Should we stand at the door and greet people, Mum? I've never done anything like this before. Granny Summerhill's funeral reception was just us and a few friends, for sandwiches, tea and cake. And I don't know any of these people.' Panic was setting in.

'Neither do I,' Julia said, looking almost as flustered as Sophie felt.

'If you'll allow us,' Tony said. 'I believe you'd be more comfortable in the sitting room. Veronique and I will filter your guests through to pay their respects. They'll say a few words and then they'll move on to the dining room where the caterers have provided a rather fine spread.'

Veronique clicked her fingers and, as if by magic, two elegantly dressed female serving staff and two similarly dressed males, walked, procession-like towards the front door. Each one was carrying a tray: one with soft drinks, one with tea, one with coffee and lastly and by far the largest, one with champagne.

'This way,' Tony said to Sophie and Julia, taking them by the elbows and propelling them towards one of the sofas.

Moments later, two glasses of champagne appeared on the small tables either side of them. Sophie blinked several times. This was all rather surreal, she thought and when Silas jumped up onto the sofa and sat to attention between her and her mum, she almost burst out laughing.

Exactly what Tony said would happen, did. Person after

person came in, said how sorry they were for the loss of Silas Summerhill and disappeared into the dining room. Some even said that he would be missed, which Sophie thought was taking proprieties a bit too far, but she smiled and gave her thanks.

Everything was going smoothly until she saw Timothy Richards standing before her.

'Hello, Sophie,' he said. 'Sorry for your loss. I wonder if I could have a few words with you when you have a moment.' He glanced across to Julia, ignoring Silas, the cat, completely. 'You must be Sophie's mum. The resemblance is striking. I'm sorry we have to meet on such a sad occasion. I'm Timothy Richards.'

Sophie couldn't find her voice but Julia smiled up at him.

'Hello, Mr Richards,' she said. 'Sophie's told me all about you.'

He glanced from her to Sophie and back again. 'Not all bad, I hope. We had a bit of a misunderstanding yesterday. That's why I'm here. I wanted a chance to put things right.'

'There was no misunderstanding,' Sophie said, glaring at him. 'I think we both understood each other perfectly.'

'Sometimes what you think you hear is not what is meant. I wanted a chance to explain. Please, Sophie. Give me that chance.'

People were hovering at the sitting room door, Sophie noticed. 'All right,' she said. 'But later. I'll come and find you when we've finished here.'

Timothy smiled and winked. 'Thanks,' he said. 'See you in a bit then.'

'Ooh!' Sophie said through gritted teeth when he walked away. 'Now I see why Thaddeus dislikes that man so much.'

'Speaking of Thaddeus,' Julia said, nudging Sophie's

arm. 'Is this him? He does look like Barnabus, doesn't he? Far more handsome though and what a body!'

Now Sophie really couldn't speak. She turned her head in his direction and met his chocolate-brown eyes, which seemed to be appraising her from head to toe; once they'd stopped burning into Timothy Richards' back.

'Hello, Sophie.' It was Oliver's voice.

'The house looks fabulous,' Cleo said.

'I didn't recognise the place,' added Poppy.

Thaddeus just stared.

'Hello, Sophie,' Clara Pollard said. 'I'm so sorry about Silas. He'll be missed. It's a pity we meet under such sad circumstances but it's lovely to see so many people here to say their final goodbyes. And you must be Julia. I hope you don't mind if I call you that. I'm Clara. Clara Pollard. We met years ago but you won't remember, of course.'

'I do remember,' Julia said. 'Hello, Clara. It's good to see you again.'

'These are my uncle Jim – or GJ as everyone seems to call him these days, and my aunt Miff. They knew Silas well.'

'Very pleased to make your acquaintance, Sophie, is it? And Julia?' Miff said. 'These old eyes aren't what they once were. He'll be missed you know, old Silas. He was a one, he was.'

'I'd as like he's not gone far,' GJ said. 'Hardly left this place for more than one hour for as long as I can remember. And that's a fair few years, I'd as like. Grumpy old sod he was but sad he's gone all the same. End of an era, it is. End of an era.'

'Take Oliver's arm, Great-aunt Miff,' Cleo said.

'What does she want his arm for? Got two of her own,' GJ quipped.

'Get away with you, you old fool,' Miff scolded and

linked her arm through Oliver's. 'I need to sit. These old legs can't hold me for longer than a second these days.'

'Please,' Sophie said. 'Make yourselves at home. I'd love to talk to you about Silas sometime if you have a minute.'

'I'd as like that's all we has,' GJ said. 'So don't you be leaving it too long or you might be coming to our own little shindig like this one. Now where's the drink? I'd as like I need to wet my whistle before too long.'

'Come with me,' Oliver said. 'Excuse us, Sophie and Julia.'

'Of course,' Sophie said, watching GJ and Miff shuffle slowly away with Oliver.

'This is Paul,' Clara said, introducing the Reverend.

'It's a pleasure to meet you both,' Paul said. 'I know Silas wasn't religious but I did meet him once or twice. He was a real character and will be sadly missed. If either of you need a friendly ear, I'm a good listener, whatever your beliefs.'

'Ben will be here later,' Cleo said. 'Oliver was supposed to tell you. There's been some sort of emergency at the pub and he had to stay and sort it out but he said he'll be here come hell or high water.'

'He's probably run out of champagne,' Poppy said. 'That's about the only thing that constitutes an emergency in his eyes.'

'I thought he said it had something to do with the gallery,' Cleo said.

'Who cares,' said Poppy. 'He'll get here when he gets here. You look really good, Sophie. Your hair is fab. I'm so jealous. Wish I could do mine like that. What? Don't give me that look, Cleo. She does.'

'You don't compliment people on how good they look at a funeral,' Cleo said, turning to follow Oliver and her relatives. 'It isn't polite.'

'Sod polite,' Poppy said. 'We all like to hear we look good, especially when someone's died.'

'I think it's time we got you another drink, Poppy,' Thaddeus said, his gaze still locked on Sophie. 'Sorry for your loss, Mrs Summerhill. And yours.'

His eyes travelled the length of Sophie's body and she thought he was about to say something else but he turned away without even a smile and, taking Poppy's arm in his, he led her towards the dining room.

'I could certainly murder a drink,' Poppy was saying, 'but you don't have to drag me away like a naughty child.'

'Someone had to,' Thaddeus said.

'See you later, Sophie,' Cleo said. 'If there's anything we can do, just shout. Sorry for your loss, Mrs Summerhill.'

'Please,' Julia said, 'call me Julia. Any friend of Sophie's is a friend of mine.'

'The same goes for us,' Clara said. 'If there is anything Paul or I can do, please don't hesitate to let us know.

But Sophie was still staring at Thaddeus until he disappeared from view.

'I know we didn't have much time to talk when I arrived,' Julia said to Sophie. 'And who knows when we'll get a chance to be alone this afternoon but why didn't you tell me there was something going on between you and Thaddeus Beaumont?'

Sophie met her mother's questioning look and could feel herself blushing. She fiddled with the hem of her skirt.

'Have you slept with him?' Julia added.

'How did–'

'How did I know? Because I'm your mother, darling and mothers know these things. Why aren't the two of you speaking now? Didn't it go as planned? Or was it a complete disaster you both wish hadn't happened? Do you regret it?'

A long sad sigh escaped Sophie's lips and she shook her head, now staring at the open door as if she thought he might return at any minute.

'I can't speak for Thaddeus,' she said. 'But it was the best thing that's ever happened to me… and the worst, now it's over. He thinks I slept with Timothy too and I don't know how to tell him I haven't. And I'm not sure he even cares. Although I think he does because I think he was jealous. I think that's why he behaved like such a shit.'

Julia squeezed Sophie's hand. 'This will soon be over and then I think you need to tell me exactly what happened between you two. We must see if we can sort it out. But plaster a smile on your face now, darling. Unless I'm very much mistaken, here comes Betty. She's hardly changed a bit in twenty-one years.'

Chapter Twenty-Nine

'Thaddeus?'

Thaddeus spun round and glared at Timothy who had come up behind him whilst he was standing on his own, lost in thought and staring out to sea, near the edge of Summer Hill cliff.

'What do you want?' Thaddeus said. 'I've got no interest in talking to you, especially not today.'

'I have a feeling you might be interested in what I have to say. It affects you and Sophie.'

Thaddeus prickled at the mention of her name. He'd been thinking of nothing but Sophie since the moment he'd arrived. What he didn't need right now, was to have to think about Sophie and Timothy… together. He might just throw the man off the bloody cliff, he thought.

'Not today.'

He moved away but Timothy shadowed him.

'I've been doing some research on Sophia Summerhill, Sophie's ancestor. Sophie and I were talking about her and I've discovered some interesting facts.'

Thaddeus bristled. 'Then tell Sophie. Don't tell me.'

'But they affect you. Well, your family at least. I'll be putting them in my book. I've already spoken to Sophie about it and I'm seeing her later to discuss it further but I wanted you to know too.'

Thaddeus stopped in his tracks. He clenched his fist and took several deep breaths. So it was true. Sophie and this shit were collaborating on his sodding book.

'I'm really not interested. Don't you get that? I'm not sure how you'd feel if some bastard came along and dug up all the dirt he could find on your family, and then wrote about it for anyone and everyone to read. Believe me, it's not something I'm thrilled about. And the less I have to hear from you, the better. So, just run back to Sophie and talk to her. Leave me out of your sordid gossip.'

He walked back towards the house, making a valiant effort not to flatten the guy as Timothy followed him.

'Sophia and Barnabus were lovers. Sophia had his child. That's where Sophie's line comes from. So you're distantly related. Not that that means anything. But Sophia was accused of being a witch and she died at the hands of your ancestor.'

Thaddeus stopped for a split second before quickening his pace.

'Did you hear me, Thaddeus? Barnabus was responsible for Sophia's untimely death and he left his bastard child to be brought up by the Summerhills. He didn't even so much as give his son his paternal family name. And I hear your dad had a mistress. Want to tell me about her?'

Thaddeus was in front of Timothy before the man had hardly finished the sentence. He didn't even think; couldn't think he was so overcome with anger. Without hesitating for a moment, he punched Timothy hard on the nose.

'No fucking comment,' Thaddeus said.

Timothy lay sprawled on the grass, blood streaming from his clearly broken nose. Thaddeus didn't bat an eye.

'You hit me!' Timothy screeched, holding his nose.

'First with breaking news, as ever,' Thaddeus replied with a sardonic smile. 'Now write about that.'

He turned and marched back to the house. That felt so good, he thought. Bugger the consequences. His knuckles hurt so he knew how bad Timothy must be feeling but he really didn't care. He almost wished he could do the same to Sophie, but he'd never dream of hitting a woman, no matter what she did.

At least now he knew for sure. Sophie had lied to him completely, thoroughly and utterly. And what's more, she'd told Timothy about his dad's mistress. Something she'd sworn she wouldn't do. She clearly wasn't the woman he had thought she was when he'd seen her on Saturday. And definitely not the woman he'd thought he'd made love with.

She was just a lying bitch. And one he would make sure he avoided now at all costs.

'Hi Thaddeus,' Poppy said. 'I was just coming to look… What's wrong? Your face is like thunder? Ooh! Is that Timothy Richards staggering back there? She pushed her sunglasses down to the tip of her nose. 'Is he drunk? He looks drunk. Is he bleeding?' Grabbing Thaddeus's arm, she looked up at him with anxious astonishment. 'Thaddeus! What have you done?'

'Something I should've done a long time ago, Poppy. Now let me go. I need to get drunk and then I need to go home. Or vice versa, I'm not really sure.'

'Oh Thaddeus!' Poppy laughed, much to his surprise. 'You've thumped him. Good for you. I hope it hurt like hell. Him that is, not you.'

Thaddeus flicked his hand and stretched out his fingers. 'I think it hurt us both but I can safely say, he came off worse. I think I broke his nose.'

'Really?' Again she laughed. Louder this time.

'I considered breaking his neck.'

'You should've pushed him off the cliff and let the gulls pick over his bones.'

Thaddeus looked at her and he couldn't help but smile.

Poppy always made him smile. Well, nearly always. When she wasn't irritating the life out of him.

'I thought about that too. But there's enough rubbish on the beach these days as it is.'

'Yeah, bloody tourists. They come here for the summer and just want to have a good time with no consideration for the environment.' She linked her arm through his. 'Let's go and tell Cleo and Oliver. Best not tell the Reverend. He'll probably give you some long sermon about "Thou shall not punch bastard journalists".'

Which reminded him of what Timothy had said. In his blind rage he'd almost let that slip right by him. Was it true? Had Sophia and Barnabus been lovers? Did Sophie know? Obviously, she did. She'd discussed it with Timothy. Did she know about the child? Did she hold Barnabus responsible for Sophia's death? Was Sophia really a witch?

His head swam with questions and he almost felt as if he was the one who'd been punched… but in the head.

'Let's get a drink before we tell them,' Poppy said.

'Let's get several,' Thaddeus said.

'A man after my own heart.'

Thaddeus glanced at her smiling face and wished he was – but not in the way she meant it. He wished he wanted her heart. Why couldn't he fall in love with Poppy? She was beautiful. She was fun. She was caring, thoughtful and kind. She was passionate and he had no doubt she'd be great in bed. So why didn't he want to be with her? Why couldn't he be with her? Perhaps he could. Perhaps he could fall in love with her if he really wanted to.

He spotted Sophie heading across the hall. In that moment he knew. It was too late for him to fall in love with anyone. He was already head over heels in love with Sophie.

That lying, cheating, deceitful bitch, Sophie.

Gorgeous, gentle, passionate, Sophie.

Arghh!

'Hey Thaddeus! Slow down,' Poppy yelled.

But he quickened his pace and almost dragged her across the hall towards the bar.

Chapter Thirty

'Have you heard, darling?' Julia asked. 'It seems your Thaddeus has broken that handsome reporter's nose.'

'What?' Sophie couldn't believe her ears. 'He's not *my* Thaddeus – but are you telling me he hit Timothy? When? Why? Where?'

Julia arched a perfectly shaped brow. 'Let me see. Just a few minutes ago. I don't know why. And on the cliff, apparently.'

Sophie pulled a face as Julia grinned at her. Then panic took hold. 'Where is he?'

'Which one? Thaddeus or Timothy?'

'Thaddeus. No! Timothy. Is he all right?'

'I believe so. Veronique's with him in one of the bathrooms upstairs. He's in a bit of a mess and his shirt's covered in blood but he'll survive. She's given him some painkillers but I suspect it hurts like hell. We thought it best if he lie down for a while so she's told him he can use one of the bedrooms.'

'Oh great! That's simply marvellous.'

'Don't worry, darling. He won't be staying. It's only until the bleeding stops and he's well enough to leave.'

'I'd better go and see him. Wh-where's Thaddeus?'

'Last time I saw him, he and the beautiful blonde… Poppy, yes that's her name, were propping up the bar.'

'Perfect. Absolutely perfect.'

'Well, what's wrong with that? At least he hasn't

punched anyone else.'

'Nothing's wrong with that except... nothing. I'm going to check on Timothy.'

'Okay, darling. And I think I'll go and check on Thaddeus. Perhaps he'll tell me what it's all about.'

Sophie walked towards the stairs and peeked into the dining room. She could just see the edge of the bar which the caterers had set up in the corner of the room and her mother was right: Thaddeus and Poppy were propping up one end – or it was propping them up – she wasn't quite sure which.

She ran up the stairs and found Veronique leaning over a prostrate Timothy who was now flat on his back with his head tilted backwards on a pillow in one of the bedrooms. Veronique was pressing a wet cloth to his nose.

'Is he okay?' Sophie asked.

Veronique pulled a face and nodded. 'He'll be fine. I had to set the break though and he'll doubtless have a black eye, coupled with other bruising but there'll be no permanent damage.'

'I am here you know,' Timothy said, sounding as if he had a very bad cold. 'There's no need to talk about me as if I can't hear you.'

'Would you like to tell me what happened then?' Sophie asked.

'That Neanderthal boyfriend of yours punched me in the face, that's what happened,' he moaned.

'He's not my boyfriend. Why did he punch you?'

'Because he's a thug, like the rest of his family.'

'He's not a thug and nor are his family,' Sophie snapped. 'He must've had a reason. What did you say to provoke him?'

'What makes you think I provoked him?'

'Because you seem to provoke a lot of people, Timothy,

me included. Now, what did you say to him?'

'I told him about Sophia and the witch thing and about her having Barnabus' bastard. And that Barnabus was involved in her death. Just the stuff I told you. I wanted to get his comment.'

'I think you got it,' Veronique said, her lips twitching.

'You did what?' Sophie shrieked.

'I told him about—'

'Yes, I heard you. What I want to know is why? Especially as I told you yesterday that you needed to check your facts.'

'I wanted to see what he knew about it all.'

'And what did he know?'

'From the look on his face, I'd say nothing. It came as a complete surprise to him. I thought you would've told him. You know, the whole: your ancestors were lovers, now you're repeating history, thing. But when I told him we'd discussed it, he seemed even more surprised.'

Sophie closed her eyes for just one moment. She could imagine Thaddeus' reaction when he'd heard they'd discussed it and the thought of it made her head hurt.

'And what did you mean about Sophia having Barnabus' bastard? Where did you get that from?'

'Well, she was the only surviving Summerhill at the time – of childbearing age at least – and the Summerhill line continued. Otherwise, how would you be here? Sophia and Barnabus were lovers and when she died, she left a son. You don't need to be a brain surgeon to put two and two together and I've also found some papers that seem to indicate Barnabus was involved in her untimely death.'

Sophie exhaled her frustration in a long, loud sigh. 'It's a good thing you're not a brain surgeon. You've just built yourself a model Frankenstein. I can assure you, Timothy, Barnabus Beaumont was not the father of Sophia's child but yes you're right, the child was hers. That I won't try to deny. I can't see why that would've made Thaddeus punch you though. Unless it was the final straw as far as he was concerned.'

'So who was the father then?'

'That's no concern – or business – of yours.'

Timothy propped himself up and smiled gingerly at Veronique. He was clearly in pain. 'Thanks,' he said. 'I think I can take it from here.'

Veronique shrugged, patted Sophie on the shoulder and left them alone.

'You can stay until you feel better but I want you out of here by this evening,' Sophie said turning to follow Veronique.

'I'll be gone before that, don't worry. I've got Jeremiah Beaumont's mistress to go and have a friendly chat with.'

His words stopped Sophie dead. 'What did you just say?'

He beamed at her then clearly wished he hadn't. 'Ouch!' he said. 'That hurt. Jeremiah had a mistress. I'd just found out about her when I was on my way here. I asked Thaddeus to comment on that too but he wouldn't. In fact, that's when he hit me.'

Sophie gasped. She was very tempted to hit him herself. 'How did you…?' She managed to stop herself. To ask how he found out would be confirming it as fact and she wasn't going to do that.

'How did I find out? I have my sources,' he said.

'I was going to ask how you managed to come up with such an absurd notion, actually,' she lied.

'It's not absurd, it's a fact. She's been in court every single day of the trial. She was there again this morning and I saw the way Thaddeus looked at her when he left. I'd seen it before but assumed he just fancied her. She's about our age and she's sex on legs. That's why I spotted her in the first place. But it struck me today that he wasn't lusting after her. He was glaring at her as if she disgusted him. Then I paid more attention and I saw Jeremiah look round at her once or twice and I knew. So I did some digging.'

'Something you clearly enjoy,' she said.

'I do. This book is going to be a sure-fire hit. There's more sex, passion, intrigue and criminal activity than any bonk-buster on the bookshop shelves.'

'And most of it will be your fantasy fiction, I suspect.'

She stormed out of the room and ran down the stairs as a thought suddenly occurred to her.

Did Thaddeus think that she'd told Timothy about his dad's affair?

She really, really hoped she was wrong but somehow she just knew that was exactly what had happened. She had a gut feeling about it. Just like Timothy had had in court today.

'Thaddeus!' She almost knocked him flying as he came out of the downstairs cloakroom and walked across the hall, in front of the stairs. 'I… I want to talk to you.'

Thaddeus glowered at her. 'I wanted to talk to you, too. That's why I stayed. Now I don't because there's nothing left to say.'

'Timothy—'

'Oh I see! You want to have a go at me for thumping your boyfriend. Well forget it. I'm glad I did it and I'd do it again in a heartbeat.'

He moved away but she reached out and grabbed his arm, quickly letting it go when he glared down at her hand.

'And I'd like to do the same,' she said. 'It's not about you thumping Timothy. It's about what he told you.'

'Yeah, about that.' He crossed his arms and leant against the newel post at the foot of the stairs. 'I was pretty sure you promised me that you wouldn't repeat a word I'd told you but hey,' he shrugged. 'I was also pretty sure that you liked me as much as I liked you and look how wrong I was about that.'

'I do like you! I… I like you… a lot.'

'Humph. I feel sorry for those you don't like then, if this is the way you treat people you say you like.'

'I didn't tell Timothy, Thaddeus. He didn't find out about your dad and… you know who, from me. I swear to you, that's the truth.'

He tilted his head to one side and narrowed his eyes. 'And why should I believe you?'

'Because I wouldn't lie about something like that.'

'But how do I know that? You could be lying now. You told me your mum wasn't coming to the funeral, yet she's here. You told me Timothy wouldn't find out about Dad's mistress, yet he knows. You told me you weren't friends with that shit, yet he calls you sexy and babe and says he can't wait to kiss you again. Again, Sophie. That tells me that he's kissed you before, but you told me you only met him on Saturday.'

'I did only meet him on Saturday! That's the truth. I only met you on Saturday and I slept with you!'

Tears sprang to her eyes but she could see the conflict in his.

'I'm not sure that helps your case,' he said. 'That means you could've slept with him too, based on that reasoning.'

She blinked the tears away. 'But… but I didn't! Thaddeus, I didn't.'

He pushed himself away from the newel post and turned to walk away. 'So you say,' he said. 'Where's Poppy? I need another drink.'

Chapter Thirty-One

'Don't look now,' Poppy said, half an hour later, 'but here comes Ben.'

'Coo-ey!' Ben called out and waved.

Thaddeus was lying on his back on the grass with his eyes closed and Poppy was sitting next to him with Oliver and Cleo sitting opposite. They had left the house and were basking in the early evening sunshine, on the cliff, a few feet away from the front door. It was getting on for five p.m. but the sun hadn't lost any of its heat and the air was still and sultry.

'Don't be mean, Poppy,' Oliver said. 'He looks excited. As if he has some news.'

Ben rushed up with one hand on his heart and sucked in several deep breaths. 'Is it true?' he asked, breathing in and out like a pregnant mother giving birth.

Poppy said: 'That Thaddeus broke Timothy's nose? Yes, it's true.'

Ben looked shocked. 'You broke the man's nose? How did I miss that? When? What happened?'

'This afternoon,' Oliver said. 'Thaddeus punched him, that's it. Wasn't that what you were going to say?'

'Na-uh, darlings!' Ben shook his head. 'I was asking if it's true about Sophie.'

'If what's true about Sophie?' Thaddeus asked, opening his eyes.

'That she was swanning around in a chauffeur-driven

limo yesterday and today. I see the mother's here but I could've sworn someone told me that they couldn't afford for her to come over for the funeral.'

'That's exactly what I said.' Thaddeus closed his eyes again. 'Perhaps the solicitors provided the car and paid for the flight.'

'Why would they do that?' Ben asked. 'And let's not forget the house! Have you seen the difference, darlings? Why it's positively sparkling. It's so bright and shiny that I needed to wear my sunglasses just to look at it. Now when did that happen? We were here on Sunday and the place was a tip!'

'Has Sophie inherited Silas' estate?' Cleo asked.

'Wow!' Poppy said. 'I wonder if he was rich. He must've been if they could afford to have the place spruced up and then there's this little do. The drinks' bill alone will cost a bomb, and that food is divine. Not as good as yours, Oliver. That goes without saying but even so, pretty bloody good.'

'She told me she didn't,' Thaddeus said. 'Inherit, that is. She said he was leaving it to charity. But I guess that was possibly just another lie.'

'Unless she was the charity,' Ben said. 'Silas always did think he was way above the rest of us and we were all just scum grovelling around on our knees.'

'Oh come on,' Oliver said. 'He wasn't that bad.'

'Humph! You didn't know him the way I did, nephew dear. And you only have to ask your father about Silas and the old days. He could tell you a thing or two. Where is my dear brother by the by? And the other one too? Old Jed. Have you seen them? I know they wouldn't miss this.'

Oliver nodded. 'They're inside. They were talking to Sophie and Julia with Mum, Clara, GJ, Miff and Paul, the last time I saw them.'

'Yeah,' Poppy said. 'They were all huddled together like some old witches' coven.'

'Thanks,' Oliver said. 'I'll tell my mum you called her an old witch.'

'Sophia Summerhill was a witch. According to that shit, Timothy,' Thaddeus said.

'What! You are joking, darling.' Ben sounded astonished. 'Aren't you?'

'Nope. That's what he told me. Before I punched him.'

'Is that why you did it?' Poppy asked.

'One of the reasons. But not the main one. He said several things I didn't like.'

'Like what, darling? Do tell,' Ben coaxed.

Thaddeus sighed, half drunk, half not caring anymore but he wasn't drunk enough to mention his dad's mistress. Not in front of Ben. The others knew. He trusted them with his life, but Ben – Thaddeus wouldn't trust him to keep his wallet safe from thieves, and he definitely wouldn't trust him to keep a secret.

'He told me that Sophia was a witch. That she and Barnabus were lovers. That she had his child – which incidentally is Sophie's ancestor. And that Barnabus was somehow connected to her death. Sophia's death, not the child's.'

'No!' Ben's hands shot to his face and his mouth formed a perfect 'O'.

'Yep.'

'What did Sophie say about it?' Cleo queried.

'I didn't ask,' Thaddeus replied. 'It's got nothing to do with me. Whatever our ancestors did is in the past.'

'And the present,' Poppy said. 'Barnabus and Sophia, your great-aunt Serenity and Silas. And now you and Sophie. What? Don't look at me like that. You slept with the girl, Thaddeus, so don't blame me for pointing out that history is repeating itself.'

Thaddeus sat upright. 'That's what Timothy Richards said. Just before I broke his nose.'

Chapter Thirty-Two

'Well, that went off without a hitch,' Tony Hardman said once the last of the guests – bar himself and Veronique, had finally left around seven o'clock that evening.

'As long as you don't count Thaddeus Beaumont breaking Timothy Richards' nose as a hitch, you're right. It did,' Julia pointed out.

'I have a feeling several people would count that as a blessing,' Veronique said.

'Amen to that!' Sophie added, with passion.

'It was beginning to feel like a party,' Veronique said. 'If you'll forgive me for saying that. Everyone seemed to be having a good time.'

Julia laughed. 'More like a wedding reception. No wedding bash is complete without a bit of a punch-up.'

'This would make an excellent venue for a wedding reception,' Tony added. 'Envisage a large marquee on the cliff with room enough for a sit-down meal, a bandstand and a dance floor, in case of rain. This is England, after all. Outside, under the stars an extra dance floor, with rows of twinkling fairy lights for that added sparkle. Plus a few bistro-style tables and chairs placed beneath the trees at the rear of the house, for those more interested in chatting quietly than dancing the night away. Oh! I do apologise.'

'Please don't apologise, Tony,' Julia said after a moment. 'You should've been a wedding planner. That sounds perfect.'

Veronique was looking at him as if she'd seen a side to him that she didn't know existed; Sophie was picturing the scene.

It sounded heavenly, she thought. It would be a night like this... In June with a full moon and a sky full of stars... the gentle lapping of a calm sea below promising a life of plain sailing for the happy couple. She could see them now, standing at the edge of Summer Hill cliff, arm in arm, kissing, smiling euphorically and exchanging promises of eternal love. She would be wearing a dress made of white silk with a pearl-embroidered bodice and a train made of the finest lace, starting from waist height at the back and skimming the floor. Her yellow-gold hair would be as it was today with a matching lace veil attached by a pearl-beaded comb. Thaddeus would be wearing…

Thaddeus! And her! What was she thinking?

'Sophie? Are you listening?' Julia was saying.

'Sorry. What did you say?'

'I was asking if you thought it sounded perfect too.'

Sophie nodded. 'Yes. Yes it does. Absolutely perfect.'

'Perhaps we'll bear that in mind for the future,' Julia said. 'Thank you, Tony. And you'll be guest of honour. Along with Veronique, of course, who'll no doubt be turning your vision into the reality.'

'Just let me know the time and date, and I'm your girl,' Veronique said.

'On that note...' Tony stood and grabbed the suit jacket he'd discarded some while ago. 'I think it's time we left you both in peace. Unless there's anything else we can do for you?'

'No. There's nothing else, thank you,' Sophie said. 'You've both been absolutely fabulous. I would never have been able to organise all this or do any of the things you've done. Thank you so much.'

'It's our pleasure,' he said. 'Now don't forget you're coming to the office tomorrow to discuss the details of Mr Summerhill's estate.'

Sophie nodded. 'We'll be there. And please call him Silas, Tony.'

He shook his head. 'No, no. I couldn't possibly do that. Mr Summerhill was always Mr Summerhill to me, and so he shall remain. He was very 'old school' and I respected that about him. I think he was a man who always had one foot firmly rooted in the past. Well, we'll see you tomorrow then. Sleep well.'

'Call me if you need anything, Sophie. You have my number.'

'Yes. I've saved it in my phone. Thanks for everything, Veronique.'

'We'll show ourselves out,' Tony said. 'You sit there and relax.'

Julia smiled and watched them leave. She then put her arm around Sophie and cuddled her.

'He's such a nice man' she said. 'I wonder why he and Veronique aren't a couple.'

'What?'

'Don't look at me like that, darling. It's clear that they like one another. And not just in a friendly, co-worker way. I know he's her boss but he's attracted to her and she's attracted to him. I'll have to have a quiet word.'

'Mum! You'll do no such thing. They may be lovely and I think we'll all be firm friends but he's still the family solicitor and you can't start talking to the family solicitor about his sex life.'

'Nonsense. I can talk to anyone I want to about their sex life. It's a free country, or haven't you heard?'

'And it's a civilised one, where people don't talk about sex just because they want to. There are other things in life,

Mum.'

'But none that are as much fun. Speaking of which, what happened with you and Thaddeus? I think it's time you told me everything. And I do mean *everything*. Every last little detail. I bet the man is really something in bed, isn't he? And not just in bed.'

'Mum!'

'What? We always tell each other everything. We always have. Don't go all coy on me now. Especially not about him. I was looking at him earlier and he has the most sensual, smouldering eyes, I've ever seen. He was looking at you at the time of course and—'

'He what?' Sophie looked her mum directly in the eyes. 'Did you say he was looking at me? When?'

'I think it may be easier to tell you when he *wasn't* looking at you rather than when he was, darling. The man couldn't keep his eyes off you.'

'I suspect he wanted to punch me like he did Timothy.'

'Hmm. You've got a lot to learn about men, darling. He wanted to do something to you but not punch you, I can assure you of that. I don't know what's happened because you still haven't told me. But that man is seriously keen on you and if you feel the same about him – which I happen to know you do – then my only question would be: Why are you sitting here with me when you could be wrapped in those strong arms of his right now?'

Chapter Thirty-Three

It was going to be a very busy day. Sophie knew that. She wished she'd gone to bed earlier last night but once she'd started telling her mum about what had happened between herself and Thaddeus, she found she couldn't stop talking. It all just poured out. She'd always told her mum everything. That was true, and telling Julia about Thaddeus actually helped. It made her think about it differently. See it from another person's perspective.

Now, as she sat in the kitchen this morning, drinking coffee and stroking Silas whilst waiting for her mum to come down so that they could get to Tony's office, she was forming a plan of action. Her mum had told her last night that no problem is insurmountable if you love someone. Sophie had only known Thaddeus for a couple of days and perhaps it was too early to say she loved him but that's what her heart was telling her. And not just her heart. Every fibre of her being. So if that were the case, then she needed to try and put things right between her and the man she loved.

The only problem was, did Thaddeus feel the same about her? That was a question only he could answer and it was one she had decided she was going to ask. She wasn't quite sure how but she was going to do it.

As her mum had said last night: 'What've you got to lose? If he says no, we find the treasure, sell the house and get on a first-class flight out of here. And you tell yourself to never look back. It may not be easy but you can do it. As your great-uncle Silas was always banging on about, you're a Summerhill, Sophie. And you only have to look at your name-sake Sophia to see what a Summerhill woman can do if she sets her mind to it. Not forgetting you've got my genes too. And they don't take any bullshit nonsense from a guy, no matter how gorgeous he is.'

'I'm ready darling,' Julia said, stretching and yawning as she came into the kitchen. 'What time are we supposed to be at the solicitors? I've forgotten again and you only told me an hour or so ago.'

'Eleven. And then we're all going for lunch – you, me, Tony and Veronique. After that, I thought you and I could do some shopping. I want to buy another new dress. A really sexy little number for tonight. They're all still coming this evening. I've just had a text from Cleo saying she'll make sure Thaddeus comes too. I asked her to let me know. When he left here yesterday he said something along the lines of: "I really hope I don't see your face again" but he had had a lot to drink by then and Cleo says he'll be here, so…'

'That's good. GJ and Miff said yesterday that they may not come because two nights out in one week is too much for their old bones. But they told us everything we needed to know yesterday, so that's okay.' Julia yawned again. 'I slept really well last night but I still feel tired.'

'It's the sea air.'

'Hmm. I live on an island, darling. I'm surrounded by sea air.'

'But not this sea air. This is different.'

'Of course, it is. It's England and it's usually foggy and rainy but I see it's another beautiful morning. The view from here is spectacular, isn't it? So have you decided how to 'Get Your Man'? That's what the dress is for, obviously.'

'Yes, obviously. But no, I don't know how I'm going to 'Get Him'. I think I'm just going to tell him how I feel and the truth about why I'm here and leave the rest to Fate. He either feels the same or he doesn't and if he doesn't, I'm not sticking around here mooning over him like a love-sick cow. There's a big wide world out there and I'm a wealthy woman now. I don't need Thaddeus Beaumont to make me happy. I can manage without him.'

Julia poured herself some coffee and eyed her daughter. 'Of course you can, darling. And I even think you can believe that if you say it enough times.'

Sophie was shocked. 'What's that supposed to mean? You said last night that I shouldn't take any nonsense from any man no matter how gorgeous he is!'

'Did I, darling? Yes, that does sound like me. But we must remember I'd had several brandies, and let's not forget I was jet-lagged after a thirteen-hour flight – if you include the two-hour plus stopover, which I do. I probably said all sorts of things.'

'So… what are you saying now then? That I shouldn't tell him? Or that I shouldn't just walk away?'

'I'm saying, I think I need a painkiller.'

Sophie got one from the cupboard and handed it to Julia with a glass of water.

'Thank you, darling. Okay. I think the man does feel exactly the same about you as you do about him and I think you're right to tell him how you feel. But if he doesn't declare his undying love for you today, I wouldn't give up on him immediately. He's got a lot going on, what with his dad and cousin on trial, his mum and his sister hundreds of miles away, his family possessions being sold off willy-nilly and a reporter telling the world his entire family history. 'Love' may be the last thing he wants to admit to feeling right now.'

'But… if you love someone and you've got all that awful stuff going on, surely it helps?'

Julia shook her head. 'Not always. Don't forget, he may feel he has nothing to offer you but scandal and money problems at the moment. He may need to come to terms with his new position in life. He's got to earn a living on his own now with no family business to support him.'

'That's true I suppose, but it's the 21st century, Mum. He doesn't have to support me. We can support each other.'

'Yes, and with any other couple I'd agree. But he's a Beaumont and until recently, a very rich man. Now he's broke. He thinks you're broke but now you're very rich. He may find that a bit difficult to come to terms with. Plus… there is the other little matter. The fact that you came here planning to find a treasure and sell it without telling him that he may, technically, be part owner of that treasure. That may not go down well. In fact, I'm wondering if perhaps you shouldn't mention that bit. You could tell him you've only just found out about it from you great-uncle's will.'

Sophie shook her head. 'I'm not going to lie to him, Mum. He may be angry about it but if he loves me, he'll forgive me. Won't he? Anyway, I can't start a relationship off with a lie. He'll have to know.'

'You're right. And yes, if he loves you, he'll forgive you. After all, his part ownership is questionable and all the paperwork points to it belonging to the Summerhills, so…' Julia shrugged. 'Just break the news gently, darling. In case he doesn't like what he hears.'

'I'll try. I think I do have one piece of news that may cheer him up.'

'Oh. What's that? Apart from you being loaded now of course and the fact that neither of you need ever work again.'

'Not that. The fact that Barnabus wasn't involved in Sophia's death. Well, that he didn't kill her I mean, as Timothy Richards is trying to make out.'

Julia blinked several times. 'Yes. I'm sure he'll be thrilled to hear that, darling. Um… his life has fallen apart, I'm not sure that knowing his Elizabethan ancestor didn't kill yours, is something that'll help him sleep better at night. In fact, I'd be surprised if he even cares.'

'Oh, he cares. I don't know how to explain it, Mum, but when you come from a long, established bloodline like he does – and like I do, come to that – you do care what your ancestors did.'

'We all have ancestors, Sophie. But I do understand. Your father felt the same. And Granny Summerhill. Forever going on about the family name.'

'It's weird. I never really 'got it' before. I knew being a Summerhill made me… not special, but part of something much bigger than me, but I didn't feel strongly about it until now.'

'Yes. I suppose inheriting the ancestral home and a huge estate can do that to a person, even if that home is falling down around one's ears. Speaking for myself, the Summerhill treasure is the only thing I feel strongly about – other than my darling daughter, of course.'

Sophie laughed. 'Let's get going and find out exactly what this "huge estate" consists of. And what the "little oddities" are that Tony mentioned.'

'I think he meant the family. All the Summerhills were a 'little odd' if you ask me. Present company excepted, naturally.'

Chapter Thirty-Four

'Wh-what do you mean, I own Beaumont Boats? How can I own Beaumont Boats?'

Sophie was more surprised by this piece of information than she was by all the other things Tony Hardman had just told her – and some of those were fairly incredible, if Julia Summerhill's reaction was anything to go by. Julia had said: 'That's incredible! Are you serious?' on at least five occasions during Tony's detailed breakdown of Silas' estate.

'Because you own all of Mr Summerhill's assets, Sophie and as I've just explained, when the bank enforced its various possession orders and put the Beaumont properties and assets up for sale, Mr Summerhill bought them, lock stock and… yacht.' He grinned. 'That particular business wasn't part of the investigations in connection with the criminal proceedings and Mr Summerhill paid market value, so no matter the outcome of the trial, or any police or government action, the purchase isn't affected. Nor are any of the others he made. Some of the purchase monies may since have been frozen but that's not our concern. That's a problem for the Beaumonts, the bank and the authorities to sort out.

'The yacht too? He owns… I mean, I own the Beaumont yacht? Their family yacht?'

'The Summerhill yacht now, yes.'

'But… why doesn't Thaddeus know?'

‘Why should he? He wasn’t a party to the transactions. Mr Summerhill has, sorry, had many companies and businesses. Thaddeus Beaumont wouldn’t recognise any of the names. I don’t think anyone knows your great-uncle was involved, other than those concerned, and the authorities.’

‘I’m sorry but I really don’t understand. Why did Silas buy it? Any of it. And why close Beaumont Boats?’

‘Ah. That I can’t answer. Except to say that Mr Summerhill asked me to purchase any and all available Beaumont assets, businesses and properties. Several of the acquisitions were sound investments. Some, not quite as sound.’ He shrugged. ‘But caveat emptor, as we say. Mr Summerhill knew what he was getting into. His mental faculties were still as sharp as ever until just a few days prior to his demise.’

‘The house? Did he buy Beaumont Hall?’

‘Sadly not. Or thankfully not, in my opinion. I advised against buying it as it’s a bit of a white elephant. But he was adamant. He intended to turn it into apartments, I believe. Not the best use of his funds but there it is. The bank wasn’t in a position to sell immediately though due to some administrative errors on their part and when Mr Summerhill suddenly became ill a few weeks ago, negotiations were put on hold. We expected him to recover. Sadly that wasn’t to be. So you don’t own Beaumont Hall, I’m pleased to say.’

Sophie wasn’t sure whether she was pleased or not. In fact, she didn’t think she was sure about anything anymore.

‘So you’re telling us that Sophie now owns not just Beaumont Boats and the family yacht but other businesses formerly owned by the Beaumonts?’ Julia said.

‘Yes. There’re several residential properties in Goldebury Bay. There’s the freehold of Sutton’s restaurant and—'

'Hold on,' Sophie interrupted. 'He owned Sutton's restaurant too? Was he trying to take over the town or something?'

'No, no. And he didn't own the restaurant, just the freehold of the building – which is now yours. He was merely interested in properties owned by any members of the Beaumonts, the Suttons or—'

'Don't tell me, I know… the Pollards,' Sophie added.

'Precisely. But other than the freehold of the restaurant, he didn't own any Sutton properties. Or any Pollard properties either. It was an ongoing instruction to let him know the moment I became aware of any transactions affecting those families.'

'Why?' Sophie asked. 'I mean, why just those? We know about the feud between the families of course, but why was Silas suddenly interested in buying things they owned?'

'It wasn't a sudden interest. As I said, it was an ongoing instruction. It's been ongoing since the death of Serenity Beaumont several years ago.'

'Hmm,' Julia said. 'I think you'd better tell us what you know about Silas and Serenity Beaumont. That little love affair came as a complete surprise to us.'

'There's not very much I can tell you. They fell in love, planned to marry; she changed her mind and moved abroad for several years. When she eventually returned, they met a few times I believe, and then she sadly passed away. Mr Summerhill had a red rose delivered to her grave every day until yesterday – the day of his funeral. Those were his instructions and that's all I know.'

'So it was true about the rose,' Sophie said, thinking that there was clearly a great deal she didn't know about Silas Summerhill.

But she couldn't think about that. Speaking to Thaddeus and finding the treasure were top of her 'to do' list. Although she also had to find a way to tell him that apparently, she was the owner of the thing he missed the most – Beaumont Boats.

'Well,' Tony said. 'Now shall we discuss the matter of Sophia Summerhill's original codicil and the little oddities I mentioned? I think you'll find this fascinating. I know I do. And not just because of the legalities involved. I mean to say, isn't it everyone's dream to find a long-lost, family treasure?'

But Sophie wasn't listening. She was still wondering how she could tell Thaddeus about this latest twist of Fate. She had a very strong feeling that this piece of news would go down like a ship with a hole in it.

Chapter Thirty-Five

This was the last place Thaddeus wanted to be and he still had no idea why he'd let Cleo and Oliver talk him into coming to this sodding, stupid supper at Summerhill. With Sophie looking so bloody hot that all he could think about from the moment she'd opened the front door, was how much he wanted to take her to bed.

She'd had pretty much the same effect on him yesterday, of course, and he'd had to virtually drink himself to oblivion to stop remembering the things they'd done together on Sunday night, their naked bodies entangled in positions even he hadn't tried before – and he'd tried most things.

He'd told himself repeatedly that a funeral reception was hardly the place to be thinking about what he'd like to do to the chief mourner but every time he'd seen the stairs, he'd remembered racing up them with Sophie in his arms.

Even when he'd lain on the grass outside, all he could think about was how much it felt like the crumpled sheet on Sophie's bed; the only remaining sheet on Sophie's bed, the pillows, duvet and quilt having long been tossed to the floor in the heat of passion. He'd even pictured her lying on the cool, green grass beside him, panting for breath, beads of perspiration on her breast bone and forehead; her cheeks flushed and a smile so wide that the mere thought of it made him want to kiss those sensuous lips and do it all over again… and again… and again.

'Wow!' Poppy said, just loud enough for him to hear. 'Sophie looks so bloody sexy that even I fancy her – and I'm not that way inclined by any stretch of the imagination. Shit, Thaddeus. Good luck resisting that.'

'Bugger off, Poppy. I need a drink,' he replied.

'It didn't help you yesterday,' she reminded him. 'It sure as hell won't help you tonight.'

'Thank you all for coming,' Sophie said. 'Especially after yesterday. I know you, Oliver and you, Ben, have businesses to run so thanks for making the time to come here again. I…I've got a few things to tell you all. Some explanations really. And some stories from the past but I'm not sure where to start and there are still a few questions I don't have answers to. Sorry, that sounds rather mysterious. Shall we just get the BBQ going and eat and drink? After that, perhaps we can all sit down and have a chat.'

'Oh yes,' Poppy whispered to Thaddeus. 'Nothing quite as nice as a friendly little chat, is there?'

But Thaddeus could – and was – thinking of several things he could do with Sophie which were much, much nicer than having a chat.

'What d'you think that means, darlings?' Ben asked, huddling close to Thaddeus and Poppy.

'I'm not sure I care,' Thaddeus said, watching Sophie's every move. 'I'm going to get a drink. Stay here, Poppy.'

'You're going to talk to Sophie, is what you really mean,' Poppy said. 'But fine. Just don't punch anyone, okay.'

'I've never hit a woman in my life and I'm not starting now… however much she annoys me. And I'm not going to talk to her. I'm going to get a drink, okay?'

'Of course you are,' Poppy said. 'Good luck with that too.'

'Why talk to her at all if she annoys you, darling?' Ben

asked.

But Thaddeus didn't answer. He was heading for the kitchen where he'd just seen Sophie go. Not that he wanted to talk to her; he was just getting a drink. He had nothing to say to the woman. Nothing she'd want to hear anyway. He had no idea what he was going to say if he did bump into her. Absolutely no idea at all.

'Hello Thaddeus,' Julia said. She was coming out of the kitchen as he marched across the hall towards her.

'Hello,' he replied. 'I'm just getting a drink.'

'There's plenty on the table outside and… Oh, I see,' she said with an odd, little smile. 'I'll make sure you have ten minutes alone.'

He frowned but kept walking. What did she mean by that? Why did he need ten minutes alone?

He shoved open the kitchen door, saw Sophie standing at the table and, as her eyes met his, he covered the distance between them in a millisecond, pulled her into his arms and kissed her as if his life depended on it.

'Thaddeus!' Sophie gasped when he finally released her.

Her eyes sparkled like sapphires and granite and he could see her passion matched his own. But he could also see surprise in those incredible eyes.

'Sophie, I… I don't know why I did that. I hadn't intended to.'

He made himself take one step back, in case he did it again. And he thought that was a distinct possibility.

'I'm glad you did.'

'Are you? Are you really?'

She nodded.

The deep red lipstick on her perfect mouth must be made of some magnetic compound, he thought because his lips felt as if they were being pulled towards hers by an invisible force he couldn't resist. So he stopped resisting, stepped forward and kissed her again.

This time, he didn't step away. He lifted her onto the kitchen table and stood pressed against her legs. She parted them and he moved closer, kissing her again. And again. And again. His hand reached up and caressed her breast and his body revelled in the knowledge that his touch affected her as much as hers affected him. He wanted her. He wanted her now. Right here on the kitchen table. He forgot about the others just feet from the door. Forgot that he was angry with her. Forgot that she may have lied to him, may have repeated things he'd said in confidence, may be playing games and keeping secrets. None of that mattered. All that mattered was here and now. He wanted to be inside her; needed to be and it was clear that she wanted him there; needed him there as desperately as he did.

'Thaddeus!'

To his ears, that sounded like a plea; he could feel her hands gently tugging at his hair. Her legs wrapped around his thighs and pulled him closer, deeper. Her kisses were urgent; pleading; giving; needing and, her orgasm sent shudders through his entire body just as deeply and as all-consuming as he knew they'd passed through hers.

It took several seconds before either of them could breathe normally again, let alone speak. They stared into each other's eyes, neither wanting to look away, neither wanting to break their embrace. As if they both had some dreadful worry that if they did, they might not come back together again.

'Sophie,' Thaddeus finally said, reluctantly zipping up his jeans and pulling his T-shirt back down with one hand, his other still resting on Sophie's bare leg. 'I'm sorry for behaving like a jerk. I'm sorry for not trusting you.'

'No, Thaddeus,' she replied. 'I'm the one who should apologise.'

She blushed the prettiest shade of pink as she reached for her panties which he'd tossed on the table beside her. She blushed crimson as he took them from her and eased them up her legs; legs that quivered at his touch and made him stop dressing her and start kissing her again.

'Thaddeus, no,' she sighed, gently pushing him away. She giggled softly; guiltily. 'Not again. Not here. We can't. We shouldn't have. Someone might come in at any moment.'

'I don't care,' he said. 'You're driving me insane, Sophie Summerhill. All I can think about is you.'

'You do the same to me,' she said, sliding from the table into the narrow space between it and him and wriggling her panties back in place. 'But my mum is just outside and although we have no secrets, I don't want her to see me having sex on the kitchen table.'

'Then let's move to the worktop,' he said, kissing her again and sliding his hand back to her breast.

'Thaddeus, stop! Please stop,' she moaned, sounding as if that was the last thing she actually wanted. 'Please. Stop.'

He sucked in a breath and slowly let it out. 'Okay. I'll stop for now.'

She blushed again and began buttoning up the front of her dress. Each button she did up, he promptly undid.

'Stop it!' She slapped his hand and grinned.

He kissed her. 'I can't help myself.'

She pushed him away and dashed around to the other side of the table.

'Stay there,' she commanded.

He grinned. She looked so beautiful trying to control not just his passion but also hers. It made him want her even more.

'Can't we sneak upstairs?'

'No, Thaddeus, we can't. I've got guests. Besides…'

She looked him directly in the eyes and his blood suddenly ran cold. He knew something had just happened. It was as if a door had just slammed shut and he was on one side of it; Sophie was on the other.

'Yes?' He could hardly get the words out of his mouth. 'Is there something you want to tell me?'

She nodded. 'Yes, Thaddeus. There is. And… I'm not sure how to say it.'

He stiffened. And not in a good way.

'Just say it, Sophie. Just talk to me.'

She wet her lips and he could see she was nervous.

'I didn't lie to you about Timothy, Thaddeus. Everything I told you concerning him was the truth. But… he did come here – to the house – on Sunday lunchtime and he told me something he'd found out about Sophia.'

'About Sophia and Barnabus, you mean? Yes, he told me all about it yesterday.'

He saw her swallow. Saw her eyelashes flutter and a tiny crease form between her brows.

'He did kiss me, Thaddeus. And I kissed him back but that was it. That was all. Nothing else happened between us, I promise you. And I haven't kissed him since. I don't want to kiss him. Ever again. Please believe me.'

Was that all she was worried about? Was that what she had to tell him? That wasn't so bad. He could deal with that.

He nodded. 'I do believe you, Sophie. And… well, despite the fact that we spent Sunday night together… and have just had sex on the kitchen table, it's not as if I own you. I can't tell you who you can and can't kiss.' He took a deep breath. 'Listen, Sophie. I don't know if you remember me telling you, but it's the Midsummer Parade on Saturday, followed by the Summer Fete on Sunday. Would you like to go with me? And I don't mean as a friend.'

‘Are you… are you asking me out on a date? Or strictly speaking, two dates as they’re on separate days’.

‘Yes and no. I was thinking that the date would start when I pick you up on Saturday… and end when I bring you home on Monday.’

‘Monday?’

‘Yes, Monday. Because, Sophie Summerhill. I no longer believe in one-night stands. If you say yes, you’ll be spending Saturday night and Sunday night with me. So, do you want to go on this date with me, or not?’

‘Yes Thaddeus, I do. I most definitely do.’ She beamed at him.

‘Good. That’s that then. Oh. Except… I would like to think… no, I need to believe that from now on, you’ll only be kissing me. Only be making love with me.’

She blinked several times, her lips parted and she smiled the sexiest smile he’d ever seen.

‘Are you asking me to be your girlfriend, Thaddeus? As in, you want to have a relationship with me. A proper relationship? An exclusive relationship?’

‘Um… I’m not sure what’s tripping you up here, Sophie. I’ve asked you out. I’ve told you I’d rather you don’t have sex with anyone other than me. I’m not sure what more you need me to say.’

‘Well, you could say it. You could tell me you want a relationship with me. You could tell me that… that you… like me.’

‘I thought I’d just done that. I thought I’d just *shown* you how much I like you. If it wasn’t clear, I’m more than happy to show you again.’

He stepped towards her, and grinned when she stepped away, blushing even more than earlier. God. How he wanted this woman. It was unbelievable.

‘And I’d like nothing more, believe me but we can’t,

Thaddeus. We mustn't. You… you could just *say* it though. You could just say—'

'I like you, Sophie Summerhill. I like you a lot. I want you to be my girlfriend and I want to have a proper relationship with you. A real relationship. There. Is that okay? Now, if you're really not going to have sex with me again this evening, we may as well go and get a drink. I'm suddenly very thirsty.'

He held out his hand to her and she went to him and took it.

'And I like you, Thaddeus Beaumont,' she said, staring up into his eyes. 'I like you a lot more than I think I've ever liked anyone. Remember that. Please, please, remember that. Because... before we go and get a drink, there's something else I need to tell you.'

This time, Thaddeus had the feeling that it wasn't merely a door being slammed shut. It was an iron gate.

Chapter Thirty-Six

Sophie didn't know where to begin. She couldn't quite believe that she and Thaddeus had just had mind-blowingly sensational sex on the kitchen table, with friends and family only feet away. Or that he'd just told her he liked her. And especially not that he'd just asked her to have a relationship with him.

Now she ran the risk of ruining everything and for one brief moment, she'd wondered whether to take her mum to one side and tell her not to mention anything about the inheritance, or the Beaumont properties, or Sophia or the treasure... To make this evening simply a night to chat with friends about days gone by, without mentioning witches, or family curses, betrayal or murder, mystery or revenge.

But deep down, she knew that was impossible. She knew she had to tell Thaddeus the truth, the whole truth and nothing but the truth. Somehow though, it all seemed ironic as it was Thaddeus' dad who was on trial, not her. And she wondered if she should at least wait until the trial was over, so that Thaddeus would have something pleasant to occupy him for a while instead of yet more evidence of lies and deceit from people he cared about and throughout his family history.

'Well?' Thaddeus said, still holding her hand and staring down at her. 'Are you going to tell me or do you expect me to read your mind? Because reading women's minds isn't something I'm known for.'

'Do you know much about Barnabus?'

'Oh, it's not about him again, is it? Are you going to tell me that we're very, very distant relatives because it doesn't matter, does it? And I don't care. And in the bigger scheme of things, everyone on the planet is related by some extreme link or other.'

Sophie saw the relief in his eyes but she shook her head. 'It's got nothing to do with us being related and anyway, we're not, as far as I know. Not even remotely unless you believe in Adam and Eve, which I don't. Sophia didn't have Barnabus' child. I know that's what Timothy probably told you but it's not true. And I know that for a fact because… Sophia left a journal... and some letters. And more importantly, a will… and a codicil to that will. But I'll get to that later.'

'So whose child did she have? And why was the kid brought up as a Summerhill?'

'I'll get to that too. That's not what's important for now. What's important is that I… well, I didn't lie to you, but I didn't exactly tell you the truth.'

She felt his hand tighten on hers.

'Oh? Which part wasn't the truth?'

'I didn't tell you the truth about why I came here. Everything I told you about me and Trent Godly was the truth and about my mum. I was almost broke when I arrived and I did ask the solicitors if I could stay, but it wasn't so that I could go to Silas' funeral. It was because I was looking for something – the same thing, in fact, that I was looking for all those years ago when you rescued me from the sea.'

'When you fell from the cliff? What is it then? Some sort of buried treasure or something?'

He looked as if he wasn't sure whether to laugh or take this seriously. She reached up with her free hand and brushed a lock of blue-black fringe away from his deep, brown eyes.

'Yes,' she said. 'But it wasn't buried. It was hidden. By Sophia. And all the Summerhills have tried to find it ever since. But none of them have. Until now. I'm going to find it, Thaddeus. That's why I came here. I planned to sell it and move to the Caribbean to live with mum and Hugh, her boyfriend. Now though, I want to find it and share it with you.'

He stared at her. Just stared at her and didn't say a word. Suddenly, he burst out laughing. 'You're serious, aren't you? A hidden treasure?' He frowned. 'Why? I mean, why do you want to share it with me? And it's not just because you… like me... is it? There's more to this story than you're saying, isn't there?'

She nodded. 'Strictly speaking, it could be argued that you're entitled to half of it. I have letters that indicate you're not. That it belonged to Sophia but there is an element of doubt and one you could probably argue. If you wanted to.'

She could tell from the look in his eyes that his mind was racing, that he was processing this information.

'So, I take it that means that you hadn't planned to tell me about it, originally. In case I tried to… argue that half of it belonged to me. And how exactly could half of it belong to me? Ah. Because half of it belonged to Barnabus. Is that what you're saying? So I would 'inherit' his share.'

'Yes. But that was before I knew you. You were just a name before I came here. I didn't think of you as… as a friend.'

'Hmm. And now that you do think of me as a *friend*, you've suddenly decided today that you want to share it with me. How kind. I was sort of hoping that you thought of me as a lot more than a friend but it's a start, I suppose.'

'I do. You're much more than just a friend to me, Thaddeus. You must know that. You must *feel* that. And it wasn't today that I decided. It was on Monday. Actually, I think I knew I'd want to share it with you from the minute I got in your car. No. From the moment I saw you in Betty's Pantry on Saturday. Something was telling me that I had to tell you about it. I couldn't stop feeling guilty. That's why I was blushing. You saw me do that, remember?'

'And I thought it was because you were attracted to me, not because you were feeling guilty about hiding a hidden treasure from me. If it's possible to hide something that's already hidden. Hmm.. I'm not sure what to do with this little nugget of information. How do you know the treasure even exists? Or that someone else hasn't found it already?'

'I know none of the Summerhills have because details of it pass down through the generations. And although I can't be certain of course, no one else knows about it as far as I'm aware. Unless Barnabus told his children...or anyone else. That's why I invited everyone here this evening. I wanted to ask about the feud between the Beaumonts, the Suttons and the Pollards because somewhere in that feud, I think there's a clue about the treasure.'

'Are you telling me that the bloody stupid feud that's been going on for centuries is somehow connected to a buried – sorry, hidden – treasure? And if so, why weren't the Summerhills included in it?'

Sophie shrugged. 'Possibly because Sophia died and her son was just a child at the time. After that, I think it's because the Summerhill family have always kept their distance and made sure we weren't.'

'Oh, I get it. Your lot let our families fight amongst themselves and stood on the side lines and watched.'

'Sort of, yes. But I think when Silas fell in love with Serenity... well after she died, really, he got involved and it started again.'

'Well, you're wrong there. The Beaumonts, Suttons and Pollards haven't had a row for years. Not since my grandfather's time. Possibly slightly before. And now we're all the best of friends.'

'Yes, thanks to you and Oliver, and now you, Oliver and Cleo. But Silas was starting his own little bonfire, I think.'

'Silas? How?'

'Please don't get angry about what I'm going to tell you and please understand that this has nothing to do with me. Except, it sort of does now. And I can put things right. I can give you back Beaumont Boats. Well, not *give* you exactly because there are tax implications, so Tony says, but we can become partners. Business partners and—'

'Hold on. What? What're you talking about? You've lost me now.'

Sophie took a deep breath and looked Thaddeus directly in the eyes. 'Silas bought Beaumont Boats from the bank. And not just that, but also your family's yacht and some of the other businesses. He tried to buy the house too but—'

'What? Silas did what?'

'I asked you not to get mad.'

'I'm not mad. I'm… gobsmacked. I'm astonished. Amazed. You name it, I'm feeling it. Why? Why did he do that?'

'I think it still has something to do with the feud and Sophia's death and the accusation of witchcraft and—'

'So that was true? Sophia was accused of being a witch? Actually, I don't care about that.'

'Well, you should care because Barnabus saved Sophia.'

'Good for him. Let's get back to Silas and Beaumont Boats. What did you mean about us becoming partners? Are you saying you own Beaumont Boats now? I thought he left his money to charity? That's what you said.'

'It seems I was wrong. He did leave ten per cent to charity but the rest he left to me. And although you'd never know it from the state he left this house in, it seems Great-uncle Silas was rich. Very, very rich. I'm going to re-open Beaumont Boats and have a partnership agreement drawn up between you and me.'

Again, Thaddeus stared at her in silence.

Sophie added: 'You told me that was the thing you missed the most. Now you can have it back.'

'From you? I don't think so.' He let go of her hand and turned away, shaking his head. 'I can't believe any of this. None of it's sinking in... but if you think that I'm going to accept some sort of charity job from my new girlfriend, you're wrong. This is crazy. God! I really, really need a drink.'

He pushed the kitchen door open and walked away.

'Thaddeus? Thaddeus come back! It's not like that. That's not what I meant.'

She raced after him just as GJ, Miff and Clara Pollard, Reverend Paul, and Christopher and Mary Sutton were heading back outside from the sitting room towards the BBQ.

'Hello, Thaddeus,' Clara said by way of an exuberantly, friendly greeting. 'We were wondering where you'd got to. Oliver and Cleo have said the food's ready. Come and get some before GJ eats it all.'

'I'd as like Thaddeus'll be the one to eat it all. Strapping young man like him needs to keep his strength up to kiss all the pretty young girls, don't you, lad?' He chuckled heartily as he slapped Thaddeus on the back.

Thaddeus offered his arm to help GJ outside and Sophie heard him say: 'Our ancestors must be turning in their graves.'

Chapter Thirty-Seven

Earlier that day, Sophie and Julia had placed some tables and chairs on the grass, to the left of the house, together with blankets, rugs and a parasol or two. The evening was warm with the gentlest of breezes skipping across Summer Hill cliff, and the setting sun, hanging low in the west, painted the grass a variety of greens and the sky a vivid hue of orange over cobalt blue.

There were still some leftovers from yesterday's reception, and coupled with the steaks and chicken wings that Oliver had marinated, the burgers and sausages he'd handmade, plus the salad he'd brought, there was plenty of food to go around.

There was also plenty to drink, which was just as well because all of the guests seemed to require copious quantities of alcohol as they listened to Sophie and Julia tell them the real story of why Sophie was here – a story that Thaddeus had just heard; but he still drank more than most and he continued to look surprised by it all. The only part Sophie didn't repeat was that she had, effectively, offered him a job.

But as twilight fell and grasshoppers chirped, and Sophie switched on the strings of party lights she'd purchased after Tony's inspiration of yesterday, she and Julia went on to tell their guests the rest of the story. When they finished, Poppy burst out laughing.

'Really? So let me get this straight,' Poppy said, whilst

everyone else was clearly trying to absorb what they'd been told. 'Sophia Summerhill was a witch *and* a pirate! There's a family curse because of her and you're looking for a long-lost treasure that she hid. No way! You're making this up, Sophie. You've got to be.'

'She's not,' Julia said. 'My husband told me about it before Sophie was born and I've seen the evidence with my own eyes. The Summerhills kept extensive records regarding the family. I think they thought that one day they'd be as famous as the Beaumonts. But we shouldn't really call Sophia and Barnabus, pirates. They were privateers – at least Barnabus was. He had letters of marque from Elizabeth I, which meant he could get away with piracy under the 'respectable banner' of a royal licence. Sophia, of course, shouldn't have been allowed on board. Most privateers wouldn't dream of letting a woman sail with them.'

'There's no evidence that she was a 'real' witch either,' Sophie said. 'It's mainly the letters from Barnabus to her, calling her one and even he used the term affectionately. They were love letters, don't forget.'

'How could we?' Thaddeus said, with a hint of sarcasm. 'But I thought you told me they weren't lovers.'

He was sitting as far away from Sophie as he possibly could; at least that's the way it felt to her but she'd been aware of him watching her constantly throughout the evening.

'I didn't say they weren't lovers. I told you she didn't have his child. They *were* lovers and Barnabus named his ship after her.'

'*The Sea Witch*?' Cleo queried. 'That was named after Sophia? Or did he have another ship?'

'He had two or three ships before *The Sea Witch* but it was that ship he named after Sophia, and that's the one he's most associated with. That's what he called Sophia and that's where the whole 'witch' thing started, we think. In the family history, it says that when she was on board a ship – any ship – the seas were perfect for sailing but when she wasn't, they weren't. So instead of Sophia being thought of as unlucky, as women generally were, she was welcomed on board Barnabus' ships. She always dressed as a man though, never a woman. From her papers, the letters and the later family records, we believe she first 'stowed aboard' when she was about twelve. Barnabus – who was seven years older than her, seemed to think it was amusing. They became lovers a few years later.'

'Is there something in the water in Goldebury Bay?' Poppy said. 'I only ask because everyone in this place seems to be bonking everyone else and most of it seems to go on between the families sitting here tonight!'

'It certainly does seem that way,' Paul Temple replied. 'Although not in our case.' He smiled lovingly at Clara and she nestled closer to him on the rug they shared.

'So why did they stop being lovers then? Barnabus and Sophia,' Cleo asked. 'Who's the father of her child? Your great-grandfather several times removed.'

'A man named Robert Cole. All I know about him is that he was an officer on a brigantine that was wrecked near here. Sophia found him washed ashore in Summer Hill cove and nursed him back to health. She seems to have fallen in love the minute she saw him. Barnabus was jealous and heartbroken when she dumped him but I think he was more upset that she stopped going to sea. He'd lost his lucky mascot.'

'Because he couldn't possibly have just been head over heels in love with her and wanted to be with her, could he?' Thaddeus said. 'It had to be because she gave him something – in addition to sex, of course.'

'I didn't mean it like that. I meant he wasn't the sort of man who would sit and mope over a woman.'

'Because another one would come along and replace her, you mean. I don't know how you can make a judgement about someone you hardly know and plan out their future for them.'

'No. I meant—'

'Darlings!' Ben said. 'I think we're drifting off the topic here. We're talking about Sophia and the treasure, not the present day.'

'I wasn't… oh, forget it,' Thaddeus said.

'So what happened to Robert and why didn't they marry?' Poppy asked.

'I'm not absolutely sure. He just seems to have disappeared at some stage. Sophia sent her young son away in secret to a distant relative and started seeing Barnabus again, so something had gone wrong. There're letters from Barnabus that indicate they resumed their affair. But I think she… went a bit mad around that time. That's when she was 'officially' accused of being a witch. By the woman Barnabus abandoned to go back to Sophia. Then Barnabus hastily married another woman, a family friend called Elizabeth Pollard, who happened to be the daughter of the then, Justice of the Peace, and the Assize Judges were known to have stayed with them. All trace of the accusation against Sophia disappeared. At least, most of it did. Timothy Richards found a line about it but nothing more. The woman who accused Sophia of witchcraft continued to do so. She was found dead at the foot of Golde Cliff just a few weeks later. Her name was Jane Sutton and she was eight months' pregnant with Barnabus' child, it was said. That's how and why the feud began. What I don't know is why Sophia hid the treasure. But I think the feud had something to do with it.'

‘Bloody hell!’ Poppy shrieked. ‘Is this really true?’

GJ fidgeted in his chair. ‘The parts about the Pollards are,’ he said. ‘I’d as like Barnabus got them to cover it all up. Can’t speak for Sophia’s part or for the Sutton’s, exactly.’

Christopher nodded. ‘I remember my great-granddad telling us Sutton boys that a Beaumont murdered one of ours and the child she was carrying, back in the old times and that the Pollards helped cover it up.’

‘Well, that’s all very interesting,’ Thaddeus said. ‘It seems Sophia was the cause of all the trouble, and my ancestor murdered a Sutton and married a Pollard to save her. What does she do in return? Hide a treasure which he partly owns. Now there’s gratitude for you.’

GJ chuckled. ‘And she’s not even blamed for the feud, neither. I’d as like she *was* a witch, and a cunning witch at that.’

‘I second that, darlings,’ Ben said. ‘Well, well. And Sophia and the Summerhills got away scot-free. And... with a hidden treasure.’

‘She didn’t exactly get away scot-free,’ Sophie said. ‘She died a few weeks after Jane Sutton. She was found in Summer Hill cove with a dagger in her chest. It missed her heart but she died… it’s said, in Barnabus’ arms. The dagger belonged to her.’

‘She killed herself!’ Poppy sounded cross. ‘That’s disappointing. Why would such a strong, independent woman kill herself?’

‘Especially when she had a young child,’ Clara added.

‘We don’t think she did,’ Sophie said. ‘Again, Barnabus is believed to have covered it up but the family history suggests she was murdered. There’s no mention of it anywhere else, so I don’t know.’

‘They thought Barnabus killed her?’ Oliver asked.

Sophie shook her head. 'There were rumours and speculation but I don't think he did. The family history doesn't say. It only says she had a mortal wound to the chest. It could've been anyone. I think Sophia made a few enemies.'

'I'd as like it was one of our lot,' GJ said. 'Elizabeth Pollard, the one Barnabus wed. She'd be none too happy to know he married her to save Sophia from some accusation. And even less pleased knowing they were up to their games again.'

'Or ours,' Christopher Sutton said. 'For the part she played in Jane Sutton's death.'

'Or Robert Cole,' Thaddeus pointed out. 'You said Sophia hid her child with a relative. Why? And you said the guy just disappeared. Perhaps she dumped him to go back to Barnabus, and Robert wasn't happy about it. Maybe that was even why she hid the treasure. From him, not from Barnabus. Perhaps Robert was trying to get his hands on it.'

'You're right!' Sophie said. 'That hadn't even occurred to us, had it Mum? But it's possible and it would explain why she didn't leave details of where it is.'

'So, where does this Summerhill curse stuff come from then?' Poppy queried. 'She didn't curse anyone. And she was supposed to have been the witch, no one else.'

Julia said: 'She supposedly said something about it being better to die young than to die alone. That story must have been repeated and embellished as stories often are, and over the years, it got extended to: All the Summerhills will either die young or they'll die alone. Even before Sophia, several Summerhills met early deaths, so people said the Summerhills were cursed. And there were probably rumours still circulating about her being a witch. Barnabus and the Pollards may have removed nearly all the written evidence of the accusation but you can bet that tongues still wagged.'

'And have they?' Poppy asked. 'I mean since then, have they all died young or alone?'

Sophie nodded. 'Pretty much, yes. Her son died when he was twenty-three and all four of his kids died young except one.'

'Bullshit,' Thaddeus said. 'That has nothing to do with some stupid curse – which wasn't even a curse. But I know how superstitious and idiotic some people were in those days. That has more to do with the conditions people lived in. Death rates were high even amongst the wealthy. I don't know about the rest of them but as for the present-day Summerhills, Silas chose to live the life of a hermit. His sister, your gran didn't die alone; she was with you, and fairly elderly. And your dad, well, I'm sorry to say this but if you're going to climb mountains, you are dicing with death... curse or no curse. Sorry, but it's true. And sorry, Julia.'

'I agree, Thaddeus,' Julia said. 'But he died doing something he loved, so there's comfort in that. And I've told Sophie repeatedly that the Summerhill curse is nonsense. But you don't really believe in it anyway, do you darling?'

Sophie shook her head. 'Most of the time, no, but sometimes…' She shrugged. 'Well sometimes, I wonder what Fate has in store for me.'

'I can tell you what it doesn't have in store for you,' Thaddeus said. 'And that's dying alone. There's no way that'll happen, believe me.'

She had no idea what he meant by that but it was the first time he'd smiled at her since he'd walked out of the kitchen… even if he did look rather grumpy just one second later.

'So what exactly is this treasure? Do you know?' Oliver

asked, handing Thaddeus and Paul each another beer and passing a bottle of champagne to Ben.

'Part of it's in the portrait of Sophia in Ben's gallery,' Sophie said. 'The jewellery she's wearing. The girdle belt in particular, is important because we think that holds the key – well one of the keys. It's the brooch on the girdle in the shape of a key and encrusted with rubies. If you look at Barnabus' portrait, you'll see he's wearing it too and the rest of the jewellery he's wearing matches the jewellery Sophia wears in hers.'

'The key opens a chest or something then, does it?' Christopher Sutton queried.

'We think so, yes,' Sophie said.

'And the chest is what you're looking for?' Mary Sutton spoke for the first time.

'Yes,' Julia confirmed. 'That's what we believe anyway. All the codicil says is that the treasure will belong to the Summerhill who finds it. We don't know why Sophia didn't mention her son by name.'

'But you have no idea where this chest may be?' Thaddeus said.

'I think it's in this house,' Sophie told him.

'Then why were you scaling the cliffs all those years ago?'

She pulled a face. 'Because I found a secret passage in the house but the other end seemed to be sealed up with a huge rock. I thought I could get to it via the cliff. Plus, I was nine years old, and every child thinks treasure will be hidden in a cave or buried in the sand.'

'That depends what you think is treasure,' Miff said. 'For me, it's this old fool.' She nudged GJ's arm and squeezed his hand.

'I'd as like it's the same for me. Miff's given me more happiness than gold ever could.'

Poppy grinned. 'I think I'd take the gold.'

'I think darling Sophie wants both,' Ben quipped, glancing at her and then Thaddeus.

'So where d'you go from here as far as finding it's concerned?' Cleo asked.

'I'm not sure. I was hoping one of you may know something else about the feud that we don't,' Sophie said. 'But if what Thaddeus said is true – that she hid it because of Robert Cole – then the feud has nothing to do with the treasure, after all. Except… didn't the feud also say that the Beaumonts accused the Suttons of stealing treasure from them?'

Thaddeus said: 'If you subscribe to Miff and GJ's philosophy, perhaps that particular 'treasure' was Sophia's life. Perhaps Barnabus thought one of them killed her, just as we've discussed and it has nothing to do with the treasure you're looking for.'

'That's possible, I suppose,' Julia said. 'After all, most of the records were written in Elizabethan English and the people who rewrote them possibly didn't do so with complete accuracy. I know it was English and not Latin but have you read anything from that time? Some of it's like double Dutch. Well, I'm assuming the originals were English. Who knows? It's said that Sophia could speak several languages. It could've been in French or German for all we know.'

'That's true. Although her will and codicil are in English,' Sophie added.

'Well. I think you know more about the feud than we do,' Clara said. 'So I definitely can't add anything. Can anyone else?'

They all shook their heads simultaneously.

'Back to square one then,' Julia said.

'Not entirely.' Thaddeus stood up and stretched his legs.

'You said she left a codicil which says that the treasure belongs to the Summerhill who finds it, so she wanted it to be found. I'd reread all the papers but with fresh eyes. Forget about the feud and just go from the basis of someone hiding something that they want someone to find. If Barnabus wrote letters to her, I assume she wrote letters back. I don't think we have them, although… if he loved her as much as this tale indicates, I would've thought there's a chance he kept some. Because of his fame and the fact he was involved in the sinking of *The Armada*, I would imagine my lot kept anything they could find. Of course, Dad has probably sold it but I'll ask. Now though, I'm going home to bed. It's been a bloody long day and I'm sorry to say, I'm knackered.'

'Oh!' Sophie was surprised, both by his suggestion, which made a lot of sense and also by the fact that it was ten-thirty. 'I didn't realise it was that late.'

And, as if she'd asked them all to leave, everyone got to their feet, said their goodbyes and gave their thanks. Within half an hour, they had all piled into various cars and headed home.

'He didn't even say goodbye!' Sophie complained to Julia when they bolted the front doors and walked arm in arm up the stairs.

But as she settled herself in bed, her mobile rang. It was Thaddeus.

'I'm still mad at you,' he said, 'although I'm not sure why. I love Beaumont Boats but there's no way I can let you re-open it just to give me a job. That's not—'

'Thaddeus! Please listen to me. I'm not offering you a job out of charity or anything. And I'm not trying to plan out your future either, in case that's what you think. It was wrong of Silas to close the business and I want to re-open it. The Summerhills made their money from boats, don't forget. Well, ships, but a boat's a boat as far as I'm concerned. And as you can tell, this particular Summerhill knows nothing about boats or ships. You do. That's why I'm suggesting a partnership. An equal partnership. I'll re-open the business and provide the finance to restart it. You provide the experience and the expertise. We share the profits. That's only fair.'

'Oh,' he said. 'Well, put like that, it does make some sense, I suppose.'

'Will you think about it? Can we discuss it at least?'

'Yes. Yes, we can discuss it. But that wasn't why I'm calling. I'm calling to say I'll pick you up at ten on Saturday for our date. Unless you've changed your mind.'

Sophie snuggled down in her bed. 'I haven't changed my mind, Thaddeus. I thought you'd changed yours.'

'I haven't. And as for that stupid curse... you can forget it, Sophie. Because no matter what happens from here, there's one thing I can promise you. If I have any say in it, you'll never be alone for long. Goodnight and pleasant dreams. I'll see you on Saturday.'

'Goodnight, Thaddeus,' she said. And she understood what GJ and Miff had meant about what one thinks of as treasure.

Thaddeus was becoming more precious to her than any amount of gold or jewels.

Chapter Thirty-Eight

'Have I been asleep for two days?' Sleepy-eyed, Julia walked back into the kitchen having left it only moments earlier to go upstairs and take a shower. 'I only ask because you told me that you weren't seeing Thaddeus till Saturday morning and I'm pretty sure I've just seen his car coming down the road. It is Thursday today, isn't it? And it's only eight a.m.'

'What?' Sophie wasn't sure whether to be excited or worried. Then she realised her hair was a mess and she didn't have time to be either one or the other. 'Stall him, Mum! I need to make myself look half decent.'

She raced upstairs and jumped in the shower. It would only take her two minutes to have a quick wash and then she'd put some perfume, lippo and mascara on – another two minutes; blow-dry her hair – five minutes, and find something sexy to wear – that could take all day.

A few minutes later, having just turned off the shower, she heard him call her name; heard his footfall on the stairs and realised he was coming up. She hastily grabbed a towel and wrapped it around her.

'Can I come in? Your mum said it was fine for me to come up.'

Did she now? Sophie thought.

'Okay. But I'm not decent.'

He opened the door and stopped, letting out a long, low whistle as he eyed her up and down.

'I don't know,' he said with a wicked grin. 'You look pretty decent to me. Bugger. I don't have much time.' He threw off his Gore-Tex jacket and covered the distance between them, pulling her into his arms and kissing her passionately. 'Good morning, beautiful. Now listen. I was thinking about you all last night and—'

'You were?' She wrapped her arms around his waist.

'Of course I was. And about this treasure. And I remembered something. I told you that there were a couple of pieces of furniture that I'd wanted from Beaumont Hall and was lucky enough to be able to keep, didn't I?

'Yes,' she said, unbuttoning his white shirt.

'Well, one of them was a desk. And it's a desk that was supposed to have belonged to Barnabus.'

'Really? Wow!'

Her hands stopped. He looked down at them and with his fingers over hers, he helped her undo the rest of the buttons in record time. Then he kissed her neck and in between kisses, he helped her unzip his trousers and pull them off. He kissed her on the mouth and gently eased her back onto her bed.

'What was I saying?' He looked into her eyes and smiled. 'Oh yes. The desk.'

'What desk?' Sophie rolled him over and climbed on top of him, grinning seductively.

'Barnabus' desk! Are you listening to me?'

'Yes. But I'd much rather be doing something else to you. Is the desk important?'

'Very,' he said as she leant forward to kiss him. 'But we can talk about it later.'

He tugged at her towel and tossed it to the floor where it lay discarded for at least fifteen minutes.

Chapter Thirty-Nine

'Now I'm going to be late,' Thaddeus said. 'I don't know what you do to me but at this rate, I'll be the one who dies young. I came here to tell you about the desk.'

'Barnabus' desk,' Sophie said, grabbing his hand and pulling herself to her knees. 'You see. I was listening. Did you find something?'

'Yes. Just as I suspected, Barnabus did keep Sophia's letters. Well, some of them at least. I found them this morning in his desk.'

'What? Just like that? You opened a drawer and there they were? That's incredible! Why didn't you say so?'

'I was trying to. Then something else came up.' He winked and kissed her again. 'And no, I didn't just open a drawer and find them. I wish it'd been that easy. I had to search for them. I rang my uncle Theo after I spoke to you last night and asked him if he knew anything about the story. He did as it happens and he told me a little something you may not know. Barnabus named one of his daughters Sophia. The man was definitely besotted with your ancestor. Anyway, Uncle Theo didn't know of any letters but like all sea captains, Barnabus kept a log, and Uncle Theo has it.'

'Wow! Can we read it? Does it say anything about Sophia?'

'I'm not sure what it says but yes, we can read it. That got me thinking. I thought he'd keep Sophia's letters with him on the ship but then I realised that was unlikely. He'd want to keep them safe but he wouldn't leave them lying around for his wife or anyone else to read. He'd hide them. The desk I have is one he kept at home, not the one from *The Sea Witch* so I did some online research on antique furniture and cabinet makers and secret compartments and—'

'Last night? You did all this last night?'

'Yes. I told you, I couldn't stop thinking about you so I thought I may as well do something useful. Now listen,' he said, kissing her yet again. 'It took me ages to find it and I had to break the lock because I didn't have the key but eventually, I found a secret drawer hidden behind an ordinary drawer. And guess what I found inside?'

'The letters!'

'Yes. But not just the letters. This was with them.' He picked up his jacket and pulled out a small, intricately carved and jewel-studded, oak box from one pocket. Handing it to her he continued: 'It's locked and I didn't break this one open but I think it could possibly contain the key. The girdle brooch you were talking about. Or something else fairly important... at least, to Barnabus.'

'The key!' Sophie gasped.

Thaddeus nodded and beamed at her. 'It's a lovely box and probably quite valuable but that isn't why I didn't break into it. I thought we should open it together. Except now I've got to go, so…'

'I'll wait for you to come back,' Sophie said. 'I agree we should open it together.' She shook the box. 'But it doesn't sound like it contains a key. Perhaps it's more letters.'

He smiled and handed her a bundle of letters that he'd pulled from the other pocket of his jacket. 'Perhaps it is. I haven't read these, either, other than checking that they're from Sophia. I thought you should read them first.'

'I think we should read these together too,' she said, even though, now that she was holding Sophia's original love letters to Barnabus, in her hands, she was yearning to read them right away.

'Are you sure? I won't get back here for at least two hours. Can you wait that long?'

'For you, Thaddeus?' She smiled and kissed him firmly on the mouth. 'I'd wait for you forever.'

He gave her an odd little smile, kissed her deeply then glanced at his watch. 'Bloody hell I'm so late. I really have to go', and he ran out of her room and down the stairs in less than ten seconds.

Sophie put the letters on the bed and turned the box over and over in her hands. It is beautiful, she thought. The carvings were so intricate, so detailed and the jewels... well, the emeralds and pearls were stunning. There was even an indented little crescent moon but the jewels, which had clearly been there once, judging by the tiny indents, were missing from that.

A crescent moon? A sudden thought struck her. She studied the box more closely. It was definitely a crescent moon. Was this box…? Did it belong to…? She raced to her bedroom window and called down to Thaddeus who had just reached his car.

'Thaddeus! I think this is Sophia's box, not Barnabus'.'

He glanced up at her, one hand on the handle of the car door. 'What makes you think that?'

She held it in the air and pointed to the crescent moon although she knew he couldn't see it from where he stood.

'There's a crescent moon on it. Sophia's crescent moon.' She touched her cheek. 'My crescent moon.'

He glanced at his watch. 'Bugger it,' he said. 'I'll meet you in the hall.' He headed back towards the house.

Sophie ran downstairs as Julia came out from the

kitchen and Thaddeus opened the front door and stepped back inside. Sophie waved the box in the air.

'We think Thaddeus has found a box belonging to Sophia, Mum!'

'Good heavens! What's in it?'

'We don't know. It's locked,' Sophie said. 'We thought it belonged to Barnabus and may contain the key or something because Thaddeus also found Sophia's letters, so we didn't think it held those. But it doesn't rattle as a key would so now we have no idea, other than perhaps more letters. Except I think it was Sophia's. We're going to have to break into it.'

'But it's such a gorgeous box!' Julia said. 'Do you really want to do that? Perhaps we should look for a key. But where would we start?'

'It doesn't have that sort of lock, Mum. Look.'

Sophie handed her the box and Julia turned it over several times.

'You're right. There's no keyhole, darling. It must be like one of those Chinese puzzle boxes. Perhaps you push something. Or twist. Or pull. Oh look! There's an indent in the shape of a crescent moon. It's just like your birthmark.'

'I know,' Sophie said. 'That's why I think it's Sophia's. It's just like the ones on the rapier and dagger in Ben's gallery. You remember he told us about them on Sunday, Thaddeus? I went back to have a look because I knew they were Sophia's and I'd never seen a picture of those, either. Apart from being beautiful, they have the same crescent moon shape. Except, the ones on the rapier and dagger stand proud and are embellished with rubies, whereas this one's indented and the stones are missing.'

Thaddeus' dark brows came together and he took the box from Julia.

'Sorry' he said, 'but I've just had a thought.' He studied

the crescent moon, looked at Sophie and smiled. 'I think I know where the key is.'

'You do?' Sophie was astonished.

'So do you,' he said. 'You've just told me. And now I need to cancel my appointment and we need to go and wake up Ben.'

Chapter Forty

Ben was definitely *not* a morning person, Sophie soon discovered but when Thaddeus explained about the box even Ben got excited. He threw on some clothes and they drove to The Artful Fisher where he retrieved the dagger and rapier from the exhibition cabinet – and all in less than half an hour.

Thaddeus took the rapier and Ben handed the dagger to Sophie. She took a deep breath and slotted the raised crescent moon on the dagger's hilt into the indented crescent moon on the box and pressed.

Nothing happened.

'Turn it, *darling*,' Ben gasped. 'Twist the dagger.'

She did so. First one way. Nothing. And then the other. Suddenly a click. She glanced up and saw the sparkle in Thaddeus' eyes. He was as excited as she was.

'Well, open it!' Ben said in an even higher pitch than normal.

Julia squeezed Sophie's shoulder and nodded. 'Yes, darling. Open it. Don't keep us in suspense.'

Sophie gingerly tried to ease it open. It creaked under the strain of being sealed for so many centuries but finally, it revealed its contents to four pairs of anxious eyes.

Resting inside, neatly folded and bearing a broken, red wax seal was another handwritten letter from Sophia Summerhill to her *Beloved Barnabus*. Although some of the words didn't make sense in today's English, it told

Sophie, Thaddeus and Julia – and also Ben – almost everything they wanted to know about the Summerhill treasure.

'You were right, Thaddeus,' Julia said when Sophie had finished deciphering the hasty scrawl. 'Sophia was hiding the treasure from Robert Cole and this was clearly written just days before she died.'

'And only shortly after she'd taken her son, in secret, to live with her distant relative,' Sophie said. 'To think that Robert physically assaulted her makes me furious. And yet, I can't see her being a victim for long. I wonder if that's how she died. Perhaps she fought with Robert and he turned her dagger on her and then fled.'

'Leaving Barnabus to find her in Summer Hill cove,' Thaddeus said. 'That's very possible. But we'll never know the answer to that – unless Barnabus has written about it somewhere. I don't think that'll be in his ship's log though.'

Ben frowned. 'But darlings, why didn't she just tell Barnabus in this letter, where she'd hidden the treasure. She says she wants it to go to her son and she effectively tells him about the will and codicil. Why not just say, "This is where it is, if something happens to me, go and get it and give it to him." I simply don't understand it.'

'Perhaps she was afraid the letter might not reach Barnabus and that Robert might find it,' Julia suggested. 'She wanted to tell him in person.'

'Then why write the letter? And why put it in the box?'

'In case the worst happened and she didn't see Barnabus again, perhaps?' Thaddeus suggested. 'And don't forget, all their letters would have been delivered by hand by someone each of them trusted. Perhaps Sophia wanted to be doubly sure that no one but Barnabus read this one.'

Sophie nodded and smiled. 'I think that's right. But I

also think she did tell him where it was. When she says the part about seeing him again where the crescent moon sets beyond the fire rock.'

'You've lost me, darling,' Ben said. 'Is this some sort of code?'

'Sort of. I think I mentioned that when I was nine, I found a secret passage in Summerhill. I followed it but it seemed to be a dead end. The exit appeared to be blocked by a huge rock. A rock, that when the light from my torch shone on it, almost glowed red… like fire. I think that's the fire rock. The crescent moon is the lock and key to the treasure. In this case, of course, it's the treasure itself.'

'You're saying the treasure's on the other side of that rock?' Thaddeus queried. 'In a secret passage in Summerhill?'

'But that's so simple!' Julia said. 'And if Barnabus knew where it was, why didn't he go and get it? Or perhaps he did. Perhaps the treasure's gone.'

'I don't think so,' Sophie said. 'If Barnabus had gone and got it, the Summerhills wouldn't have been looking for it. They knew of it because of Sophia's will. I know Barnabus would never have got the treasure and kept it. I just know he wouldn't. He loved Sophia too much to do that. I think he left it there and meant to pass it on when the child returned to Summerhill.'

'But Barnabus died a year later,' Thaddeus said. 'So he didn't get the chance. Is that what you think?'

'Yes,' Sophie said. 'That's exactly what I think. It's the only possible explanation.'

'But darlings, why hasn't anyone found this secret passage thing before now?' Ben asked.

Sophie shrugged. 'Perhaps they were looking in the wrong place. I only found it because I was poking around. It was clear that no one had been near the place in a very,

very long time. Sophia may have been the last person to use it prior to me finding it that day. I asked Silas about secret passages and he told me to mind my own business, so when I found it, I didn't tell him. Of course, that was the day I fell from the cliff and when I recovered, Silas told us to leave, so although I told you where it was, didn't I Mum, I didn't get a chance to show you.'

'And are you going to tell us?' Thaddeus asked with a smile and one raised eyebrow.

Sophie grinned. 'Yes of course. It's in a panelled wall in the bedroom I'm sleeping in. It's the smallest bedroom in the house and the plainest, and it's not really somewhere you'd look for a secret passage. The only one mentioned in the family history is one behind the fireplace in the Great Hall. That one leads down to a small cave in Summer Hill cove. The one in my room opens on to a long flight of stairs leading down to an underground cavern and an even longer tunnel. The 'fire' rock's at the end of it.'

'Or clearly not at the end of it if the treasure's behind it,' Thaddeus said. 'There's a cave leading onto the Firehills that has a rock at the back of it. When you enter the cave, you think there's no other way out but if you get up close to the rock, you can see it hides an exit. You can squeeze around the rock and it leads out onto a path. The Firehills are to the right and Golde Cliff is to the left. The smugglers used to use it. I think we should go and take a look at your 'fire' rock. Perhaps it does the same.'

Chapter Forty-One

The sitting room at Summerhill was full to bursting. GJ and Miff, Clara and Paul, Christopher and Mary, Ben, Oliver and Cleo, Poppy, Thaddeus, Julia and Sophie were all huddled together staring at a large, carved oak chest sitting in the middle of the room where the coffee table usually stood.

'*Darling*!' Ben pleaded. 'Please don't keep us in suspense. I'm dying to see what's inside. Open it! Please, please, open it.'

'In just one more second,' Sophie said. 'I'm nervous. I've been thinking about this moment for most of my life. Imagining… wondering what it would feel like to find the Summerhill treasure and now that I think we have, I'm almost too scared to look.'

'I feel the same,' Julia said. 'I mean, what if it's not what we're expecting? What if it isn't jewels and gold?'

'I hope there's not a body in there,' said Poppy.

'Trust you to think of that,' Cleo said.

'I'd as like it don't matter much what's inside unless you open the damn thing,' GJ mumbled.

'He's right.' Thaddeus squeezed Sophie's hand in one of his and passed her the rapier with his other hand.

The chest had the same crescent moon indent that the small box had but this one was larger, just as the ruby encrusted crescent moon on the rapier's hilt was larger than the ruby encrusted crescent moon on the hilt of the dagger.

Sophie took a deep breath, put the rapier in place and closed her eyes.

Poppy giggled and said: 'Wouldn't it be funny if you opened it and there was a piece of paper inside that said: "Sorry. You're not a winner this time. Good luck on your next attempt", or something like that? Like it does in competitions.'

'No, Poppy, it wouldn't,' Thaddeus said.

Sophie took another deep breath, grabbed Thaddeus' hand and placed it on top of hers and together they turned the rapier. Just as the small box had, the aged wooden chest creaked when they opened it.

Sophie let out a little scream and burst into tears.

'Shit!' Thaddeus said, wrapping his arms around her.

'Bloody hell!' Poppy said. 'Congratulations! It looks like you're a winner, after all.'

'You're not joking! Oliver said.

None of the others said anything for several minutes. They just stared at the glistening, gleaming, tangled heap of precious stones and jewellery... emeralds and rubies, pearls and opals, diamonds and sapphires. Necklaces, belts, buckles, rings, earrings, even single stones the size of peas and larger, vied for space in the crammed-packed chest.

'Well,' Julia finally said. 'I think you've found the Summerhill treasure.'

'And what a treasure!' Christopher Sutton said.

'Yes,' said Sophie. 'And it's far beyond my wildest dreams.'

'Mine too,' Thaddeus agreed.

But Sophie and Thaddeus weren't looking at the treasure. They were looking at each other.

Thaddeus pulled Sophie to him and, oblivious to everything around them, their lips met in a long, slow, binding kiss.

They both knew they'd found something far more valuable than gold and priceless jewels.

They had found each other.

Fate had thrown them together and the future looked very bright.

Very bright indeed.

THE END

Thank you so much for reading, *Ninety Steps to Summerhill*. I do hope you enjoyed it.

COMING SOON

Ninety Days to Christmas

Book 3 in the Goldebury Bay series

Poppy can't buy what she wants for Christmas.

Poppy Taylor is tired of playing gooseberry to her loved-up friends. She wants a man of her own to snuggle up with in time for the holidays – and Christmas Day is only 90 days away.

She's set her sights firmly on the new man in town: property developer and all-round nice guy, Toby Blackwood. Poppy's hoping it won't just be the wood burner in her cottage keeping her warm as the cold, dark nights draw in…

But Toby's obnoxious, older brother Ryan, a self-made millionaire, makes it abundantly clear that he has other plans for Toby and he's not going to let Poppy get in his way.

***

To see details of my other books, please go to the books page on my website or scan the QR code, below. http://www.emilyharvale.com/books.

***

Scan or tap the code above to see Emily's books on Amazon

To read about me, my books, my work in progress and competitions, freebies, or to contact me, pop over to my website http://www.emilyharvale.com. To be the first to hear about new releases and other news, you can subscribe to my newsletter via the 'Sign me up' box.

Or why not come and say 'Hello' on Facebook, Twitter, Google+ or Pinterest. Hope to chat with you soon.

Love,

Emily xx

CPSIA information can be obtained at www.ICGtesting.com
Printed in the USA
LVOW07s2331310716
498507LV00035BA/536/P